Books by Conor Corderoy

Heat

A Love to Kill Fc
The Deepest Cut
In Hot Blood

I0658890

In Hot Blood

ISBN # 978-1-78686-186-3

©Copyright Conor Corderoy 2017

Cover Art by Posh Gosh ©Copyright 2017

Interior text design by Claire Siemaszkiewicz

Totally Bound Publishing

Heat

IN HOT BLOOD

CONOR CORDEROY

Dedication

This book is dedicated to Stella Vegas
Without her love and support, I would not have made it
this far.

Chapter One

The overhead sign was broken. It was dark green and the right corner was missing. I leaned forward over the steering wheel to look up at it. The drizzle had washed most of the dust off, but what was left had painted muddy streaks across the words. I made out Suzano, Poa and F Vansconcelos, with an arrow pointing left. My windshield wipers squeaked to a slow rhythm, washing water across the words and making them warp.

It was Sunday in the Itaquaquetuba district of Sao Paulo and everyone was hiding from the rain. The road was empty, so I spun the wheel and turned into the Rua Primero de Maio. I could hear the tires on the wet blacktop and it sent damp shivers up my back. Primero de Maio ran along the east bank of the Tieté River where it opened out into a broad, slow flowing expanse of water that was more like a lake than a river. Along the right there was a long row of slums, not quite *favelas*, but close. Most of them were cheap, two-story construction of brick in pale blue, white and dirty orange. They had big steel gates on the ground floor and covered terraces above with satellite dishes, bikes and strings of washing elbowing each other for space.

Along the left on the river bank were the real *favelas* – lean-tos made out of wooden pallets, boxes and torn tarpaulins. Hungry, half-naked families huddled inside and stared with frightened, incurious eyes at a world whose best offer for them was indifference. There had always been extreme poverty in Brazil – in much of the world – but this had the look of an ugly, infected sore, one that was going to spread.

I drove past houses that doubled as shops, selling

sweets, cigarettes and beer. I was looking for number three hundred twenty, but the numbers seemed to jump around a lot. I finally found it three or four hundred yards down the road, headed west. I drove past it then pulled into a patch of wasteland on the banks of the river, climbed out and walked the short distance to the house. I hunched into my shoulders with my collar turned up. There was a crude, dirty-gray plastic intercom outside the gate. I pressed the call button, and after a couple of seconds, a voice that could have been male or female said, "*Alô*...?"

I said, "Igor sent me." That was Russell's idea.

The gate buzzed and clanked and I pushed through into the shelter of what I could now see was a carport. The patter of the water outside echoed in the enclosed, tiled area and a damp breeze snuck in around my ankles. I crossed the floor where small puddles had accumulated from the windblown drizzle. There was an imitation-wood door that looked as though it were made of aluminum. I was about to hammer on it when it opened.

I had been told I was meeting a man, but there was a woman standing there looking at me. She had no expression, the way no expression can be a hostile expression. She had straight black hair, black eyes and the kind of checked, button-down overall that women wear when they want to look really unattractive while they clean houses. I said, "Who are you?"

She turned and disappeared up an invisible staircase. She left the door open, so I figured I was supposed to follow. I stepped in. It was a steep, narrow stairwell. When I got to the top, I was in a large, shabby room with broad windows and glass doors looking out onto a large terrace and the river-lake beyond. Ugly clouds bellied low over the trees and the water.

The guy was sitting on an old sofa that had collapsed back when the world was young. He had something on his face that might have been a beard. He was wearing baggy pants with stripes of many colors, and he had one of those bags that men who wear sandals like to sling across their shoulders to make themselves look like Christian carpenters. It was open by his side, and he was rolling a cigarette and watching me while he did it. There was an empty glass on the table and a half-empty bottle of rum.

I said, "Are you —?"

Before I could finish, he said, "Agostinho, I am Agostinho Pereira."

I paused, then said, "You are Perkins. I don't want to know your real name."

He rolled his eyes, crossed his legs and licked the paper. "*Estúpido!* Like an es-spy es-story!"

He wasn't Brazilian. He was Portuguese. I could tell because he sounded Russian when he spoke. I said, "You have something for me."

He glanced at me over his rollup. "I haff time to roll a cigarette?" He showed it to me, as though I might not know what a cigarette was. I decided I didn't like him. It was an easy decision to make. I said, "Who's the woman? Does she speak English?"

He froze, gaped slightly and raised his eyebrows in an 'excuse me?' kind of gesture, like my stupidity had momentarily paralyzed him. "Joelma? English?" He gave a small laugh that was as mirthless as it was ugly. He got to his feet with an effort and walked quickly to a peeling blue door at the back of the room. He pushed through it and I saw a darkened, filthy bedroom. I heard the sound of a wardrobe door opening and he came out again, carrying a black attaché case. It was covered in leather, but I knew it was steel. He stopped in front of me and cocked his hip as he handed it over. I took it, but he didn't let go. He narrowed his eyes and gave me something that looked like the inbred cousin of a smile.

"*Try* not to be conspicuous. Don' handcuff it to your wrist or always be lookin' over your shoulder." He did an exaggerated demonstration of a person looking over their shoulder.

I said, "Let go of the case."

He screamed like a parakeet, and after a second, I realized he was laughing.

Again, I said, "Let go."

He stopped laughing and eyed me then let go of the case. "Have a drink before you go."

I shook my head. I had a bad feeling and suddenly I wanted to be out of there. I was about to say so when there was a buzz from the kitchen where Joelma was knocking pans around. I said, "Who is that?"

He shrugged, dropped onto the sofa and reached for the bottle. "People visit me. I have friends."

I was getting mad. I said, "Now? *Today?*"

Joelma came out of the kitchen and went down the stairs, muttering. I reached for my piece. Agostinho sighed and rolled his eyes. He said, "Relax, chill. Is probably my friend, Paolo." There were quiet voices downstairs, then two soft *phut!* sounds. Agostinho went pale and stared at me. I swore. There were feet tramping, running on the stairs. They erupted out of the stairwell. There were two of them, and they were *not* human.

They moved fast and without fluidity. They both wore black suits and Wayfarer sunglasses and had no expression at all on their faces. Their skin was pale, almost like china — and they were identical. I raised my Smith & Wesson and shot the nearest one point blank in the chest. He staggered back two steps then strode forward and punched from the hip. I acted without thinking and raised the attaché case. The punch connected with the steel, lifted me off my feet and threw me across the room. I landed in a heap, badly winded, and all I could think was that I mustn't let go of the case or my revolver.

The freak was staring at me. I cocked the Smith & Wesson. He turned his head to Agostinho, who was on the sofa looking real sad and shaking his head. They both advanced on him. The one who'd hit me grabbed him and dragged him to his feet. He was moaning and saying, "*Nooo, ay nooo…!*" like a kid who doesn't want to go to bed. The other freak took hold of his head, twisted and ripped it off. There was a geyser of blood that hit the ceiling as his hands and legs thrashed and jerked.

I may have shouted incoherently. I know I scrambled to my feet. I fired, but not at them. I knew that was pointless. I fired at the plate glass, and as it shattered and crashed to the floor, I ran through the shower, covering my head with the case then vaulting over the terrace. I landed on the roof of a parked car. Sprawling, I slid off and landed in a heap in the mud. I staggered to my feet and ran across the wet blacktop. Frightened eyes watched me from the *favelas.* I could hear my breathing rasping in my throat. My heart was wild. My mind raced.

I was fumbling in my pocket for the key. I had a spasm of pain in my chest from the blow. My legs were bruised and shaking from the fall. I had the key out and was sliding across the mud to my car when I heard the dull thump behind me. One of them had followed my example and jumped onto the car roof. Then I heard another. I glanced over my shoulder as my car flashed and beeped. They were running, closing on me fast.

I clambered in, hit central locking, slotted in the key and pressed the ignition. The engine roared then the window shattered and a large, hard hand was trying to grip my collar. I slammed into reverse and hit the gas. The tires spun in the mud. The car didn't move. I could feel myself being dragged toward the shattered window. A second hand was reaching in. I bellowed something incoherent. I knew I needed less gas. With my left hand, I pushed against the door, resisting their pull. They were immensely strong. I could feel myself slipping. I eased off the gas. The car jolted and began to move, pulling them with me. I felt the rear end bump onto blacktop. I floored the pedal and spun the wheel. I saw one of them thrown clear and sprawled across the road. He still had no expression on his damned face. The other was dragging and scrabbling, still gripping my collar.

I slammed on the brakes and felt him hit the rear wing. As he scrambled to his feet, I pulled the Smith & Wesson from my pocket and blew two rounds into his elbow. He didn't loosen his grip but he ripped half my collar off. I slammed into first and hit the gas again as the other guy was getting to his feet. I rammed him hard and sent him bouncing over the roof. I took the corner in third. In the rearview mirror, I could see them on their feet, climbing into the car with the dented roof.

I found a pack of Camels in my pocket, shook one halfway out and poked it into my mouth. I lit up and inhaled deep. My hands were shaking. I kept seeing Agostinho's head ripping off and his blood hitting the ceiling like a crimson fire hydrant. I took random turns left and right, not heading anywhere in particular except vaguely south and west, forcing myself to cool down. Here and there were stretches of wasteland or parks—Juiz de Fora, Villa Monte Belo and either side of the Mal, Tito Avenue where vast shanty towns of makeshift dwellings had sprung up. The misery and hunger had reached such vast proportions that they'd become invisible.

Eventually I found a car park near the Jardim Cotching area. I dumped the car and took three taxis to three different locations scattered around the city. I was pretty sure I'd lost anyone who was trying to tail me, so I caught a fourth cab to the Tivoli Hotel in the heart of town.

I had a long, hot shower followed by a longer cold one then toweled myself dry, dressed and called Russell. Even on the secure line, he insisted on talking code. I think he enjoyed it.

"Did you meet Perkins?"

"Yeah. He wasn't in good health."

"I'm sorry to hear that. What was it?"

"He had diarrhea. Verbal."

"I see. How bad was it?"

"Pretty bad. It seemed to annoy his neighbors."

"Did you—?"

"I got what I went for, but you know what he's like. He's an excitable guy. He lost his head."

"What?"

"Literally."

"That's unfortunate."

I couldn't agree. "Yeah, well, you know, that's a subjective judgment, Russell."

"I trust you weren't infected."

"No. I quarantined myself. But at the risk of taxing the metaphor, Russell, I don't know how far the bug may have spread. Let's talk when I get back. Is there anything I need to know?"

"Agreed. Like what?"

"Like what's in the case?"

"Shut up, Liam. No, you don't need to know that. I'll see you tomorrow."

"Day after. I land at seven-twenty a.m."

"Good. Have a good flight."

* * * *

I found the cocktail bar and ordered a large Black Bush. I was halfway through it and about to order another when she sat next to me. I felt her climb on the stool and I felt her watching me. I ignored her. I was missing Maria and was feeling in need of her special brand of loving right then. The last thing I needed was a pick-up. I heard her order a Bradford Martini and the exquisite, cut glass voice was strangely familiar. Then she said, "Hello, Liam. It's been a long time."

I still didn't look. I didn't need to. I said to my glass, "Catherine. Catherine Howard." Now I turned to her. "Or is it Mary Jane Carter? Or was that fake, too? What's your name now? Anne Boleyn? Scarlet O'Hara?"

The barman poured her drink and moved away. She bobbed the olive a few times and glanced at me. She had her hair cut short. It was very black. Her eyes were still green. She was stunning. She said, "I don't blame you for being angry."

"That's big of you. What the hell are you doing here?"

She picked up her drink and sipped it, watching me. She set it down, centering it carefully on the mat. "Looking for you, Liam."

I shook my head. "No."

"You need to hear me."

"Uh-uh. No, I don't."

I signaled the barman for the bill.

She said, "I know you are working with Professor Whittering—with Russell. I know why you're here."

The barman put the bill in front of me. I glanced at it, unseeing. I said, "I don't know what the hell you're talking about." I signed the bill and stood.

She said, "Please, sit down. We need to talk."

"*You* need to talk. I don't."

"You need to listen."

"Forget it!"

"I know what's in the case."

I stared at her a while. I said, "Okay, talk."

She made a small gesture with her head and her eyebrows at the stool I'd just vacated. I suddenly felt unreasonably mad—madder than the situation called for. I leaned on the bar and told the waiter to give me another Bushmills. We were quiet while he poured it. Then she said, "I've missed you."

"Cut it out."

"Why? It happens to be true."

I turned to face her. "Listen, Catherine. Every word you ever said to me was a lie. Everything you ever did was to try and manipulate me, just like you manipulated Rupert and then killed him. So, cut out the bullshit. It's not going to work."

She spent a moment tracing shapes on the bar with her finger. "That's what you remember, Liam. But there was a time when you felt something for me. That was also real."

"For me or for you? Maybe I felt something once—briefly. But the woman I cared about didn't exist. She was a lie, one of your many. So, no, you're wrong. It wasn't real."

"Are you so sure you know me, Liam?"

"What do you want, Catherine? Does Sinead know you're here?"

She didn't answer straight away. Then she said, "She sent me. She asked me to come. I didn't want to. I didn't want to see you again."

"Why? Why are you here? Why did she send you?"

She took a long time to answer—like the words were going to make a big difference and she didn't like the difference they were going to make. Finally, she said, "Sinead is working with Russell. *We* are working with Russell."

"What the hell do you mean? Why hasn't he told me this? Is this more of your bullshit, Catherine?"

"He can't tell you about it. It's classified and highly sensitive. It's not just me and Sinead. There is a group of us now. After we broke away, more followed. We are working—cooperating—with Russell and his..." She left the word unsaid.

I studied her face, thinking hard about what she was telling me. Joanna had said the same thing, that more and more were defecting. I said, "So, if Russell isn't telling me because its sensitive and classified, why are *you* telling me? And what did Sinead send you for?"

She glanced at me then down at the bar again. She was having real difficulty saying it—or she was giving an Oscar-winning performance. Both were possible. She said, "Because this concerns you. It concerns you directly. It's something you need to know."

"If that's true, Russell would have told me."

"I told you. He *can't!*"

"Why?"

"Maria is pregnant!"

My skin went cold and I felt the hair on my neck stand up.

I said, "*What?*"

"She is pregnant."

"Bullshit!"

"Liam, please—"

"How the hell would you know?"

"Please, *listen* to me!"

I could feel the rage building inside me. I was fighting to keep my voice under control. "You are *lying!* If she were pregnant, she would have—"

"She doesn't know herself yet."

"*What?* Why am I even talking to you? *God dammit! You're lying!* We've been using—"

"It's not yours."

The room moved. My head throbbed. My heart pounded once against my ribs. I felt sick. I said, "I am *not* going to listen to you. You are a lying, manipulative monster. Get away from me and *never* talk to me again. Stay *away* from me!"

The barman had stopped what he was doing and was watching. A couple of the patrons had paused in their conversation to look. I threw some money on the bar and left.

Chapter Two

I didn't sleep. I lay staring at the ceiling. The lights and sounds of Sao Paulo far below seemed to reflect off it in strange, distant echoes—broken voices, car engines and horns. They were snatches of lives that had traces of meaning like shreds of mist hanging from them but didn't touch me—the return of a shout that might be of rage or joy, left only a memory on my ceiling of a tragedy or a triumph in somebody else's life down in the street.

I knew Maria better than I knew myself. She was real and honest, and the notion that she was seeing another man was absurd. So why had Catherine disturbed me so much with what she'd said?

My mind went back to when I had first met Catherine in Noddy's Diner, when she'd first fed me her story about being blackmailed. She was a damn good liar. She had been convincing. But even then, I'd seen through her. I remembered her at the station as the train for Paris had pulled out. I remembered her in my apartment and in the hotel in Competa. She was a consummate liar. But every time she lied, I had seen through her. Even if I hadn't known what the truth was, I had known she was lying.

And, though I struggled not to admit it, this time I knew she wasn't.

I thought of Maria and of the life we had together. We'd had our problems, but we had overcome them. We'd found the way. I thought of her direct, honest gaze, of her lying in my arms at night. I tried to imagine her in another man's arms, and I couldn't. I couldn't because it wasn't real. We were together. We were solid.

I may have slipped into an uneasy sleep. I can't be sure. I thought I was awake, but it isn't always easy to tell. Consciousness can play tricks on you. I remember moonlight—a strange kind of blue moonlight—filtering in like a mist through the window. And there was a knocking at the door. I ignored it, because I was thinking about Maria, trying to kill the images that Catherine had seeded in my mind. I told myself they weren't real, that they were lies. So, I ignored the knocking.

It didn't seem to matter because she came in anyway. And, by then, I must have been dreaming because a voice in my head said, "*You must have left the door open.*" She was standing by the side of my bed, looking down at me.

I said, "*Catherine? What the hell are you doing?*" But when I said it, I realized I hadn't spoken.

And when she answered, "*I need you, Liam…*" she wasn't speaking, either.

Then she was naked.

Her skin looked cool and pale in the moonlight. Her nipples looked pink and sweet and her bush was very black in the strange light. I felt myself stirring, growing hard. I said, "*No. I don't want to do this.*"

She smiled. I heard her voice, disembodied. "*You have always wanted me. We need some candles, to bring the flame.*"

Then it was dark and she had gone. I wanted to sit up. It had been a strange dream and I wanted to switch on the light and get some water but I couldn't move. My body was heavy and paralyzed.

There was movement in the room—a rustle, a movement of air. A drawer opened and closed. A scratch and a flare of flame, and there was a warm glow of orange light at the end of my bed. I saw Catherine holding a candle and the warm wash of the amber light on her bare skin. Her eyes looked very black in the gloom. Her short hair was very black, too, and her long shadow seemed to dance on the wall behind her. I could feel my penis rock-hard pushing against my pants and the hot flood of adrenaline in my belly. I gritted my teeth and fought to move. I said, *"No! I don't want this. I love Maria. I won't betray her!"*

She turned and placed the candle on the chest of drawers.

There was another scratch and another flame flared on my right. It danced and wavered, illuminating her belly in orange light and making deep shadows under her breasts. Behind her, a black shape swelled and loomed on the wall.

A moment later, too soon for her to have moved, another rasp like a match and a flame bloomed on my left. In its dull glow, I saw her face, lit from below, smiling down at me. Behind her, the passage to the door looked very black and deep. I realized she was holding two candles now, and as the flames wavered, shadows moved around her face and eyes like living ink. She placed one on the floor, then leaned across me and placed the other on the headboard above me. Her breast was inches above my face, washed in the burnished copper of the candlelight.

She moved and her face was almost touching mine. I could see small flames dancing in her eyes. She was astonishingly beautiful, but her beauty was inhuman. It was too perfect. Her voice, unspoken, said, *"You have too many clothes on, Liam. I need you naked."*

And, somehow, she was sliding her hand over my naked chest, over my belly. Then her fingers were closing over my penis. I looked down and there was a madness in my mind. She gripped and began a gentle motion, up-and-back. I felt myself swell and grow harder. She squeezed and her rhythm grew faster.

I peered at her face and said, *"No..."*

But she wasn't looking at me. She was staring at my penis, watching it grow as she thrust down with savagery. Its size seemed crazy — too long, too thick and too hard. Then she was straddling my legs, slowing her rhythm. I could feel her bush brushing my skin. I kept repeating, over and over, *"No! No..."* She smiled at me and her face was both exquisite and evil. She leaned over real slow and the candlelight washed the skin on her back. Her hand squeezed gently, pushing down, and her lips parted. I was engulfed by the warm moistness of her mouth. I groaned, forcing my mind to think of Maria, of her sweet, beautiful face, of her deep, beautiful, trusting eyes, of her gentle sweet lips.

But dark images kept forcing me back. I could hear myself groaning as waves of intense pleasure consumed me. I opened my eyes, fighting the pleasure, and saw her watching me, smiling as she moved her mouth, taking me deep inside. I felt a strange electric tickle inside my cock. It spread through my skin with an intensity that was insane. I gasped. I heard her moan as her rhythm grew faster and she tightened her lips. The electric waves of pleasure grew more intense with every movement of her mouth. A voice in my head was screaming, "*No! No! No!*" but I couldn't tear my eyes away from her.

Then she stopped. And though my mind was praying she would leave me now, my body was screaming for relief, for the climax.

She had an ornate, blue glass bottle in her hands. She tipped oil from it into her palms. The smell was intoxicating and fogged my mind so that all I could see was her golden body in the wavering light of the candles and all I could feel was the smooth silk of her skin. I heard her voice whispering, "*You want me.*" Then her hands were on my cock, rubbing the oil into my skin, slipping and sliding, making me still harder. My brain was on fire. My breathing was ragged. Then she had her breasts on either side of my penis, smothered in oil, rubbing them. I felt a roar welling up in my chest. I kept saying, "*No! No! No!*" but the pleasure was like a raw fire. I was staring at her full breasts. The nipples were long and hard. My cock was like stone, pushing up through the fullness of her cleavage.

Then she was astride me, holding me with her fingertips, guiding me. I slipped inside. My eyes were locked on her face as the walls of her vagina pulsed against me. She was rising, pausing, then dropping. Her rhythm was growing faster and I was growing harder as she pushed down on me. I was gritting my teeth, holding my breath, fighting the feeling—fighting the raw pleasure, but there was a voice in my head telling me I had never seen anything so beautiful as her face. Her eyes were huge, dark pools. Her lips were intensely red. Her skin was like fire-lit porcelain. With a suddenness that overwhelmed me, the strange, electric tingling in my cock swelled into a rush that flooded my skin and I was roaring like an animal, pounding up into her, hearing her scream, watching her grind on me, clawing at my chest, digging deep with her nails—and the pain was exquisite.

She fell on me. I could feel her tongue on my neck, licking my sweat, as her body thrashed against mine and her hot vagina clenched and pulsed on my penis in slowing, throbbing spasms. She twitched, breathing hard in my ear. The pulsing slowed. My breathing was ragged. We pushed and slipped against each other and slowly she slid her face up, brushing her cheek against mine. Her short black hair was ruffled and stuck to her face with perspiration. Her lips brushed mine and she kissed me. I tried to turn away, but I couldn't move. Then she ran her tongue over my chest and slowly climbed off me.

My body and skin were aching, pulsing. The candles went out, and I plunged into a deep, black sleep.

* * * *

I woke up and a sleepy sun was filtering through the window. Different sounds were now rising from the street below—sounds that spoke of coffee and *bolo de fubá*, of a new day, of rattling steel blinds and squeaking awnings, of early sunlight stretching and yawning across a fresh blue sky.

I levered myself onto one elbow and wondered why I was relieved I could move—wondered why I was surprised I was dressed. I noticed I had not got into bed and remembered I'd come up without having dinner. Then memories started to seep back.

Catherine.

I sat up. It had been a dream.

It *must* have been a dream.

I got to my feet. I was unsteady. I walked to the bathroom and pushed open the door. I turned on the shower and started to undress, throwing my clothes on the floor as I went. I turned on the cold tap in the basin and bent to splash water on my face. It was then, as I was toweling myself, that I saw the claw marks on my chest.

Chapter Three

There was dense fog on the South Downs. I crawled from Gatwick to Chichester and the fog didn't let up. I'd never seen anything like it. But unprecedented weather was becoming the norm these days. In fact, the unprecedented in general was the norm these days.

My instinct, when I'd climbed into my car at the long-term parking lot at the airport, had been to go straight to London to see Maria—not just because I hadn't seen her for almost a week but because of Catherine's unexpected visit in Sao Paulo. There was an unarticulated need in me to touch base and make sure everything was okay.

But that wasn't possible. I had no idea what was in the case, and I kept telling myself that if Russell hadn't wanted to tell me, he had a damn good reason. I knew I had to get it to him before I did anything else, however much I needed to see Maria. Progress was slow and frustrating. I switched on the radio, but it wasn't much help. Drought and steadily climbing temperatures worldwide had killed two years of wheat crops and crippled the economy of the Ukraine. Now they were hitting hard in the prairie states of the USA, especially in Kansas. The wheat market had gone into crisis. Reserves were exhausted. There was not enough production to replace them and prices were spiraling out of control. If a solution wasn't found, it looked like bread would become more expensive than gold in the next twelve months.

Meanwhile, China was talking about halting rice exports because her paddies were drying up. The climate change lobby was shouting about the greenhouse effect, but the hawks were talking about discredited alarmists and the environmental conspiracies of the liberal left. Even Sir Jeremy Luff, the father of the Living Earth theory, had gone on record as saying that early predictions on climate change had been alarmist. I wondered how different the forecasts would have been if they'd been accurate.

But the headlines belonged, as always, to the Middle East. With world agriculture in crisis, the Arab countries were desperate to import food and the price of Middle East oil was in free fall. Overnight, in what had been some of the richest countries in the world, hunger had become a stark reality. After years of crippling armed conflicts, now famine and scorching temperatures in the high fifties Celsius were killing the old and the very young alike in the thousands. The mullahs raged that it was Allah's punishment for straying from the true faith. Their jihadist warriors waged their imbecilic war of atrocities on the weak and the vulnerable with weapons sold to them by blameless billionaires in London, Washington and Moscow and US and British troops stood poised to invade Iraq, Iran and Syria. Russia watched, scowled and warned that any such invasion would lead to all-out global war.

So, distracted by the Middle East, nobody watched the CO_2 counters. The Brotherhood must be pleased with themselves — no bread, but plenty of circus.

I eventually arrived at Russell's place in Fishbourne at just after eleven a.m. It looked ghostly as I crawled among strands of mist into the narrow road by the Millpond. There was a heavy silence. On my right, the shadow of the willow seemed to drift in and out of the fog that crept from the pond, occasionally obscuring the road. Russell's house, across the road from the water, was a crooked, shadowy form with rickety chimneys, like fingers trying to claw their way back to the sunlight. It loomed and faded as the billows rolled across the road.

I parked by the willow and climbed out of my TVR Daemon. The door slammed with a deadened echo and the double beep of the lock and the tap of my heels as I crossed the blacktop seemed strangely desolate in the closed world of the fog.

I rang the bell and heard it chime a long way off inside the house. I heard hurrying feet. The door opened. Mrs. Byrd stood looking at me in a blue-and-white-checked apron with a wooden spoon in her hand. She said, "He's in the library. You know the way. I have the stew on the boil."

I went through to the library, ducking through the doorway to avoid the eight-hundred-year-old beams. He was sitting by the open fire, in a Chesterfield wingchair that looked like it might have been as old as the beams in the ceiling. The library was small, no more than fifteen foot across, and it was warm from the heat of the open fire. The only light was a standard lamp behind his chair and what little came in through the leaded windows. Russell was asleep with an old hardback open on his chest. He appeared frail, and I wondered how old he was. He could have been anything from seventy to a hundred and seventy. I peered at the book. *Den Ældre Edda, En samling af de nordiske folks ældste sagn og sange* by Finnur Magnusson

He must have sensed my presence because he snapped open his eyes and he was wide awake. His eyes weren't frail or ageless. They seemed to be about nineteen. He said, "Yes, Odin was frightfully devious, not the way people tend to think of him at all. Quite disgraceful, really. Have you asked Byrd for tea?"

I showed him the case and placed it by his side. Then I sat in the large calico chair opposite him. His house was furnished for comfort, not style. I said, "She's making a stew. And she has a dangerous-looking wooden spoon."

"Phooey!" He had a brass bell by his side and rang it. Then, without waiting for her to appear, bellowed, "Tea, Mrs. Byrd! And *biscuits!*" Then he watched me for a bit. "So Agostinho bought it, did he? Poor sod. He always was a fool. I suppose he had been mouthing off, hadn't he?"

I nodded. "I think so. He was arrogant, stupid and a

show-off. Where the hell did you find him?" I waited for an answer but he just shook his head. I said, "It wasn't pretty. I never saw anything like it before."

Mrs. Byrd brought in a tray of tea. There was also a plate of hot, cinnamon toast. She peered at Russell with a face you wouldn't want to argue with and said, "You don't want biscuits on a day like this. You want something warm. Cinnamon toast. My mother swore by it. Biscuits, indeed!"

Russell ignored her and she gave me a look as she turned to go, like we had conspired together and got one over on the old goat. I winked at her and she blushed. When she'd gone, Russell said, "What exactly did you see?"

He poured tea and handed me a cup. I told him what had happened and he listened, staring into his cup. He didn't sip till I'd finished. Then he said, "That is very troubling. It means they have introduced a new weapon into the field and one that is only very superficially disguised."

I added, "Meaning they're not too bothered anymore whether people notice them or not."

He nodded. "They are becoming bolder. I don't want to speculate about why. Have you seen the papers this morning?"

I shook my head. "No. I heard the news on the radio, but it was the same old same old, as far as I could tell."

He reached down by his side and pulled up bits of the *Daily Telegraph*. "It wouldn't have been on the radio or the television." He folded it to the right page and tossed it to me. "Have a look."

I glanced and saw a small column on the science page. The headline said, *HEAT Corporation to Experiment in Wireless Energy Transmission*. I put it on my lap and said, "There's something else, Russell. Catherine Howard turned up at the hotel."

He froze with a piece of toast half way to his mouth. He put it back on his plate and said, "What did she...? What did she want?"

I was watching him with growing interest. I said, "I'm not

sure. She said she knew why I was there. She said Sinead had sent her and she knew what was in the case. She said you were working with Sinead — with *them*."

He grunted then he eyed me a second. "Did she tell you what was in the case?"

I shook my head. "No. But she told me Maria was pregnant and that the baby isn't mine."

He folded up the toast as though it was a letter to his solicitor and slotted it into his mouth, then he chewed like he was searching for answers in the taste of cinnamon and butter. He swallowed and drained his cup. He said, "I need to talk to Reggie."

I said, "You need to talk to *me*. What's going on, Russell?"

He shook his head. "I can't tell you anything about Maria" — he paused, staring at the floor — "except that I very much doubt she's been having an affair. Women are unpredictable and unknowable. Sigmund said it and he was right, but even so, I don't see it." He stopped, like he was making a bigger effort to see. Then he made a face like impatience and said, "As to the case, I can't tell you about that until I've spoken to Reggie."

"Has it got something to do with Sinead?"

He stared into the fire. The glow made his face look orange and cast deep shadows around his eyes. He appeared diabolical. Outside, the fog was turning to drizzle and there was a wet tapping at the window, like a clock throwing away used seconds. He said, "Go and talk to Maria. Find out what it's about. That's your priority for now. I'll talk to Reggie then we'll see where we go from there."

I said I wouldn't stay for lunch. Mrs. Byrd gave Russell a look that said it was his fault I was going out into the fog and the rain. I stepped into the damp drizzle with a pit in my stomach, wanting to see Maria, wanting to know she was mine but sick at the thought of what I might find instead.

Chapter Four

The fog was lifting and the drizzle was turning to rain. The camps in Richmond Park had expanded in the few days I'd been away. They'd started as tent cities for refugees from the droughts and Middle Eastern conflicts but had swelled to take in the growing numbers of our own homeless and dispossessed, victims of the economic crash caused by what the media was now calling The Drought. North of the fifty-second parallel it wouldn't stop raining – that in itself was having a devastating effect on crops – but south of the fifty-second parallel, it hadn't rained for two years and temperatures were soaring into the fifties Celsius as far north as France. Famine had spread from Pakistan through Iran, Turkey, Georgia and the Ukraine, right across the northern Mediterranean. In the south, it had spread like wildfire to Senegal and South Africa.

All along Hammersmith Road and Kensington High Street there were shops, restaurants and even pubs boarded up. Nobody had any money to spend anymore. Instead, the people who used to be customers now slept in the doorways, because their homes had been repossessed by the banks.

I turned onto Church Street and parked outside my building. I hadn't phoned Maria to tell her I was back. I pulled out my cell and stared at it. I could have called her at any time since I'd landed, but I hadn't. I knew why I hadn't and felt sick at myself. My thumb hovered over the speed dial. The memory was big and bright in my mind's eye, when I'd walked in and found her laughing on the sofa with Stephan. It had been innocent on her part, but I could still feel the hot anger in my belly. What would I find now if I went up without calling? A sick twist knotted my gut and I put the phone in my pocket.

I took my bag and climbed the stairs, keeping an eye on the elevator to see if anybody rode it down. Nobody did. I slipped the key in the lock and was aware that I did it quietly. I stepped in and closed the door behind me without making any sound. Then I stood, listening. I'd stopped even trying to kid myself. I was listening for sounds of her with a man. There was only silence. The bedroom door was open. I got another sick twist in my belly as I saw her, in my mind's eye, lying asleep with her head on another man's chest, the way she did with me.

I hesitated then stepped through the door. The bed was empty. The *en suite* was empty, too. She wasn't in the apartment. I threw my bag on the bed and went to stand looking out of the window, turning my cell over in my pocket.

I kept telling myself I knew her and I trusted her.

I heard the key in the lock and turned. She came through the door with a couple of carrier bags. She saw me and her face lit up. She dropped the bags and ran. Next thing, she was in my arms, clinging to me and smothering my face in kisses. It took me a minute to register what she was saying. She was saying she had news, wonderful news.

I felt sick. The room moved. She was saying, "Sit down. I'll just put the shopping away. It's so wonderful. Why didn't you call? Do you want a drink? Have you eaten?"

I took the bags and followed her into the kitchen. She was talking too much, too fast, not leaving any spaces for me to answer. She kept grabbing my arm and my shirt and jumping up and down. I helped her put the things away without speaking, listening to her barrage of words. Had I gone to Russell's? Had I eaten? Was I hungry? She led me back to the drawing room and set me on the sofa. She sat next to me with our knees touching and took my hands in hers. Her face was radiant. She looked beautiful. She said,

"Are you ready?"

I laughed—forced myself to laugh—and said, "Sure. What is it? Did you win the lottery?"

She smiled a deep smile and said, "Better than that. Baby, I'm pregnant. Five weeks..."

She kept talking. She'd been feeling queasy in the morning. She'd missed her period. The room was moving. My heart was thumping hard and I felt nauseous. I was thinking... five weeks. Five weeks. *Where was I? Where was I five weeks ago? Where was* she? I must have gone pale because she was frowning.

"Are you okay, Liam? You *are* happy?"

I squeezed her hands. "Of course, I am, babe. I'm just—" I shook my head. "How? I thought you were..."

She was smiling again. "That's what I asked the doctor. Apparently, it does happen. The pill is ninety-nine-point-nine percent sure." She cocked her head, half-frowning, a little sad. "I know we weren't planning it, Liam, but now that it's happened..."

I shook my head. "You've got me wrong, baby." I stood. I went to the drinks tray and poured myself a whiskey. She was watching me, waiting. I watched her back, then said, "Catherine Howard turned up at my hotel in Sao Paulo."

She frowned. "Catherine Howard? From Çalares?" I nodded. She said, "What the hell did *she* want?"

"That's what I asked her."

She waited, then said, "And?"

"She was there to tell me you were pregnant."

Her face clenched like a fist. "*What?*" I didn't answer. She said, "How the hell did *she* know?"

I shook my head. After a beat, I said, "I told her I didn't believe her." Her expression told me she knew there was more, so I told her, "She also said it wasn't mine."

She went ashen then, like stone. I saw her reading my face. She said, "And you believed her."

It wasn't a question but I shook my head. "No. I told her I didn't believe her."

"But now you're not sure."

"I didn't say that."

"You don't need to."

"Maybe you're wrong. Maybe you're reading me wrong."

"Am I?"

I rubbed my face. I felt suddenly exhausted. I didn't want to be having this conversation. I kept getting flashbacks of Agostinho, grabbed by the two freaks, his head twisting as they tore it off. I just wanted to hold Maria and lie with her in the darkened room and know I was home.

Home.

I tried to remember five weeks back. There was just an empty space in my head. Without thinking I said, "Five weeks ago, where were we? What happened?"

She stared at me, angry. She said, "You need to ask?" She stood up. "This is the second time, Liam. If you don't trust me by now... If you can't learn to trust me..." She shook her head and left the sentence unfinished.

I said, "Where are you going?"

She didn't look at me. "Maybe I'm going to meet the father of my baby."

She walked away. I heard the door slam.

My baby. She had said '*My baby*.'

My baby.

From the window, I watched her cross the road, heading down to High Street Ken. I felt I was having déjà vu. *Stephan*. But Stephan was Rinpoche and Rinpoche was dead. I asked myself "Who then?" and realized I was assuming that what Catherine had said was true. It was the oldest trick in the trade to mix true information with lies to create disinformation. But if it was a lie, how the hell had she known Maria was pregnant?

Five weeks. Why couldn't I remember?

I pressed quick-dial on my cell and Russell answered after two rings.

"Liam..."

"She's pregnant."

"Don't jump to any conclusions."

"Quit bullshitting me, Russell. What the hell's going on?"

He sighed. "I don't know."

"I don't believe you. You know something."

He was quiet. Then he said, "Liam, have you upset her?"

"Are you kidding me? How did Catherine know Maria was pregnant, Russell? Why is Catherine telling me I'm not the father?"

I have never heard Russell shout and he didn't shout then, but he barked, "*Liam!* Shut *up!*" It sobered me a bit and I quieted and listened. "I don't know the answers to your questions, Liam, but I do know what they are *not!* Now, if your instinct is telling you to trust Maria—and I know it is—then, for goodness sake, trust her!"

It made sense and I realized it was what I'd wanted him to say. It was why I'd called him. I said, "Okay."

"Is she there?"

"No."

"She's marched off?"

"Yeah."

"Go and find her. Apologize. Tell her you support her and you trust her. Don't let Catherine come between you. I'll get back to you as soon as I can."

The phone went silent. I sat staring at it. I couldn't shake the sick feeling in my gut. I dialed her number. It rang once and she answered straight away.

I said, "Baby?"

"Liam."

"Where are you?"

"In Hyde Park. Liam, I'm sorry—"

"No, babe. I'm sorry. I was stupid. I *do* trust you. You know I do."

"No. I should have thought. I can't imagine what you must have felt."

"She's a liar. She's a compulsive liar, babe."

"Will you come and get me?"

I smiled, even though she couldn't see me. "Yeah. I'm

coming, sweetheart."

I found her by the Round Pond under her violet umbrella, watching the small raindrops make ripples on the water. I stood next to her with the rain in my hair and on my face. She looked up at me and smiled and we remained, kissing slow and deep for a long time, holding on to each other like we were never going to let go.

It was a moment I was going to remember many times over the next few days.

Chapter Five

It was four in the morning. I was sitting by the open windows, smoking and drinking whiskey. The fog had settled again and the street lamps were luminous pools of amber in a dull world of damp gray. There was absolute silence. There was the rhythmic slap of water falling from a gutter. In a secret place, hidden by the mist, a tin can fell from a dumpster and rolled. Two cats yowled and spat. But these noises, distant and muffled, seemed to knock at the edges of the silence without ever disturbing it, just like the red, amber and green lights of the pedestrian crossing slipped and rippled on the puddles without ever penetrating their liquid blackness.

I flicked the butt out of the window, watched the sparks flair and die and heard the hiss down in the street. F. Scott Fitzgerald had said something about the long, dark night of the soul, where it was always three in the morning. It would be dawn in an hour, but I'd never see it in this fog.

Somewhere, an engine whined as it climbed through the gears. At first, the mist made it impossible to locate, but then I saw two sets of headlamps staining the fog orange as they moved up the hill from High Street Ken. They were moving fast – too fast – but stopped suddenly outside my building. They looked like Land Rovers. I heard the muffled slam of doors. I counted six. Hazy figures took up positions by the vehicles, like they were on guard. Two more figures moved though the billows, running to my building's entrance. I made for the drawer where I keep my Smith & Wesson. I checked it was loaded, cocked it and positioned myself at an angle in front of the door. All the lights were out, so I'd be in shadow and they would be backlit from the landing. I waited.

I heard the elevator stop and the doors open, feet tramping. They weren't even trying to be silent. I was thinking of the porcelain-faced freaks in Sao Paulo. I was telling myself, *shoot at the eyes*. I trained the gun at head height, braced myself and the doorbell rang.

I moved to the door, stood to the side and quietly said, "Who is it?"

"It's Russell. Open up, Liam, quickly!"

I peered through the spy-hole. I saw Russell in the fisheye view and behind him, Brigadier Reggie Hook. I opened the door and they pushed in.

I said, "What the hell?"

Russell snapped, "Not now. Get Maria, pack a couple of bags with the essentials. *Quickly!*" Hook was over by the window in the shadows, staring out. In his hand, he had a Sig 9mm.

I slipped my .44 in my waistband and went to the bedroom. I knew Russell well enough to know he was serious. I woke Maria as gently as I could. She looked at me, warm and sleepy, frowning. "What's going on?"

"You need to get up, baby—fast. We need to move out."

She was frowning harder now, scratching her head. "What?"

"Don't ask questions, honey, just do it. I'll explain as we go."

I was already throwing things in a bag.

She was sitting with her feet on the floor, legs bare and hair ruffled. "Can I wash?"

"No."

She glanced at me, registered it was serious then started dressing.

We left the lights off and slipped out of the apartment. Hook led the way down the stairs as I closed the door. When we reached the lobby, he took my keys, signaled for us to wait and went to the door. There was a brief exchange with one of the guys by the car. He turned, gestured us to move out and we clambered in the lead Land Rover. Hook got in the front and we took off. The fog was still thick. Visibility was maybe thirty-to-fifty yards.

I said, "Where are we going?"

Hook raised his hand to silence me and the driver spoke, "Alfa two. They've entered Church Street, bottom end."

Hook said, "Pull over. Kill the lights and the engine."

The driver was pulling in, repeating Hook's words before he'd finished. "Pull over. Kill lights and engine."

I realized he was talking into a radio. The Land Rover behind us and my Daemon pulled in ten yards back. I turned to check out of the rear window. Hook said, "Keep still. Don't move."

We were motionless. A dull glow appeared in the mist. It grew brighter, then divided like a cell and a dark Audi emerged from the fog and halted outside my building. The lights died and the doors opened. Two men in suits and dark glasses got out. Their faces appeared luminous in the diffused light from the street lamps. The driver started around the hood and the passenger moved to the street door.

I whispered, "That's *them*."

Hook immediately replied, "Quiet!"

They stopped. They looked straight at us, scanning the fog. My heart was pounding high in my chest. I could hear my own breath rasping. I fought to control it. The seconds seemed to dilate into minutes. They glanced at each other and stepped into the lobby and out of sight. Hook raised his hand, signaling we should remain silent and immobile. I counted to thirty, then he said, "Okay. Move out. Quiet and steady."

The driver said, "Move out on ten. Quiet and steady."

We pulled away and headed up the road in the direction of Notting Hill Gate. Ten seconds later, the rear cars pulled out and followed us. As we hit the Gate, Hook said, "Okay, go!"

The car surged and we were doing fifty through the fog, flooded by the headlamps of the car behind. We ducked into Portobello, took a couple of sharp turns, doubled back on ourselves then we were crossing Ladbroke Grove down Cambridge Gardens, then Du Cane Road doing eighty miles an hour with visibility down to maybe fifty yards. We jumped the lights at East Acton and cut onto the A40, headed west to Oxford doing a hundred and twenty miles per hour.

We were speeding through a hazy yellow tunnel of cloud. Maria was holding my arm. I peered through the rear window. Powerful headlamps glared through the haze. I turned back to Russell. I said, "What's going on, Russell?"

He was staring down at his knees. He didn't answer at first. When he did, he said, "We are taking you to a safe house."

Maria glanced at me, then at Russell. She said, "Why?"

He faced her, and his expression was hard to read in the dim light and the moving shadows. He said, "You are pregnant, Maria. It's important you are kept safe."

I knew then something was wrong – real wrong. I could sense Maria knew it, too. Hook said, "We'll talk when we get to the house. Try to get some rest."

She settled her head on my shoulder and closed her eyes. We drove in silence for maybe an hour or a little more. After a time, we came off the highway, plunging into deep countryside. The fog started to turn pale as the sun rose at dawn, but it didn't lift. It just billowed and trailed across fields and hedgerows like a defeated army of over-fed ghosts. I had no idea where we were, except that it was west and a little north of London. Aside from that, we could have been anywhere.

We came to a crossroads. I could just make out some small wooden signs. One way said Chute, Oxenwood. The other said Vernham Dean, Hungerford. A third option was a dirt track. The driver spun the wheel and we went down the track between fields. Eventually, we came to an esplanade.

The fog drifted listlessly, this way and that, like it didn't know where it was going. Through it, I could see barns or stables on the left and a huge Tudor manor on the right. We climbed out into the dank air. Doors thudded and slammed. I took hold of Maria, and we made our way inside.

There was a vast walk-in fireplace in the drawing room with three huge logs burning in it. The flames danced in the leaded windows against the cloudy gray outside. The smell of burning wood was strong on the air. Russell went and stood staring into the blaze, clenching and unclenching his hands. Maria took hold of me and rested her head on my chest. Behind me, Hook came in with our driver and two other guys. They were all in jeans and leather jackets and had that look that only British Special Forces have—real tough and politely insolent.

Hook gestured with his head at our driver. "This is Captain Byrd and these are Sergeant Brown and Trooper Green. They'll be taking care of you for the immediate future."

Sergeant Brown was gaunt and wiry. He appeared hard, the way an oak tree appears hard. He was bald and had a big moustache and the slow eyes of an experienced killer. Trooper Green was younger, maybe in his twenties. He was clean-shaven and looked like he was amused but he was keeping it a secret. Hook turned to them and said, "Sergeant, you take the upstairs with Green. Captain, you take the back. Hargreaves has the perimeter. Radio silence unless critical."

They left. Hook picked up the house phone and pressed a button. He said, "On site," and hung up. Then he pressed a button on the wall, turned to Maria and me and said, "There's a bedroom upstairs. It's as secure as anywhere in the house and Brown and Green will be keeping permanent watch over it. The entire house also has a highly sophisticated electronic security system and there are armed guards inside and out. I suggest you get some sleep, Maria."

While he'd been speaking, a woman of about fifty had

come in and was smiling at Maria. She said, "Shall I show you to your room, dear?"

Maria gave me a kiss and left with the woman. I stared at Hook then at Russell, who was still gazing at the flames. I said, "Feel like telling me what's going on now?"

Hook nodded. "I wish we knew."

A young man came in with a tray of coffee. He set it on a sideboard by the leaded window and withdrew, closing the door behind him. I was aware of Maria on the other side of the door, cut off from me upstairs. Hook poured three cups, strong and black, handed one to Russell and another to me then he sat in a chair by the fire with the flames bathing his face in wavering orange light. I stood by the mantelpiece. Hook spoke with his gaze lost in the flames.

"The HEAT Corporation is installing a large dish aerial on the Lyn Celyn Fusion Reactor. The reactor is due to go online in about twelve months."

He glanced at me and sipped his coffee. I said, "What's the aerial for?"

"That was what we wanted to know as soon as we found out about it. We have" — he paused and studied his coffee, like there were words in there and he wanted to choose the right ones — "friends at Lyn Celyn, and they got information to us."

I interrupted him, "Sinead's people?"

He hesitated. Russell glanced at me. Russell said, "Yes."

Hook said, "That isn't important."

I snapped, "To you."

He gave me a once-over that told me he wasn't used to being spoken to like that. He said, "All right, we'll come back to that point. Now, hear me out. When you were in Algeria at the installations of the Kallisti Corporation, you witnessed some experiments in progress. Do you recall?"

I nodded. "Yeah, of course. They were using IT appliances, tablets, cells, computers."

He nodded. "Correct. We think the dish aerial is not to receive — at least, not *only* to receive. We think it is primarily to transmit. If we are right, it would transmit a signal to a necklace of satellites that would, in turn, transmit back to Earth. The story is that it's part of a new generation of improved telecommunications, a project called LYRE — Link-Yoked Reference Exchange, that will bring signal coverage to every corner of the globe. By a process called link-yoking, it is supposed to transmit a blanket signal that is picked up by every cell phone, every tablet, every computer — every IT appliance on the planet. There will not be a square inch of the globe that does not have coverage. But, we suspect, it may be linked to their research into passive compliance. We think it may be a way of, as it were, 'switching off' the ability for the brain to act independently, with self-determination." He spread his hands. "Effectively a way of creating slaves."

I wanted to say that it sounded like cheap science fiction, but I had learned better than that over the last couple of years. I had seen that induced passive compliance with my own eyes — that and more. Hook was talking again.

"We think they will use a signal that's encoded into a kind of computer modem. We think it was partly developed in Algeria at the Kallisti installation and partly at the LYRE research facility in Alaska. An associate of ours managed to steal the modem we think contains the codes.

I said, "The case I collected from Agostinho."

Russell turned to look at me but his face told me nothing about his thoughts. Hook nodded.

"Yes. Clearly — as you discovered to your cost — they know we have it and they intend to get it back."

I sat on the sofa opposite Hook. Russell was watching me, like he was waiting for me to say something. I watched him back for a moment then said to Hook, "They know we have it, probably because Agostinho was a bigmouth, but is there a chance we have a leak?"

Hook looked unhappy. "I can't answer that question, Murdoch."

I said what he didn't want to say. "You can account for

your people, but you can't speak for Sinead's." They didn't answer. That was good enough for me. I said, "They want the modem back. Why don't you just destroy it?"

"Because we don't know if they have back-ups or how hard it would be to replace it."

I frowned. "So?"

Russell spoke for the first time. "*So*, we need to see exactly what it is then reverse engineer it so that we understand how it works and we can protect ourselves against it. And that brings us to the next point."

"Which is?"

He sighed. "We know from you — and from other sources — that there is an elite of immensely rich and powerful people in industry and politics who have allied themselves with the" — he hesitated, like he didn't know what to call them. He settled on — "the Brotherhood. Clearly, these people will need to be protected or immunized in some way against this signal."

"How will they do that?"

"We don't know for certain yet. That's why this process of reverse engineering is so important. We assume a way must exist, but, as yet, we don't know what it is."

I reached in my pocket and took out a pack of Camels. As I peeled it and pulled one out, I said, "So you plan to reverse engineer the modem and develop some kind of defense mechanism so we end up with the same technology as them."

Hook said, "Perhaps. Apparently, the number of humans who will form this elite in the New Order is one thousand, six hundred and eighteen. They consider themselves the Elect — or the Anointed. And they are all associated in some way with the Cavendish Foundation."

I frowned. "The Cavendish Foundation?"

"It's a foundation established by the Cavendish family —"

"The ex-President?"

He nodded. "Its official purpose is to stimulate trade with third-world and Islamic countries. What they actually do is facilitate arms deals with terrorist organizations and pariah regimes in exchange for vast sums of money. But they have a still-deeper function and that is to sell seats at the top table."

I said, "What do you mean, 'seats at the top table'?"

Hook had been quiet for a while. Now, he spoke up, "Essentially, they are selling princedoms in the New Order. If you are rich enough or powerful enough, you can buy yourself a princedom. When the great, catastrophic event occurs and the Ael, the Naga—whatever you want to call them—reclaim Earth, you can be one of the Elect, one of the princes in the New Eden. All you have to do is grease the palms of the Cavendish Foundation."

Russell was nodding. "There are one thousand six hundred and eighteen places to be had. Most of them have already been allocated. The point is, these 'princes' are human, and there must be some way in which they will be protected from this signal. We need to know how."

I sucked on my cigarette and blew smoke at the ceiling. I was thinking of Maria upstairs and the unborn child in her belly and I was getting mad. I said, "You got all this from Sinead and Catherine?"

They glanced at each other. Then Russell said, "From Sinead." He paused then added, "And others who have followed her."

I looked at the tip of my cigarette. It was growing light outside and the fog was turning to drizzle. I said. "You kept me out of the loop before. Why are you telling me this now?"

Russell said, "We are working under strict security, Liam. We can't afford to get personal about this. The fact that we are confiding in you now is a measure of our trust. We want you to take the modem to a lab—"

I cut across him. I was fighting to keep the anger from my voice. I loved this guy and I'd have done anything for him, but there was a rage building inside me. I said, "These creatures are trying to kill my wife and my baby, and I want to know why. I call that pretty personal, Russell. And while we're on the subject, who is 'we' exactly? Do 'we' know whether this baby is mine or not? And if it's not, who *is* the father? Only, it would be nice to know, if 'we' think I am entitled to know, that is." They appeared embarrassed. I gave them a minute to suck it up then added, "Maybe it's not personal to you. To me, it's pretty damn personal."

Russell sighed, like he'd forgotten his keys or his wallet and had to waste time going back to get them. He said, "I didn't say it wasn't personal, Liam. I said we can't afford to get personal. You must know that anything that affects you and Maria is personal to me."

I stood and walked to the window. The fog had lifted some, but there was still a low ceiling of slate-gray clouds and a steady patter of rain. The hedgerows looked sodden and desolate. Hook said, "It's understandable, the way you feel. Of course this affects you personally in many ways."

Russell said, "But I must insist. We are talking about the survival of the human race—of the entire species. If we are going to survive, we cannot *afford* to take these things personally. We have to remain hard-headed and objective, Liam, and we are relying on you."

I nodded. "I know." I turned to face them. "So where do I have to take this modem?"

Hook said, "Gdansk, in Poland."

"When?"

"Tomorrow."

I put the coffee cup down on the sideboard and crossed my arms. "Okay, I'll do it. Now tell me what the fuck is happening with Maria."

Russell said, "We don't know, Liam."

"Bullshit! Is that the same 'we' that is showing me the measure of their trust?"

Hook turned to face me and he looked mad. "You are out of order and you need to calm down."

"I'll calm down when you tell me what the *fuck* is happening with Maria!"

41

Hook was about to answer but Russell spoke first. "Catherine has gone rogue. I spoke to Sinead. It wasn't easy. She is not an *easy* person to find or connect with, but I spoke to her. The most I was able to get out of her was that they knew she was pregnant."

"So, is the baby mine or not, Russell?"

He rubbed his face with his hands. "Look, Liam, I asked her several times and, quite frankly, she didn't seem to understand the question. They are different than us. They don't have the same values and priorities."

I spoke real quietly. "Russell, if I don't get a straight answer from somebody in the next five seconds, I am going to burn this fucking house down then I'm going to go to Gdansk and I'm going to burn your fucking lab down. After that, I'm going to find Sinead. tear her head off and shove it up her *fucking* ass, and maybe then she'll begin to understand *our* fucking values! Is the baby *mine*? Am I the baby's *fucking* father? *Yes* or *no?*"

Hook had got to his feet. He was preparing to call his guys. I was half hoping he would. Russell said, "I simply don't know, Liam. All I can tell you is what she told me. They knew she was pregnant. If it's any consolation, she told me that Maria had not had any other mate than you."

For a few seconds, my whole body was flooded with a strange mixture of rage and relief. I gritted my teeth. "Was that so *goddamn* difficult to say, Russell? Couldn't you have told me that an hour ago?"

He averted his eyes. Hook said, "Okay, Murdoch. Now you know, you can calm down and get a grip. This isn't easy for anyone."

I stared at him, trying to remember this guy was my friend and my ally. I said, "I need some sleep. I'll see you later."

I climbed the stairs and found the room. I undressed and climbed into bed next to Maria. She looked like she was sleeping. Her breathing was soft. I put my arms around her and held her close. I sensed her smile. She whispered, "We thought you were never going to come."

I kissed her shoulder and smiled. I knew the answer, but I asked anyway. "We?"

She held my arms and kissed my hands. "Baby and me."

Chapter Six

Hook had booked me on a flight to San Francisco via Casablanca, Rome, Helsinki and Ottawa. He'd gone to considerable lengths to keep the reservations off the radar. He had then dispatched a guy of my build and similar looks, armed with an attaché case, to take that long, pointless odyssey. The expectation was that the Brotherhood would pick up the tortuous journey to San Francisco and assume we were taking the modem to somebody in Silicon Valley. While they followed the decoy, he had provided me with documents in the name of David Price and booked David Price on a direct flight to Gdansk from Heathrow airport.

Hook and I had driven alone to the airport through torrential rain. The wipers had beaten a rhythm like a panicking heart. I had asked him, "You have a Tudor manor in Wiltshire and four guys from the world's most elite special ops corps assigned to the protection of a young woman who is not a diplomat or a politician. How much is that costing?" I'd peered out into the hiss of spray as we overtook a truck. "You want to explain that to me?"

Something like a smile had creased his face for a few seconds, then gone back inside where I couldn't see it. He'd said, "Not really," and added, "You are both valuable to us, Murdoch."

I'd thought about that for a mile or two and eventually had asked him, "Who's 'us' — the British Government?"

"You're not cleared for that yet." He'd gone quiet then until we'd arrived at the terminal. He'd driven down into the underground car park, pulled over and left the engine running. Before I'd gotten out, he'd said, "Concepts like the British Government, the US government, the EU... They have no meaning anymore, Murdoch. You need to understand that the whole structure of human society is disintegrating. There are other" — he'd paused then and turned away into the darkness, like he had been searching for a word in the shadows, a word that hadn't been invented yet — "*other* forces are at work now, with *other* priorities and objectives." He'd looked me in the eye. "Will you accept that for now? We will protect Maria with our lives, Murdoch. You can rely on that — not just because she is valuable to us and our cause, but because you are both our friends." I had drawn breath to ask a question but he'd shaken his head. "No, don't ask. When the time is right, you will be introduced to the cause and its leaders. Until then" — he'd shrugged and smiled — "don't trust us. Trust your own experience. Has Russell ever let you down or acted dishonorably?"

I had sat watching him, thinking. Then he'd held out is hand and we'd shaken. It had felt odd. It had only been later, on the plane, that I'd realized it had felt more like a welcome than a goodbye.

Now I was headed down *Juliusza Slowackiego* in a rented Ford, driving through dense woodland toward *Mysliwska*. There was no rain here, but there was a low ceiling of clouds — a ceiling that seemed to be sitting over the whole of northern Europe. It made a landscape that should have been green and vibrant, dull and oppressive.

I took a right at the big roundabout onto *Bulonska* and five minutes after that I was pulling up outside a terrace of five blocks of post-Soviet apartments that backed onto a dense woodland just outside the city. I killed the engine, lit a Camel and sat for a while smoking and keeping my eye on my mirrors. Nobody drove up. Nobody appeared. Nobody showed. After five minutes, I got out, dropped what was left of the butt on the ground, trod on it and pulled the attaché case out of the back of the car. Nobody followed me into the building, and nobody followed me up to the fifth floor.

The guy who opened the door must have weighed three hundred and thirty pounds at least. He was six foot three and could just about carry the weight. He had a thick black beard and black hair down to his waist. He had black eyes that looked right through you. He didn't say anything. He just looked at me.

I said, "You ordered a pizza?" It was what Russell had told me to say. The big guy said, "Is it pepperoni?" He was American. I figured Boston. I said, "No, pineapple and sauerkraut."

He stood back and let me in, saying, "I'm Tiny. Come meet the guys."

It was a small apartment overcrowded with a huge number of computers. Narrow aisles made a maze among the hardware. You had to step over cables and pizza boxes to find your way to a chair where you could sit.

The guys were Ivan and George Chang. Ivan was an orphan from the Ukraine with acne and a dirty T-shirt that had once been yellow. Underneath the food stains, I could make out Jimmy Hendrix. Underneath his greasy fringe, I could make out pale blue eyes that observed me and didn't smile. George Chang was a Chinese Californian with a PhD from Stanford. He might have been thirty or he might have been fifty. He had an easy smile and shook my hand while Ivan watched from behind his hair.

George said, "Were you followed?"

I said, "I wouldn't be here if I had been."

"Cool. Can we see the modem?"

They all gathered around and I handed him the attaché case. He flipped the switches and pulled out a black box the size of a small laptop, only four times as thick. He glanced at Ivan and said, "You want to get the shutters?"

Ivan and Tiny both went and started fitting what looked like fly-nets over the windows. George stood and carried the black box into a darkened room. Here, there was less chaos. There was a bench that ran around the room, up against the wall. It was covered in computer equipment. George was talking as he walked. "I worked on a CIA project back in the sixties and seventies that was attempting to discover what happens to thoughts when they go into the unconscious."

I stopped in the doorway and watched him sit down and place the modem in front of him on the bench. I said, "You worked with the CIA in the sixties? How old are you?"

He didn't look at me. He was fitting a cable to the box. "Don't ask."

My skin went cold. I said, "Are you a hybrid?"

"I said, don't ask." He flipped a switch on a tower and a screen to his left lit up. "The point is that ideas flow in our brains because somehow we trigger positive and negative poles that make streams of electrons flow in particular patterns. Those patterns make thoughts." He turned and pointed at my leg. "Until I say what I am about to say, you will be completely unconscious of the back of your left knee."

I was suddenly aware of the back of my left knee. I reached in my pocket and pulled out my Camels and my Zippo. "Okay." I pulled one out and offered it to him. He shook his head. While I lit up, he said, "So, where was the thought of your left knee before I said it?"

I inhaled deeply. It was an interesting question. "I don't know."

He turned back to the computer. "We've got some of the theory. The brain learns how to create certain patterns of positive and negative poles that make the streams of electrons flow through the neurons in particular patterns. Those poles are always there, *potentially*. When they are triggered—fired up—that's when we get consciousness, memory, imagination."

I nodded then shrugged. "Makes sense, but it still leaves the question, how does the brain remember where to fire the positive and negative poles?"

He gave me a strange look and said, "Yup. It may be some

47

kind of residual imprint. The thing is, if we could find a way of controlling what stays in the unconscious and what is fired into consciousness, we would be much closer to controlling how and *what* people think."

The screen that had lit up started flickering with a mass of black and white dots. I said, "And?"

He was staring at the screen, doing something with a keyboard. "We didn't have the technology. As far as I am aware, we — *they* — still don't."

"Who's 'they'?"

He spoke without looking at me. "That's something you would have to ask Russell." He turned in his chair and stood up. "The thing is, what we have here in this modem is looking like a medium for broadcasting instructions to the brain to shut down certain types of polarities."

"Anything related to protest, rebellion, resistance?"

He stared at me a while, then shook his head. "Much more than that, Murdoch — anything related to asserting the idea of 'I'. Think about it. Every time you say 'I' or 'me', you create some kind of idea in your head of what kind of person you are — *who* you are. Try to imagine what you would be like if all of those thoughts were forced into your unconscious and were unable ever to surface into your conscious mind."

I did it. I tried to imagine it. I felt sick. "You'd be nothing more than—" I couldn't find the word.

He provided it for me. "A biological robot?"

I stared into his eyes. "Yeah."

He nodded. "I know all about that, Murdoch — so does Sinead and so did Joanna." He sighed. "Look. I have to get to work. This shit" — he gestured at the computer behind him — "is going to play havoc with your brain. Check in to your hotel. Grab something to eat. Come back tomorrow. I'll probably have something for you to take back to Russell by then."

I went down and sat with my ass on the car, smoking and looking at the puddles. I kept thinking of Maria back at the safe house with Hook and Russell. I kept thinking of Hook promising me that Maria would be safe. And everywhere I looked there were more hybrids showing up as our allies and friends. I wanted to phone Russell and tell him I was flying back and I was taking Maria where I could care for her myself and she would be really safe, but I knew that would put us all at risk. I flicked the butt into the wet grass and climbed into the car.

As I drove into town—to the docks and my hotel—I turned over in my mind what George had said to me. He'd mentioned Sinead and Joanna. In Algeria, Joanna had tried to sell me a line about how a lot of hybrids were defecting. They wanted to break away from the Brotherhood and integrate with humanity. I hadn't bought it then and I didn't buy it now, but it looked as though Russell and Hook were.

I shook another cigarette out of the pack and poked it into my mouth. According to Russell and Hook, Catherine had gone rogue. The more I thought about that, the more it sounded like bullshit. Catherine had always been rogue, and if she and Sinead had become lovers—or whatever hybrids became—it was because they were both rogue and always had been. Nothing had changed there, which meant that Catherine was as closely tied to Sinead now as she always had been. Russell and Hook couldn't see it because they didn't know Catherine the way I did.

And that meant one thing—that Sinead was deliberately misleading Russell and Hook. And that led me to the billion-dollar question. Were Maria's pregnancy and the codes connected in some way, or was Maria's pregnancy a separate, parallel issue? I went back in my mind to the hotel in Sao Paulo. I could see Catherine with her short black hair, her green eyes looking at me, watching me. She had said, "Sinead is working with Russell. *We* are working with Russell."

She'd told me Sinead had sent her. She had taken pains to tell me she hadn't wanted to see me but that she missed me. And she'd laid it on real thick that she didn't want to give me the bad news—like she cared about my feelings, like she *had* feelings, like we'd had something special.

Why would she do that? Why would Sinead send her to do that?

And the answer was suddenly real clear. They would do that to separate me from Maria. And, right now, I was one thousand miles away from her. I was one thousand miles away from her, delivering a modem that Sinead had arranged for Russell to collect, knowing he would send me. And I had collected it from one hybrid and delivered it to another, on information provided by a third. My mind was reaching, straining, but I couldn't see clearly.

I was approaching my hotel, a dubious dive deep called the Blue Studio in woodlands off the *Rakoczego* roundabout and down *Ferdinanda Magdallena*. I pulled over to the side of the road, took out my cell and sat staring at it. To call Russell was a risk, but there was a growing unease in me that we had walked into an ambush, and I couldn't shake the feeling that Maria was the prey and I had left her exposed.

I kept telling myself that she was at a secret location surrounded by some of the toughest special ops men in the world, but there was this other voice telling me the location was only secret if you didn't know about it. Did Sinead know about it? Did Catherine? I didn't know. I didn't know because the whole thing had been taken out of my hands. I had been sidelined. I had been sent a thousand miles away.

Then I remembered my conversation with Hook in the car. Maria was valuable to them. *Why?* Why was Maria, and her pregnancy, suddenly so important to everybody? But I knew in that moment that Maria and her baby were key, and I had been gotten out of the way so that somebody else could move in and take them.

Large drops of rain had started to spatter the windshield. They triggered the automatic wipers and the loud squeak of rubber on glass snapped me out of my thoughts. I felt the beginnings of panic in my gut. I thought of Maria in bed not more than thirty-six hours ago, kissing my hands and whispering, *'We thought you'd never come.'*

'Me and baby.'

I dialed Russell's secure number. He answered almost immediately, "What's the matter?"

"I have to talk to you."

"Don't waste time. What is it?"

"Is she okay?

"Of course. What's this about?"

"I've got a bad feeling. We've been led into an ambush."

"Watch your language. Get to the point. We can't stay on the line much longer."

"They want her to themselves. They got me out of the way."

"You're being paranoid."

"Paranoid? Are you kidding me? Look at who gave you the information. Look at who gave me the package. Look at who I just gave it to. They are all—"

"I know."

"That doesn't worry you?"

He didn't answer for a long moment. Then he said, "We have to get off the line."

I said, "Send somebody to replace me. I'm coming back."

"Don't—"

I cut across him. "I'm not asking you. I'm telling you."

"Listen to me!

"No! *You* listen to *me*. You got too damned cozy with the neighbors. I don't know why, but now they're going to pay you a visit and try and take my girl. I intend to be there when they show up. And Russell—?"

"Don't use *names!*"

"You boys had better stay wide awake, and she had better be there when I get back!"

I hung up. I hated talking to Russell that way, but I had a hot rage building in my belly. I knew Maria was at risk, and as far as I could see, Russell and Hook weren't only doing nothing to protect her, they were opening the door and inviting the enemy in.

I spent a frustrating half hour in the cyber café at the Blue Studio, trying to buy a ticket back to London, but the afternoon flights were cancelled due to fog and the first flight was at six the next morning. I booked a first-class seat.

Maybe Russell was right, and maybe I was getting paranoid. I didn't care. I knew we were being set up and I knew I was being watched. I drove into town, dropped the hire car at a multi-story car park and caught a cab to the Radisson Blu, a five-star hotel on the Motlawa River, opposite the Basilica of St. Mary of the Assumption. I figured if they already knew I was here, I may as well be comfortable, and if they didn't, a five-star hotel would be the last place they would look for me. People never hide in five-star hotels.

I dropped my bag in my room, had a shower and stepped out for a walk and some late lunch.

The pedestrian area outside the hotel was deserted. It was only half past three, but the heavy cloud made it seem later. The gray paving was wet from the recent rain and the light that spilled from the hotel windows behind me and from the shops and restaurants opposite, made luminous liquid runnels among the cobbles. I turned right, feeling hungry and in the mood for a drink.

The buildings looked seventeenth century and alternated white, pastel green and pastel blue. Ahead of me, there were three arches in an ancient red brick building with tall leaded windows. Small billows of mist were creeping in through the arches. I walked through them and found myself on the banks of a river. A heavy fog was rising from the water. A cobbled bridge spanned the river ahead of me. To my left, I could see warm light glowing through the mist, so I walked that way, following my elongated shadow as it pushed ahead of me, hoping it would lead me to a restaurant or at least a bar where I could find some food and a stiff whiskey — or maybe two.

I was engulfed by the twists of vapor that rose like slow snakes from among the boats and barges. The silence became oppressive, broken only by the lapping of the invisible water and the stark echo of my footsteps. Warm windows loomed occasionally, showing silent scenes of laughing drinkers huddled around tables and bars. A dark archway opened ahead, leading into a narrow alley. I went through and found myself on a cobbled street with only one lamp. Beneath the lamp was a wooden sign hanging from a chain. It looked medieval and had gothic script. It made me smile and I stepped closer. Through the coils of mist, I saw that it said, *La Taberna Vasca* — The Basque Tavern. Wrong country, but it sounded about right for what I needed just then.

It was like a cave. There was a short flight of steps going down. Everything was wood and stone, and the walls and the ceiling were irregular, like they'd been hewn out of living rock. There was an open fire at the far end, burning logs and wooden booths along the left wall. The bar was along the other and the tables were like heavy benches. There were only two or three couples in quiet conversation — no music and no fruit machines. I went and sat at the bar. The barman was five foot six with six-foot shoulders and a face like a bad dream covered in black sandpaper. He was polishing a glass and asked me with a nod of his head what it would be.

I asked for a large Bushmills and sat looking at it instead of drinking. He dropped a menu in front of me and I ordered a plate of lamb chops and *patatas a la pobre*. There was a table by the fire and I took my drink over there. The smell of charcoal-grilled meat followed me. I watched the flames dancing in my whiskey for a while then took a long pull. It felt good.

My mind was on Russell and Hook, on Maria and the baby and the house in Wiltshire. So, I was paying no attention when the door must have opened behind me. There were voices at the bar — a girl and the grating rasp of the barman. I wasn't aware I had heard them until I felt the presence by my side.

I looked up. She was young, between eighteen and twenty-four or five. She was cute, but it was hard to tell under the woolen hat, the scarf and the shapeless jacket. She had dirty jeans and a pair of Timberlands that may have been somebody else's. She had big brown eyes, and under the hat, she had thick dark-blonde hair. She reminded me of somebody, but I couldn't place it. When she spoke, she sounded American, probably West Coast. She said, "Buy a girl a drink?"

I glanced back at the bar. The hulk was eyeing her and wiping down the counter. I did something that should have been a smile but had no soul and said, "Sorry. I'm not in the market."

She cut across me and dropped into the seat opposite. "C'mon, man. I'm not selling my body for the price of a drink." She shrugged. "It's cold and damp outside. I could use a warm place to sit and some company."

I spread my hands. "How can I say no? What'll you have?"

She turned and shouted at the barman, "Iker, gimme a beer, will ya?" She turned back to me and grinned. "Sure smells good. You gonna eat?"

I watched her pull off her hat and shake out her hair. She wasn't cute. She was beautiful. She undid her jacket and pulled her chair up closer to the fire. The hulk came over with a jug of black beer. He paused before putting it on the table and looked at me. "She bothering you?"

I shook my head and smiled. "I think I can handle her. You better make that two plates of lamb, though."

He raised an eyebrow at me, like he thought I was a sucker, and went away. Maybe he was right. Maybe I was, but I figured if she could use some company, so could I. She gave me a smile that might have been embarrassed and said, "Thanks. You're a pal. Name's Maggie Meigh."

"Maggie Me?"

"Yeah. How about you? You got a name?"

"Murdoch. How old are you, Maggie?"

"You going to get paternal on me?"

I thought about it. "Maybe. I get the feeling somebody who should have, didn't."

She looked away, at the fire. "I'm twenty-four."

"What are you doing here? You a student?"

She took a long pull on her beer, belched, wiped her mouth on her sleeve, glanced at me and shrugged. I knew who she reminded me of. The air of self-reliance, tomboy femininity and the vulnerability just below the surface were all Maria. We were quiet for a bit, listening to the crackle of the logs, watching the sparks jump above the flames. The food arrived and she pulled her chair up to the table.

She ate ravenously, like she hadn't had a hot meal in weeks. When she'd gotten through four or five chops, she stopped and licked her fingers, eyeing me. "You live here?"

I shook my head. "Nope."

"You're here on business."

"Yup."

She returned to her food. "Man of a few words, huh?"

I smiled. "Are we so different?" She looked up, like I'd said something important. I went on, "You talk a lot, but you don't say much." I took a pull on my whiskey and set the glass down. "I know you're hungry, I know you're thirsty, and I know your name."

She flopped back in her chair, a half-devoured chop in her hand. She shrugged. "There isn't much to tell. I'm not real interesting. Besides…" She sat forward, tore the meat off the chop, chewed a couple of times and drained her beer. She showed me the glass and said, "Can I have another?"

I nodded. "Besides, what?"

"I don't want you to get fucking paternal with me. Okay, you bought me dinner and a couple of drinks and you've probably lived a lot. That doesn't mean you can start lecturing me." She shrugged again. "I live my life my way. If you don't like it, you don't have to buy me a drink. Right?"

I raised an eyebrow and sighed. "Maybe I don't care enough to disapprove, Maggie. Maybe I don't need a lecture either. I'll stop buying you drinks when I get bored. Keep up the act and that'll be in the next fifteen seconds. We've all been there and all done it. Wanting to be independent isn't special or surprising." Her cheeks colored, so for good measure I added, "And you're not doing me a favor by letting me buy you a drink. You asked, remember?"

As I was saying it, I was wondering if there had ever been a time when human beings were not searching, struggling, fighting for freedom. It was why I was in Gdansk, and it was why she was in Gdansk — each of us fighting our own war of independence. And wasn't it what Catherine and Sinead were fighting for? And even Banks, Joanna and del Roble, when they had been alive. Maybe it wasn't just humans then.

Maggie was looking at her hands in her lap and saying, "I'm sorry. I just want to be free. I know it's naïve, but that doesn't make it any less true, does it?"

I watched her for a few moments. I saw she'd cleaned her plate and drained her glass. I decided she was a nice kid who probably had nice parents somewhere who were going through some kind of hell wondering what had happened to their cute little girl. I said, "I don't know. Free to do what?"

She frowned at me. "What do you mean?"

I shrugged. "It doesn't mean anything. If you were totally free, you wouldn't have any limitations, would you?"

She smiled and shook her head. "That's right. No limitations."

"So, you'd have no arms, no legs, no skin... Hell! You'd have no body, no brain, no thoughts, no desires, no passions..." I spread my hands again. "The only way to be free is if you don't exist. 'Free' doesn't mean anything on its own, Maggie. It only means anything when you are free to do something."

She watched me a long while and I watched her back. She said, "Like free to love?"

"Yeah." I caught Hulk's eye and signaled for more drinks.

Then I asked her, "Is that what happened? You loved somebody and it didn't work out?"

Her gaze drifted to the fire. I could see small flames dancing in her eyes. She gave her head a tiny shake. "Nah. It was the opposite. I kept trying to love, but there was no one. So, I decided to travel, to search the world and see if I could find someone — anyone — who could turn me on."

The barman brought the drinks. As she took her glass, she gestured at my plate with her head. I realized I'd hardly eaten. She said, "You gonna eat them?"

I took a chop and pushed the plate to the middle of the table. I said, "Yeah, but you can help me."

The warmth from the fire was making her cheeks flush. I caught myself thinking that if I were ten years younger, I'd find her cute. She caught the look and smiled. It was a nice smile. She was making short work of the chops and said, "My dad is rich — like, big-time rich. Couple of years ago, I dropped out" — she made a quote marks sign with her fingers — "'borrowed' some money from him, and set off to search for freedom and my soul mate."

I watched her devour the last chop and said, "So, if your dad is so rich, how come you're so hungry?"

"I ran out of cash, Sherlock. And he won't give me any more unless I go home and go back to college."

"So, where are you sleeping tonight?"

She didn't answer straight away. She wouldn't meet my eyes, but she was smiling. She said, "I don't know," then looked up. "Do you?"

I sighed. "I know where I'm sleeping. I don't know where you're sleeping. Look, Maggie. I'm married, I love my wife, and I'm not a cheat, so I'm not coming on to you."

She appeared mad. "It's something, isn't it? I'm twenty-four and pretty hot, and I get turned down by a guy ten years older than me."

"Stop it. We're not going there."

She scowled at the fire for a bit. "Next, you're going to tell me sex isn't the same as love."

I stared at the same flames as she did. Maybe I saw something different. I said, "It took me a while, but I realized it's not."

She rolled her eyes and sighed, and I checked my watch. "Look. I have a flight at six in the morning. I have to get some sleep. Where *are* you staying?"

She stared me a minute then shrugged, but she didn't say anything.

Chapter Seven

We stepped out into the alley. She had stopped scowling and now she was smiling. The fog was so dense you couldn't see more than twelve feet in front of you. It had a strange, coppery glow where the light from the streetlamps was diffused. I turned right toward where I knew the arch was and she took my arm with both of hers, like she was hugging it. I said, "You didn't answer my question."

"About where I'm staying?"

I looked down at her.

She glanced at me for an answer and I nodded. She shrugged. "I don't know. I couldn't pay the rent and they kicked me out. I'll have to find a squat or something."

The sound of our footsteps changed, became more muffled and at the same time louder, like we were walking in a narrow tunnel. I realized we'd entered the deep archway that led out to the river. She giggled and clung tighter to my arm. "It's spooky. I like it. Do you like spooky, Murdoch?"

We came out of the passage and were engulfed by the thick billows of fog rolling off the water. We were surrounded by an amber cloud with no fixed point of reference, and I was completely disorientated. I reached out with my right hand and found the wall. I said, "We need to go this way."

She whispered, "*Do* we?"

I said, "I'll call you a cab from the hotel. He can take you to a hostel. I'll give you some money."

She was quiet, walking in step with me as we made our way, real slow and cautious, along the path. After maybe ten minutes, the form of the bridge began to emerge in the dank air. I knew the three arches were opposite. She said, "I doubt there will be cabs on a night like this."

I knew she was right. I said, "Do you know of a hostel where you can stay?"

She made a face. "No…" She left the word hanging, like she was waiting for me to pick it up and do something with it. I didn't, so she said, "Can't I stay with you?"

We'd come to the arches and I could see the glow of the hotel through the billows of vapor. I paused and looked down at her. She was biting her lip and clinging hard to my arm. "Okay, Maggie, I'm going to book you in to a room at the hotel for one night. You can't stay with me. You stay in your own room. Come on. We'll have one for the road in the bar then we go our separate ways. All right?"

She clung to my arm and gave a couple of childlike hops with a big grin on her face. I couldn't help laughing, and we made our way to the hotel.

The receptionist raised an eyebrow you could describe as conspiratorial and said, "*Alors*, we eff only zee room adjoining monsieur's. Will zat be acceptable?"

I said that would do fine and we went to the bar. She had another beer and I had a small whiskey. The place was empty and we sat in a corner, secluded by a palm. I said, "Listen to me, Maggie. You can tell me I'm acting paternal, being a pain in the ass, whatever you want to call it. I don't really care. We're probably never going to meet again, so what you think of me really doesn't matter. What *is* important is what happens after you get out of bed tomorrow, put your clothes on and step out through those doors."

She shrugged, then watched my face. "Why does that matter?"

"Okay, here's the lecture. It matters because the choices you make about what you do tomorrow can make a difference to people's lives. Some of those people you already know, some of them you haven't met yet. I've been where you are, Maggie, where all I cared about was the next hundred bucks I could scam off some sucker. I was so damned miserable I didn't even know it. I thought life was a gas, and I was too damned stupid to know that I was crying out for help."

She squinted at me, like I was speaking a language she only half-understood. I knew how she felt. I had never heard myself speak like this, and the words sounded weird in my mouth. I took a deep breath and plunged on.

"I was lucky. Somebody helped me. Somebody threw me a line and I was smart enough to take it. That was ten years ago. And today, I realized something. Happiness doesn't come from what you get from other people. I have a wonderful wife, and we are going to have a baby. What makes me happy is thinking about all the things I can give them and do for them to make *them* happy.

"I can't help you the way my friend helped me. It just isn't possible. But I *can* tell you that if you don't throw your life away tomorrow morning, maybe, down the line, you can make somebody *else* happy."

She stared into her beer for what felt like a long time. Then she shrugged and said, "Okay, I'll think about it."

I drained my glass and so did she then we made our way up to our rooms. As I pushed open my door, she hesitated outside hers. She said, "You sure you don't want company?

"I'm sure."

She stood close to me and put her hand on my chest. "It can be a secret. Nobody has to know. You said we'll probably never see each other again." She frowned. "We're not doing anybody any harm."

"Except ourselves — and each other. Now, get some sleep. Goodnight, Maggie."

She pouted and went in, closing the door behind her.

Soon after, I was wearing a towel. I had showered, packed my bag and set my alarm when I noticed the dividing doors between my room and Maggie's. I noticed them because the handle was moving. I heard the soft click of the lock and the doors opened. She was standing there, a hand on each door. She'd removed her coat and her hat. In fact, she'd removed everything except a long white shirt that hung open with nothing underneath except the suggestion of her curves. She said, "I tried not to."

"They should have been locked."

"They were. I picked them."

"Go to your room, Maggie. Go to sleep."

"I'm going to sleep with you. You can't stop me." I took a step to her and she smiled a lazy kind of smile. "I'll scream and say you tried to rape me. And when I pull that towel off, you'll be naked."

I didn't think she'd do it, but I didn't know and it wasn't worth the risk. I sighed. "You can do what you like, Maggie. I'm going to sleep."

"Oh, come on!" She walked up to me and hooked her fingers into the towel. "Stop being so goddamn holier than thou. Loosen up."

I was beginning to get mad. I took hold of her shoulders and looked hard into her eyes. "Listen to me. I am in love with my wife. I don't want to fuck you—not because I shouldn't, but because I don't want to. Now go to your room and get some sleep."

I stepped away from her, pulled back the covers, pulled off the towel and got into bed. Before I lay down, I pointed at the open doors. "Go to your room, Maggie."

She watched me. She wasn't smiling. She said, "I don't want to and you can't make me. I want to sleep with you."

I exploded, "For God's sake, Maggie!"

She took her time walking around the bed, pausing every few steps to look at me, like she was defying me to stop her. When she got to the other side, she pulled back the quilt then she slipped off her shirt. Her breasts were generous and shaped like tulips. Her nipples were surprisingly long for a young girl and the areolas were wide and dark. Her skin was very pale, but it was smooth and taut, and her bush was dense and black. She was staring at me and I could hear her breath, slightly ragged as it quickened. She sat on the bed, swung her legs in, lay down and pulled the quilt up to her chest, leaving her breasts exposed.

There was nothing I could do, so I lay down, turned my back on her and switched out the lamp. I knew I had to sleep. I hadn't had a decent night's sleep for almost a week, but my eyes were wide open and I was aware of her lying motionless next to me.

I heard her voice, small, almost apologetic. "Murdoch? Can I hold you?"

"No."

I closed my eyes. She said, "I'm sorry about my behavior."

"It's okay. Go to sleep."

"I'm real scared. And you've been so kind to me."

"Forget about it. Go to sleep."

After a moment, I felt her hand, small and cool on my shoulder. It moved, by slow, hesitant stages down my back to my hip. I was about to tell her to cut it out, but I heard a small whimper. It might have been a sob, and I told myself the easiest thing was to pretend I was asleep. Then I felt her move. I thought she was going to roll over and spoon me, and if she did, I was going to drag her to the bathroom and give her a cold shower and I didn't care if she screamed the hotel down. I'd had enough. But she didn't. She moved again, then again. Small, almost imperceptible movements, and I heard her whimper again. She started to explore my hip with small, caressing movements. Her breath shuddered and I felt her tense. She gripped my hip. Her breathing was growing heavier.

Then I felt her body close to mine. She pressed her thigh against me as she spread her legs and began to writhe. I froze. She was murmuring, "Oh, baby, oh, baby…" I didn't want to, but I was swelling and growing hard. I tried to fight it, but all I could do was think of Maria holding me in bed, and that started a fire in my belly. I wanted my wife. I was hungry for her, and in the darkness, I was remembering her skin rubbing smooth and soft against mine — her lips on my neck and on my shoulder, her hand exploring.

In my mind, I was telling myself I should get out of bed, turn on the light and throw her out, back to her own room.

But all I could do was think of Maria' huge, beautiful black eyes looking deep into mine, her cool, small hands caressing my skin, holding my cock, making it swell and harden like rock. I could hear Maggie's breathing, fast and ragged in the dark. My own breathing was shallow and quick. I was having trouble telling what was my fantasy and what was real. I could feel her slipping her hand over my thigh, seeking my cock. I knew her other hand was between her legs. I could feel her rhythm growing fast and harder, her breath broken by whimpers. She took hold of me and began to move her hand up and down, in time to her own rhythm. The pleasure was insane.

"No!" I yelled and staggered out of bed, slamming on the light as I did it. I turned and saw her. Her legs were splayed, bent at the knee. Her left hand was clawing the sheet and her right was between her thighs, rubbing hard and fast. She was staring at me, her pupils dilated wide, her mouth open, as though she were about to cry out. I watched in a kind of fascination as her back arched, her face and neck flushed pink and she let out a long, whimpering groan, clenching her thighs onto her hand. Then she kind of keeled over and collapsed onto her side, with her back turned to me

I stared at her. I said, "Get out. Get out of here."

She whimpered again, said, "Leave me alone, you drip," and pulled the quilt over her head.

I went to the shower and stood under the cold stream of water for five minutes. What they say about cold showers is a myth. It doesn't work. I finally got to sleep at two. At four, I was awake and dressing to go to the airport. Maggie was still sleeping peacefully.

Chapter Eight

It was still raining when I arrived at Heathrow. I'd booked a minicab to meet me at the airport. The cab driver must have seen the look on my face because he didn't say a word throughout the trip except to ask me where I wanted to go. I gave him the address in Wiltshire. He punched it into his GPS and we drove in silence past hedgerows and fields that looked as though they'd been wrapped in damp cotton-wool. We arrived at eleven, but as I climbed out of the car, it could have been four a.m. It was a gray world of low clouds, mist and drizzle. I watched his taillights disappear and walked to the front door. Nobody answered the bell and I couldn't see light in any of the windows. A small knot twisted at my gut.

I pulled out my cell and dialed Maria. The number was switched off or unavailable. I tried Russell and got the same message, so I picked the lock and went in. The house was dark and empty. Even the echoes sounded empty. I stood in the drawing room looking out through the leaded panes at the sodden garden. Somewhere there was a steady splash and patter of water spilling from a gutter onto paving.

Maybe they'd gone to Marlborough. Maybe they'd gone out for the day. But I knew I was kidding myself. They would have left somebody in the house—a guard, somebody watching the perimeter.

I climbed the stairs to Maria's bedroom. I pushed open the door, expecting to find what I'd found downstairs—nothing. Instead, I found the wardrobe thrown open, the bedclothes on the floor and the bed saturated in a large, dark stain that I knew was blood. The whole room seemed to rock and I felt my skin turn cold and pasty. The strength drained from my legs and I began to shake. I kept telling myself, *not her, not her*.

Not Maria.

My brain switched to autopilot. I could hear my breathing shallow and quick. It felt like my heart was pounding in my head. But I had to *think!* I was staring at the wardrobe. Why was the door open? It didn't make sense. Were they searching for something? Surely they knew I had the modem. They wanted Maria – and the baby. Then why the wardrobe? And where was Maria? Where was her...? I couldn't face the word. All I could think was that she *couldn't* be dead.

Not Maria.

I went and stared into the wardrobe, a door in each outstretched hand. It was empty. All her clothes were gone. It didn't make any sense. I turned to the chest of drawers. All the drawers were out, and they were all empty. I kicked open the door to the *en suite* bathroom. The cabinet was open. All the toiletries were gone. I turned and stared at the big stain on the bed. The light from the landing gleamed on it in twisted, wet lines. In this humidity, it could have been ten minutes old or twelve hours old. It would take days to dry.

I forced myself to think. *Think!* There was hope. There *was* hope. I moved around to the far side of the bed near the door. There was no blood on the floor. Out on the landing, there were no stains, either – no spatter, no drag marks and nothing on the stairs. That meant if it was Maria's blood, she had not been bleeding when they left. That could mean she was dead or it could mean they had stopped the bleeding and taken her to a hospital.

If that was the case, it meant she was having a miscarriage.

I pulled out a Camel and poked it in my mouth.

Think!

I flipped my Zippo and leaned into the flame. My hand was trembling. I inhaled deep. I knew what I had to do, but I had a knot in my belly and my feet didn't want to move. If Maria had had a miscarriage, the only place where I was going to find blood was in her bed. If she had been targeted and killed, there would be blood in Russell's room, in Hook's and in other parts of the house. This was the SAS. They would have put up a hell of a fight. There should be carnage in the house. So far, there had been no sign of any violence but that didn't mean much. They might have been surprised in their sleep.

Unlikely.

I walked down the landing to Russell's room and pushed open the door. The bed was made and the room was tidy. I found Hook's room the same way. Then I scoured the house from the wine cellar to the attic. There was not a trace of a fight or any kind of violence.

So, she'd had a miscarriage. But then, why hadn't Russell called me? I tried his number again — and Hook's — but got the same unavailable message. I phoned the Savernake Hospital and the Chippenham Birth Center. Neither had had any pregnant women check in as an emergency in the last twenty-four hours. I could feel a rage building inside me. I tried to fight it because it was directed against Russell.

They're cutting me out. They're keeping me away from her. They're trying to steal her from me.

I didn't want to think it, but I was feeling it like someone had dropped molten lava into my belly. Russell was betraying me to help Sinead.

I slammed down the phone and walked to the drinks' tray in the drawing room. He'd known I was on my way back. If she had been taken to hospital, the first goddamn thing he should have done was pick up the phone and call me. I poured myself a stiff whiskey, picked up the glass and froze.

Something small and hard pressed into my left shoulder blade and a very calm, quiet voice said, "I don't want to shoot you. I just want to talk. So, take it nice and slow, and when I step back, you turn around with your hands in the air. After that, you can pour me a drink. Understood?"

I put down my glass and turned with my hands in the air. It was Tom. I'd met him once before. He was one of Hook's men. He'd helped me get Maria out of Algeria. He'd saved my life. He watched me, staring hard into my eyes with his Sig leveled at my chest. He said, "Are we okay?"

I sighed and turned back to the drinks' tray. As I picked up the decanter of whiskey and a glass, I said, "Put that goddamn thing away, will you? Couldn't you have just rung the doorbell?"

I turned back with a glass in each hand. He still had his automatic leveled at me and he was eyeing me with care. I said, "What's the matter with you?"

He seemed to think about it, then put his piece away in a holster under his jacket. He took the glass I handed him and said, "I might ask you the same thing. You're supposed to be in Poland. The boss is worried about you."

I said, "Who's the boss?"

"Why are you back early?" He sipped and waited for me to answer.

I said, "Where are they? Where Maria? What's all the blood upstairs? What the hell happened?"

He moved to a white armchair and sat. "She had hemorrhage—a threatened miscarriage. They called a doctor and the doctor decided to take her to hospital. Everybody decamped with her. I was detailed to wait for you and take you there. If—"

I waited. He watched me. I said, "If *what*?"

"If I was satisfied you were okay."

"What the fuck are you talking about?"

"Your behavior in the last twenty-four hours has been erratic."

"Bullshit!"

"Convince me."

"I don't need to convince you of a goddamn—"

He cut across me as smooth as an eel on dope. "Make it easy for yourself, Russell and Maria, Murdoch. You can try and beat it out of me if you like, though I wouldn't recommend it. Or you can just persuade me they haven't gotten to you. We're on the same side, me old mucker. Just take it easy and talk to me, all right? You need to cool down and remember who your friends are."

I rubbed my face, dropped into a chair and took a long pull. He was right, but I eyed him a moment and said, "What I'm worried about, Tom, is whether my friends remember who *I* am."

I saw his eyebrows twitch in a brief frown. He spread his hands. "Talk to me."

I took a drag on my cigarette. "How much do you know?"

"I know everything you know. We have the same clearance."

I told him about Agostinho, about Catherine turning up at the hotel and about Maria's pregnancy. "When I got to Gdansk, I found that the guy I was giving the codes to was also a hybrid." I gave him a moment to think about it. "We get the intel from Sinead — a hybrid. She directs us to collect the codes from Agostinho — a hybrid. And she directs us to take them to George, another hybrid. Meanwhile, her girlfriend tells me Maria is pregnant and the baby is not mine, and Russell and Hook put..." I shook my head. "How much? How much have they invested in resources to keep Maria and her baby safe?" I pulled out another cigarette and lit it while he watched me, thinking. I blew out smoke and added, "And why? Why is it even necessary to keep her safe? Maria and her baby are suddenly everybody's major concern? Why? And why are Sinead and Catherine trying so hard to separate me from her? You add those two questions together and you have a problem. *I* have a problem."

"Fair enough. I'll take you to them." He nodded.

I said, "What do *you* know?"

He looked me in the eye and said, "I know what you've just told me. And I agree with you."

I believed him. I believed he agreed with me, and I believed that was all he knew about Maria. But I also believed there was something he wasn't telling me, something he was thinking over.

We took my TVR and burned rubber all the way down the M40 to London. I drove too fast. The roads were wet and visibility was poor with a mixture of mist and drizzle under heavy, low clouds, but I didn't care. There was a craziness in my head and in my gut that was going to drive me on until I was holding Maria and knew she was safe. And once I had her, I swore I was never going to let go.

At East Acton, he told me to get off the highway. We took a couple of turns down leafy backstreets and came out on Du Cane Road. We passed Wormwood Scrubs Prison and I pulled up outside Hammersmith Hospital. As we climbed out, I said, "Where is she?"

He walked around the hood saying, "Follow me and keep your knickers on, Murdoch. If you lose it, it doesn't help anyone. All right?"

I growled, "Lose what?"

"Your cool, Murdoch. Your cool."

I didn't answer. We rode the elevator to the fourth flour and he led me down a couple of corridors to a set of doors where I saw Sergeant Brown and Trooper Green sitting reading magazines. They looked up as we approached and said, "Good afternoon, Lieutenant." They pronounced it 'left-tenant', the way the Brits do, brown-eyed me and said, "All right, sir?"

I nodded at him and we pushed through. There was a dark passage and a door on the right. Tom opened it and stood aside for me to go in.

She was in bed. She was hooked up to a machine that was monitoring her heart, making a soft, rhythmic beep. Her face lit up when she saw me. She said, "Liam!" and reached out for me. Hook was standing by the window and Russell was sitting in an armchair. They were both watching me. I ignored them and went to sit on the bed by her side. I took her hands and kissed her. I talked soft, keeping my voice quiet, keeping my mounting anger and worry to myself. I said, "What happened, baby?"

"I wasn't expecting you back for a few days."

"I cut the trip short. I'm not leaving you again till this is all over."

She smiled and I knew from her eyes that whatever had happened – whatever happened in the future – she was mine and always had been. "Do you promise?"

"I promise, baby. Now tell me what happened."

"It was in the small hours of the morning. I just started bleeding. I called Russell and he called the doctor. She came really quickly. She gave me something to stop the hemorrhage and called an ambulance." She squeezed my hand. "I'm fine. Baby's fine. Everything is going to be okay."

I smiled at her. "You bet." I turned and looked at Russell and Hook. They were still watching me with no expression. "Can I have a word with you outside?"

I stood and opened the door. After a moment, they rose and followed me out. Tom was leaning against the wall. I moved away a few paces and turned to face Russell. "You want to explain to me why you didn't phone me and tell me what had happened?"

"There is a considerable risk every time we use the telephone."

"Bullshit!"

Hook spoke up. "It's not bullshit, Murdoch. It is a very real risk, and you need to get a grip."

I stared at him and I could feel my control slipping. "*I* need to get a grip?" I shook my head. "No, pal. You two need to get a grip. I don't know what goddamn game you are playing behind my back with my wife, but friendship or no friendship, it ends today and it ends now. What kind of schmuck do you think I am?" I turned back to Russell. "I trusted you, Russell."

A flash of irritation contracted his face. "Oh, for goodness sake, calm down, Liam! You have completely misunderstood –"

"What?" I snarled. "What have I misunderstood? That you've let the hybrids move in and take over your operation? That you're receiving instructions from hybrids about what to do with my wife? What is it I have misunderstood, Russell? That they are using you to manipulate me and separate me from Maria and our baby?"

He sighed and closed his eyes. "I grant you, it looks that way, Liam. But if you don't shut up and let me talk, I can't explain, can I?"

I was too mad to shut up. I said, "You're damned right it looks that way. And any explaining you do from now on, you are going to do on *my* terms." I heard the double doors open but didn't pay any attention. I was scowling at Russell.

Hook was saying, "What does that mean?"

I cut across him and said, "It means I'm taking Maria home with me. I'll move her to a safe location and get private care for her."

Russell was shaking his head. "No, Liam. Don't do that. You don't understand."

I looked past him and saw the door swinging closed. Tom was watching me. I pushed past Russell and Hook and opened the door. There was a woman in a white coat standing over Maria, peering down at her, talking. Her voice was soft. Maria was smiling up at her, listening. My heart was pounding. My head was throbbing. I turned back to Russell and Hook. They were watching me, waiting. I said, "*This? This* is the doctor you called?"

Sinead turned and looked at me.

"*Sinead Tiernan* is the doctor you called to tend to *my* wife and *my* baby?"

Russell said, "Liam…"

I exploded, "*Don't!*" I stared at them both. "You *knew*! When I went to you after Sao Paulo, you *knew*! You have *used* us! Between the goddamn lot of you, you have *used* us!"

Russell's face flushed. He shouted, "Liam! Listen to me!"

but I was too mad to listen to him. My mind was on fire.

I shouted, "No! I am through listening to you, Russell. You lied to me and you put Maria's life at risk. You sold out."

I moved into the room. Maria was glancing from me to Sinead. She said, "What's going on, Liam?"

Sinead was staring at me. She had those weird, empty eyes, like the universe was staring at you through them. She said, "Don't do it. You don't understand."

Behind me, I could hear feet running. I said, "Get out of my way, Sinead." I pushed past her. Maria seemed scared, like she didn't know who to believe. I looked into her eyes and pointed at Sinead. "This woman is a hybrid. She was part of del Roble's organization. She is Catherine's lover, and between them, they have set us up."

She frowned. She was real frightened. She glanced at Sinead then past me at Russell and Hook. They were her allies and she was having trouble letting go. She stammered, "But Russell said—"

"She's taken them in, baby. It's what she does. You remember Pete Strickland? This is the woman who set him up to be killed by Catherine Howard. Now, get your stuff. We are leaving."

The voice came from behind me. It was cold and hard like a blade is cold and hard. It said, "You are not going anywhere."

I didn't know who the voice belonged to, but I knew in that moment that I was going to kill whoever it was. That day, people were going to die. I turned.

The room seemed to be very full—too full. There was a guy in a suit and a crew cut. He had pro written all over him. Behind him were two more of the same type. One was a six-foot-six black giant in shades, the other was a bit smaller and white but seemed to be made of granite. Hook had come in and was looking out of the room at Tom. He seemed worried. Russell was gazing past me, probably at Sinead and making small movements of his head, like he was trying to transmit a message, but I wasn't paying attention to any of that. The hot rage that was building in me wouldn't let me think. All I knew was that these men wanted to separate me from Maria, and that wasn't going to happen. I said, "Who the fuck are you?"

He said, "I represent a higher authority. I am taking charge of Mrs. Murdoch's treatment."

I said, "You better step aside, pal."

He smiled in a way that wasn't a smile and said, "Take Mr. Murdoch outside and explain to him why the girl stays."

I turned to Maria and said, "Get dressed. This won't take long."

Then everything began to happen at once. I went to push past the crew cut as the two hulks stepped forward. Russell scuttled toward the bed and Hook started to say something as he and Tom closed in. Then I made my move, and everything I did was fueled with the madness and the frustration that had been building in me since Sao Paulo.

I made to step past him, but as I did it, I reached up and grabbed his nose between my forefinger and middle finger and I twisted hard. He screamed and grabbed my wrist with both his hands, like he was supposed to. Then I stepped back and rammed my fist twice into his solar plexus. He went crimson and retched. I turned and saw the big black guy looming over me. I didn't think. I kicked hard with my instep between his legs. His face creased into a mask of pain and tears sprang into his eyes. I was still holding the crew cut's nose with my left hand. With my right, I grabbed the black guy's head as he doubled up and I rammed my knee into his face. He went down and I stamped on the back of his neck. I felt the vertebrae snap.

Tom and Hook had the other guy down, but I wasn't interested in him or in them. I pushed Crew Cut stumbling backward out into the passage. He seemed to be recovering, so I hit him again, hard, in the floating ribs. He sagged and I snarled, "Keep walking!"

I saw what I was looking for — a door to the back stairwell.

I kicked through it and pushed him up to the rail. Then I pushed a bit more so his back was arched over and he was gripping my wrist so as not to fall. I leaned forward and snarled, "So, what exactly were you going to explain to me?"

When he spoke, it was nasal and it made me want to laugh a crazy laugh. He said, "Don't! Don't do it. We can talk. I can give you money. Just don't!"

"Money? I've been made that offer before. Who do you work for? Who is this 'higher authority'? Are you with the Brotherhood?'"

"Pull me up!"

"*No! Talk!*"

His mouth was curling involuntarily. The pain and the fear were getting to him. He said, "It's the Pentagon. It's a department of the Pentagon. You've never heard of it."

I twisted harder and rammed my face close to his. I rasped, "What do they want with my *wife*?"

He was sobbing. "It's not her. It's the baby."

"What do you know about the baby?"

"Nothing! I was just sent here. It's need-to-know."

"Wrong answer, schmuck!"

I grabbed his balls, squeezed hard, lifted and threw him over the rail. There was a short scream, a sickening series of thuds — then silence.

I pushed back into the corridor. It was dark and silent. Tom was not there. I made it in three loping strides and opened the door. The room was empty except for the black guy and his pal, and they were both dead. The covers were thrown back and the heart monitor was emitting a single, high-pitched signal.

I burst through the double doors at a run. Sergeant Brown and Trooper Green were gone. I kept running. I passed a code-blue team racing in the direction of Maria's room. Sinead was not with them.

I reached the elevators. One of them was going down. I didn't stop. I burst into the main stairwell and ran down the stairs, taking them a landing at a time. I reached the reception area as the elevator stopped and the doors opened. People spilled out. Not one of them was Russell, Hook or Maria.

I ran out into the parking lot. Nothing. Nothing there and nothing on Du Cane Road. There was a dark blue van with smoked windows heading up toward Wood Lane. I knew it had to be them. And I knew by the time I'd got into the Daemon and out onto the road, I'd have lost them.

Russell had betrayed me. Hook had betrayed me. Sinead and the hybrids had Maria and I'd lost the only things that had ever really mattered to me. I watched the small red taillights of the van disappear through the gray mist and drizzle. I was up against Russell's genius, the skill of the SAS and the might of the hybrids. I didn't stand a chance. I was out of options. Game over.

I wiped the rain from my eyes. I could roll over and die, or I could dig deep, find reserves and fight. There was only one answer. There was only ever one answer. I would dig deep. The blood-letting had started. Now, the killing wouldn't stop until I had my woman, my baby—and my revenge.

Chapter Nine

I knew the cops would be arriving within minutes. When they'd disconnected Maria from the heart monitor, it had sent up an alarm that said she was flat-lining. That had been the code-blue team I'd seen. When they'd arrived, they would have found not only Maria gone, but at least two dead bodies, and it was only a matter of time before they found Crew Cut in the stairwell. He my only lead. I had maybe two or three minutes to get to him before the cops did.

I turned and ran back into the hospital. I found the back stairwell. His body was on the first-floor landing. He'd hit the banister rail and broken his back. He was twisted into a grotesque swastika, and by the expression on his face, he'd taken a while to die.

I moved fast. I pulled off his jacket then fished through his pants pockets. There was nothing there but some loose change. I grabbed the jacket and took the stairs two at a time, then ran out into the rain and climbed into my car. As I pulled away up Du Cane Road, I passed the cops going the other way.

It wasn't smart, but I drove home to my apartment. I needed to eat and rest. I needed a drink, and above all, I needed to think. Besides, I figured if anybody was looking for me, the last place they'd look was at my place. And if they did, I'd be glad to give them a special magnum .44-caliber welcome.

As I arrived at Notting Hill Gate, the rain started in earnest. It was like heavy gray sheets cascading from blue-black clouds. The underground station had been closed, but as I drove past, I could see tarpaulin bivouacs set up where the stairs led down to the entrance. The official figure for the homeless had hit five hundred thousand. The real figure must have been nearly double that. There had been marches and demonstrations, increasingly violent ones. But you can't legislate against droughts. You can't legislate to make food grow when the land is scorched and dry. The planet was no longer producing the basic commodity – food. No food, no jobs, no money, no homes.

I turned into Church Street and parked outside my main door. As I climbed out, I heard a notification for a Whatsapp. I ignored it and ran, holding Crew Cut's jacket under my arm and I rode the elevator to my apartment, shaking water from my hair and wiping it from my face.

I threw the jacket on the table and stood under a hot shower for fifteen minutes. Then I toweled myself dry, got dressed and poured myself a large Bushmills. I realized I was famished. I scrambled three eggs and fried some bacon, put it on two pieces of rye and sat staring at the jacket while I ate.

I finished, took a slug of whiskey, lit a Camel then started methodically emptying his pockets. He had a cell phone with no numbers saved in the address book. He had three pounds in change and the keys to an Audi. Two got you twenty it was dark blue or black. They always were. He also had a wallet with five hundred pounds in it and an American driving license in the name of Jonathan D'Eau. *Cute.* In his other inside pocket, I found a leather case with his real ID. His name had been Major Peter Kawalski of the Allied Executive. I'd never heard of them, but Washington bred secret agencies like rabbits breed bunnies at Easter.

AE. It had a ring of Ael about it. It sounded like Del Roble's crew back in a new disguise. The question was, what the hell Del Roble or a secret US government agency wanted with Maria and her baby – *our* baby? It was the same question I had been asking about the British government. Why the hell was the SAS deploying an entire squad and a brigadier to protect her? And why the hell had Sinead and Catherine come out of hiding to tend to her and try their damnedest to separate me from her? I crushed out my cigarette to go stand looking out at the gray rain. It was midafternoon on a summer's day, but the cars and buses already had their lights on and their reflections lay broken, spilled on the wet blacktop. The other question I didn't want to ask and I didn't want answered was why Russell and Hook had gone behind my back and stolen Maria from me—Maria and our child.

Our child.

Where had they taken her? With Russell's brains and the combined resources of the SAS and the hybrids, it could be anywhere. And with every passing hour, my chances of finding her became more remote. What the hell were Russell and Hook playing at? But I knew the answer to that. I had been on the receiving end of Sinead and Catherine's mind games in the past. I knew what they could do to a man.

I took a slug of whiskey. The warmth spread through my belly. I looked into the deep amber and saw my lamp and the gray light of the window reflected in its depths. I didn't know how to find her but somebody did—somebody who had already found her once before, despite Sinead and Hook's efforts. I turned and looked at the wallet lying on the table. The AE would know how to find her.

The Allied Executive.

I went to the table and picked up his cell. I turned it over in my fingers. There was no brand, no make. It was just sleek and black, made of steel or some kind of carbon fiber. I activated the screen and looked in the call register. There were no calls logged. I found the speed dial and pressed 1.

It rang once, and a male voice said, "Who is this?"

I said, "I'd like to know the same thing."

"If you dialed this number, you know who we are. Who are *you*?"

"I know what you call yourselves, pal. I could call myself Peter Kawalski, but that wouldn't mean jack."

"Is this going anywhere?"

"Yeah. I'm giving you time to triangulate the call and find out where I am. When you find me, things can go one of two ways. We can cooperate and help each other, or I can kill your operatives the same way I killed John D'Eau aka Major Peter Kawalski."

There was a silence that said he was thinking. He said, "Who are you?"

"I'm Liam Murdoch. I can be useful to you, but my help comes at a price."

"I'll get back to you."

He hung up.

Ten seconds later, I got another Whatsapp. I sighed and fished out my phone. There were two messages from a number I'd never seen before.

Are you there?

And the second read.

Have you forgiven me yet?

I stared at them a long time, wondering what they meant. Eventually I answered.

I don't know. What did you do?

The answer was almost instant. It was a little laughing face with tears spilling out of its eyes. Then another message.

Seriously? You don't know who I am?

In my time, I have known a lot of girls who were in what they liked to call 'the entertainment business'. That was before I met Maria. They were all casual acquaintances and most of them had faded from memory. I wondered if this could be one of them, hoping for a hand out of hard times, but the timing was too nice. I typed back.

Hairy Bob? Jack the Wire? Knuckles Wilson? Harry the Teeth?

This time it was three laughing faces with tears. Then...

You crack me up.

Then nothing. I waited. After a minute, I threw my phone on the table and went back to the window to look at the rain. It had gotten heavier and there were knots of people sheltering in the doorways with the light from the shops reflected on their wet coats. Others were running with their umbrellas bobbing or their jackets pulled over their heads, like it was somehow better to get your kidneys wet than your hair.

The Whatsapp notifier sounded again. I went and looked.

I'm outside your block. Can I come up? I'm cold and wet.

I answered

No.

It said that whoever it was was typing.

Come on, Murdoch. Gimme a break. I'm cold and wet.

There was a crying face. I was suddenly real mad at the whole damned human race.

Tell me who you are or go to hell!

I went and stared down at the people in the street. They were just huddled lumps of wet coats, scarves and hats. It could be anyone. I went to the kitchen. The light was going fast. I hit the switch. Overhead, I heard thunder. The light flickered on. I took the percolator and started making coffee. I went back to the drawing room, and in a sudden fury, I grabbed the phone and dialed Russell. He was unavailable.

I called Maria and Hook — same result. Then the Whatsapp notifier went again.

It's Maggie.

I stared at it a long time. Questions were racing around my head but finding no answers. I felt like I was in a spider's web of unanswered questions, but it was a web that was like a 3D matrix and spread out in every direction for infinity. The more I reached for answers, the more questions kept appearing like sticky entangling threads. Finally, I answered.

Yeah, come up.

From the window, I saw one, small body detach itself from the coffee shop doorway and dodge through the traffic. Three minutes later, my doorbell rang.

She still looked like a sack of wool, but now she looked like a saturated sack of wool. She was grinning at me from under a floppy, wet hat. She said, "Are you mad at me?"

I stepped aside and said, "Come in," in no particular way. She walked in and I closed the door behind her. I pointed in the direction of the bathroom. "You want to dry off? Have a hot shower?"

She beamed. "You serious?"

"Sure. Did you eat? I can make you some food."

She seemed to kind of sag, still grinning. "Man, I am so relieved you're not mad at me! I thought, if I like just turn up, after the way I behaved in Gdansk…" She rolled her eyes and shook her head.

I said, "Don't worry about it."

She hesitated. "Will your wife, like, mind?"

I stared at her, then said, "No. She's not here."

Her face brightened. "Oh, cool!" Then she laughed, "I mean, cool I can have a shower, not cool — "

"I know. Go ahead. Give me your coat and your hat."

She climbed out of her trappings and pulled off her hat.

She was neat and pretty underneath. She handed them to me and shook out her hair. She said again, "I'm famished. I haven't eaten since that night." She left the words hanging, like they meant more than just the words.

I smiled without much warmth and said, "I have some lamb chops. I'll grill them for you."

She gave a little skip, grabbed me and kissed me on the cheek, then gave me a mischievous smile and went into the bathroom. I hung her coat and hat in the kitchen, put some frozen chops in the microwave to defrost and stepped back into the hall. I listened. I could hear the water and the sounds of her moving about in the shower. I stepped in, gathered up her clothes, put them in a refuse sack and tossed them in the bedroom. I locked the bedroom door and went into the kitchen to check on the chops.

Fifteen minutes later she appeared in the doorway with tussled wet hair and wrapped in a bath towel. She looked like she didn't know whether to smile or not. She said, "Where are my clothes?"

I said, "Drying."

She glanced at the dryer. It was off and the door was open. She said, "They weren't wet."

I smiled at her and showed her a chop. "You want them grilled or casseroled?" before she could answer, I said, "There are bathrobes and slippers in the airing cupboard."

She glanced again at the dryer and repeated, "Where are my clothes?"

I repeated my smile and picked up a big Sabatier knife and started peeling garlic. "Drying." I held her eye, still smiling. Then I said, "I have another apartment downstairs with a special drying room. Didn't you know? You'll be comfortable in the robe till they're dry."

She put a frown together with a smile and stuck it on her face, then went to put on the robe. She must have decided while she was in the bathroom that I was making a play for her, because when she came back, she'd lost the frown and her smile had turned sexy. She'd left the robe a bit loose so

I could see the swell of her breasts. It was a nice swell and they were nice breasts. Not so long ago, I would have been peeling the robe off to explore the rest of her curves and swells. She leaned on the doorjamb and said, "So, we're alone?"

I gave her a smile that said we were, and asked her, "You want some wine?"

She grinned. "You got a beer?"

I pulled one out of the fridge and cracked it. I handed it to her without a glass. She drained half the bottle and licked her lips.

I said, "So how did you know my number?"

She raised an eyebrow and for a moment looked older than her twenty-four years. "I looked on your phone after you finally went to sleep."

"Why?"

She frowned. This wasn't fun anymore. "What is this, an interrogation?"

"Sure."

She stared at me then shrugged. "I wanted to see you again." Then the smile was back. "I was hoping you might decide to let me thank you."

I gave a small laugh. "You don't give up easy."

"Not my style."

I turned and finished preparing the chops. "How'd you find my address?"

"You are one suspicious motherfucker."

I gave her a second, then repeated, "How'd you find my address?"

"You're in the phone book."

"Me and a lot of other Murdochs."

She gave a cute smile on one side of her face. "Only five, Mr. Paranoid. And you're the only one in Notting Hill. I figured you for a Notting Hill type of guy. Any more questions?"

I nodded. "Yup. How'd you know I lived in London? For that matter, how'd you know I lived in England?"

She threw up her hands. "Oh, for cryin' out loud, Murdoch! What is it with you? I went through your fucking wallet, okay? Satisfied? Your address is on your fucking driving license. Way to make a girl feel fucking stupid. You trying to humiliate me to make me go away or are you on some kind of power trip? Is this how you get your kicks? Get me my fucking clothes and I'll go."

I didn't say anything. I watched her. She put her beer down and said, "I liked you – a lot. You were the nicest guy I'd met. You were kind to me. You cared about me and you didn't try to get in my pants. That turned me on. I wanted to give it one more shot before I went back to the States. Satisfied? Now I wish I hadn't bothered."

It had the ring of truth and she was convincing. The chops were beginning to smell singed and I turned to flip them over. She said, "You want me to leave?"

I shook my head without looking at her. "No."

I dished up and carried her plate through to the dining table. She sat and ate voraciously in silence. A couple of times she muttered something about it being good. When she'd finished, she wiped her mouth with the back of her hand, drained her beer and belched. Then she grinned at me.

I said, "You should know that my wife has been kidnapped."

The grin faded and her face went pale. If she was acting, it was a superb performance. She whispered, "Shit," then, "No wonder…"

"No wonder?"

She gave her head a few little shakes. "You were suspicious."

"It's not safe here for you. I'm going to meet some men – "

"What men?"

I shook my head. "Don't get involved, Maggie. They could be coming here soon, and anyone involved with me is at risk. You need to go."

She stared down at her small hands on the table then she

met my eyes. "Right now?"

I sighed. She was probably a lonely kid who was like the rest of us, just looking for a way to make sense of a world and a life that didn't make any sense. I'd made the mistake of being kind to her, and she wanted me to make sense of everything else for her. "Every minute you stay here you are more at risk, Maggie. I wish…" I hesitated. I saw a small smile in her eyes.

She said, "Yes?"

I gave a small laugh. I figured life was hard enough for naïve dreamers. I didn't need to make it any harder. "I wish I could ask you to stay, but A, I'm married and very much in love with my wife, and B, I don't want to put you at risk."

She looked down at her hands again, nodded but didn't move. I went on, "You said you were on your way home. Have you booked a flight?"

She nodded again without looking at me.

"When for?"

She hesitated then said, "Tomorrow morning. Ten a.m."

I started to speak, saying, "Maggie, I wouldn't be doing you any favors if I—" and the phone rang. The screen said, 'Private Number'. I answered, "Yeah, Murdoch."

"You alone?" It was an American, a woman. Her voice was hard.

I thought fast, weighed the possibilities, said, "Yeah."

"You killed my operative."

"What do you want?"

"You said you could help us. How?"

"Not over the phone."

"Where?"

I hesitated. "Here."

There was a long pause. Then, "No. We'll send a car for you."

"How do I know—?"

"You don't. You want to deal, you get in the car. If we wanted you dead, believe me, you'd be dead by now. We want to deal. The car will be there in fifteen."

She hung up.

Maggie was watching me. I said, "They're coming for me in fifteen minutes." I pulled over Kawalski's wallet and drew out the five hundred pounds. I gave it to her and said, "After I've gone, wait twenty minutes then leave. Don't call a cab. Hail one at Notting Hill Gate or High Street Ken. Better still, get a bus or an underground train. Book into a hotel at Heathrow and stay in your room till it's time to get your flight. Make sure nobody sees you leaving here. Make sure nobody ever connects you with me. Do you understand?"

She nodded. She said, "Are you going to be all right? Are they going to—?"

I answered without thinking, "It's not me you need to worry about."

I got up and went to the bedroom. In the wardrobe, I found the steel box where I kept my weapons. I opened it, put my Smith & Wesson in and took out the carbon polymer Sig that Hook had given me when I'd gone to get Maria back from Algeria. It was invisible to metal detectors and I had a hunch I might need it. I closed the box, locked it then stood up. Maggie was in the doorway watching me. She said, "You really love her, huh?"

"Yeah."

I slipped the automatic into my waistband behind my back and pushed past her into the drawing room. I closed and locked the door behind me. She said, "What does that feel like?" Before I could answer, she went on, "I don't think I will ever be able to feel that."

I slipped on my jacket and considered her for a while. I said, "I used to think the same way. One day, it just happens to you. I hope it will happen for you, Maggie."

She didn't answer. Ten minutes later, my phone rang. A male voice said, "Downstairs." I checked out of the window and wasn't surprised to see a dark Audi with its hazards on outside my door. I looked at Maggie. She was watching me in silence. I said, "Take it easy, Maggie. Be lucky."

As I closed the door behind me, I heard her say, "You, too."

Chapter Ten

It was growing dark. There were two guys in suits. They had the anonymous faces of people who have become drones. One of them opened the rear door for me then walked around the hood and climbed into the front passenger seat. The other got in behind the wheel. We did a U-turn and went down the hill toward High Street Kensington. Through the window, everything was doused in wet, evening light. The sidewalks were spilling people in sodden macks and umbrellas. I could hear the hiss of the tires on damp blacktop. We turned left onto the High Street and headed in the direction of Knightsbridge. I said, "Where are we going?"

I got the reply I expected. I saw the driver's eyes flick at the rearview mirror. That was it.

We turned right at the Albert Memorial and moved down through Victoria. Pretty soon, we came out on the river bank at Pimlico and turned east, headed for the Palace of Westminster. The rain was growing heavier and it was hard to make out details among the diffused lights. The only sound was the drumming of the rain and the rhythmic squeak of the wipers. The river, Old Man Thames, was a strip of blackness on my right. And ahead, through the liquid lights of the embankment, the Victoria Tower loomed, amber and massive. We were at the House of Lords, the Houses of Parliament.

The mother of all parliaments.

We turned in at the gate and stopped. The driver's window hummed down and a cop looked in. The driver showed him some kind of ID. The cop saluted and we moved on into the car park. He pulled up outside the main entrance. The guy in the passenger seat jumped out and came around to open the door for me. As I climbed out, he said, "The duke's secretary will meet you inside, Sir. He'll take you to His Grace."

I watched the car pull away, back through the gate into the rain and traffic. I had a feeling I'd stepped through the looking glass. I turned and climbed the stairs. The lobby, if that's what you call a place like that, was grand and ancient. There was a man of about fifty in a black jacket and gray pinstriped trousers standing in the middle of a very shiny checkerboard floor. He seemed to recognize me and approached me with what you could only describe as deferential insolence. You have to be English to master that kind of skill. He said, "Mr. Murdoch?" as though he thought it was in very poor taste that I should have that name.

I said, "Yeah."

He turned away from me, like I offended his sensibilities, but said, "Follow me, please."

I followed him. We went through a stone arch with an ancient oak door in it, then up a flight of narrow stairs carpeted in royal blue. I remembered that this was the part of Parliament that the aristocracy had kept for themselves, to safeguard the interests of the Crown against the commoners. That's why they called the assembly the House of Commons, because it was where the commoners met to debate and vote.

We came out into a broad corridor and I followed him around a couple of bends until we came to a short passage. Here he stopped outside one of two doors and turned to me. "Kindly wait here. In a moment, I shall present you to His Grace, the Duke of Suffolkshire. You will address him as Your Grace or My Lord. He will address you by your surname." He tapped on the door and stepped in without waiting for an answer. He said to an invisible body, "Murdoch."

The invisible body must have told him to bring me in because he turned to me and said, "Follow me."

He led me through an oak-paneled office with a sensible secretary sitting at a desk. I was pretty sure she was wearing a sensible tweed skirt and sensible brown shoes. She ignored me and I ignored her back. My guide led me to a huge arched door and knocked on it. A voice said, "Come!" and my guide opened the door, announced, "Murdoch, Your Grace!" and stepped aside to let me in.

I don't know what I'd expected, but whatever it was, it wasn't this. The guy must have been six foot three with a shock of silver-white hair swept back from a craggy, handsome face. He could have been anything from fifty to seventy, but he radiated an intense energy, and he had eyes like a pair of nail guns. He was dressed in a suit that was understated but must have cost as much as my car. He'd been standing at a leaded window looking out over the Thames. He'd turned to greet me as I came in and now moved toward me. The office was big, carpeted in blue and furnished in red leather. There was a coal fire burning. It took him five long strides to cross the room. He held out his hand as he approached and smiled.

We shook. He said, "Murdoch, how do you do?"

I said, "Your Grace."

He gestured me to a big, burgundy chesterfield that was nestled by the fire with a large sofa of the same design. "I believe Irish is your tipple, isn't it? Bushmills?"

I didn't answer. He brought me a generous measure in a hand-cut tumbler and sat opposite me in a wing chair that looked as though it had recently accommodated Sherlock Holmes. He crossed one very long, very elegant leg over another and said, "I understand you want to do some kind of deal with us."

I looked around the room—at the fire, the portraits of what I assumed were his ancestors, his vast oak desk, his Saville Row suit and his Eaton school tie. I said, "I don't know. Who is 'us'? I spoke to a woman from the AE."

Nothing changed in his expression, but his voice hardened. "What do you want, Murdoch?"

I said, "Have you taken over from del Roble?"

His eyes narrowed. "Del Roble?" I studied his face. His expression wasn't what I'd expected. Nothing about this guy was what I'd expected. He said, "Serafino del Roble?" I nodded, still watching him. "What makes you think...?"

He let the words trail off and turned his gaze to his shoe. It was a very shiny, black patent-leather shoe. I waited. He said, "What do you know about Serafino del Roble?"

I said, "A lot. But most of all I know he's dead, because I killed him."

He couldn't keep the pleasure from his face. He lifted his gaze to meet mine and smiled. "Did you, by Jove?"

This guy was all curve balls. He sat chuckling while I stared at him. I said, "If you're not from the Brotherhood, who the fuck are you?"

He nodded. "Yes, I see. I see now. You think we are the Brotherhood of the Goat—or one of their sister organizations."

"But you're not."

He shook his head. "No. Oh, no. No, we most definitely are not. I would be very surprised, indeed, if you had ever heard of us."

"So? What do you want with Maria?"

His expression became serious and he turned his gaze on his whiskey. He tipped it this way and that, examining the angles. Eventually, he said, "You phoned us, Murdoch. You said we could cooperate and that you could help us."

"At a price."

"Indeed. I suggest you tell me in what way you think you can help us and what your price is."

"You want Maria, so do I. I can get her back, but I need your help to find her. The price is, you tell me why you want her and I get to keep her."

His face hardly moved, except for a minute twitch of one eyebrow, but understanding dawned in his eyes.

"Murdoch…of course… You are her husband."

"Yeah. I'm her husband."

The realization had triggered a domino effect in his brain. You could almost hear the clicking as his gaze drifted around the room. He said, "And you killed del Roble…"

I nodded. "You are beginning to get the picture."

He narrowed his eyes and tried to nail me with them. "Who do you work for?"

I shook my head. "No dice."

"Are you employed by the renegades?"

"I told you, no dice. I'll get Maria back. In exchange, I need to know why you want her, and I need your help to find out where she is. That's the deal."

He stood and walked to the window. He stared out for a long while. He muttered something that sounded like, "It can't be," then turned and stared hard at me, like he was trying to bore holes in my skull with his eyes. He said, "For a long time, we've thought there was another" — he searched for the right word — "another agency at work. Things happened we couldn't explain. There were even those who talked about…" He trailed off again. There was some big idea in his head and he wanted to talk about it but he didn't want to say the words. I was becoming curious. I drained my glass and pulled out my Camels. I flipped my Zippo and leaned into the flame, like I had all the time in the world.

I blew smoke at the coals and spoke. "You want to know who I am? I'm the meanest son of a bitch in this valley. I killed del Roble, I killed Banks and I killed Golika — several times over." I turned to look at him. "They won't be coming back. You want to know who I work for? I work for myself. Now, the Brotherhood has my wife and I am going to get her back. If you help me, it will be easier and quicker. You want in or not?"

He nodded. He had no choice. "Fair enough, Murdoch. That's the deal. We'll help you find her and I'll tell you why we want her. But it seems to me that when you know more about us, you may want our cooperation to go a lot further."

I stared at him a while. Maybe he was right. I said, "Maybe, maybe not. Let's take it as it comes. What do you want my wife for?"

He sighed, opened a cigarette box on his desk and popped a cigarette in his mouth. He lit it with a match and frowned at me. "Do you know Dr. O'Brien, your wife's physician?"

"I know her—but not by that name."

He nodded. "You know her as Sinead Tiernan."

"Yeah."

"Do you know—?" He hesitated for a second. "Do you know *what* she is?"

"I know what she says she is. I know what del Roble said they all were."

"Oh, it's true, Murdoch. It's all true." He sipped his whiskey and stared at the glowing coals in the fire. "What I don't understand is how you came to know about him." He rose on his toes a couple of times. "How do I know you're not one of them? How do we know this is not a setup?"

I thought about it. "I guess you don't. And I can't think of any way to convince you, especially as I have no idea who or what *you* are."

He gave a little grunt.

I said, "All I want is intel on how to get to Maria, where she is right now. I haven't got the resources to find her. I figure you have. And I want to know why you're after her. If you aim to hurt her, I'll kill you, the way I killed Kawalski, Banks, del Roble and all the rest."

"I understand."

He sat and we were both silent for a long while. Then he said something that surprised me. He looked me in the eye and asked, "Is Maria human?"

I started to say, "Of course, she is…" but I went cold all over as all sorts of things started to make sense.

He waited, watching my face. Then he said, "Are you absolutely sure?"

I said, "Yeah, I'm sure. Why does it matter?"

"It matters because we think maybe the baby isn't."

It shouldn't have surprised me but it did. I felt suddenly sick. I didn't say anything and he watched my face a while, reading me like *Hello* magazine. He nodded. "You had some suspicion."

He drained his glass, stood then refilled it. He showed me the decanter and I nodded, so he refilled mine, too. As he was putting the decanter back he said, "I'm not sure how much you know, Murdoch, or how long you've been in this game, but we are at war. Are you aware of that?"

I said, "Once again, Your Grace, who is 'we' and who are you at war with?"

He gave a small, sad laugh that sounded genuine. "It used to be easy. The bad guys were always the Frogs, then it was the Krauts, then the damned Communists." For a moment he looked tired and suddenly older. "Nowadays, you don't know who the damned enemy is. The enemy could be your oldest friend, your secretary, your chauffeur..." He shook his head.

"You're either rambling or being evasive. You don't strike me as the rambling type. Cut to the chase."

He raised an eyebrow at me and laughed. "We are an alliance of groups that operate within existing governments. Our purpose is to fight the invasion. We were founded a long time ago. We operate in the utmost secrecy because we are aware that our governments and seats of power worldwide have been infiltrated by the invaders. They are very subtle and very devious, and above all, very believable. They are turning humanity against itself. Sadly, that is not a difficult thing to do." He studied my face, then went on. "We have been monitoring Sinead Tiernan for some time — among other people — and that's how your wife came to our attention. We aren't sure, but we think that her baby might be some form of" — he paused and gave the word a lot of thought. Then he sighed and shook his head — "a weapon. Some kind of hybrid weapon."

"How the hell can a baby be a weapon?"

95

"I don't know. We don't know. But you must be aware how important the baby seems to be to them."

I nodded. He was right about that. "Yeah. So, what do you want to do with my wife and my child?"

"I could lie to you, Murdoch, but I won't insult your intelligence. We want to know if it's human. If you are the father, if you and your wife have normal, human DNA and the child carries your DNA then we couldn't be less interested. But if you, your wife or the child have alien DNA, then obviously, we are concerned."

"Wait a minute! Alien DNA? What are you talking about?"

He looked surprised. "What do you think I'm talking about? If any of you is an alien or an alien hybrid."

"We're *not* aliens."

He was silent for a long time, staring at me with the smoke from his cigarette coiling up from his hand, like the ghost of a snake. Eventually, he drew breath and said, "A while ago you said you knew what they said they were. What did they tell you they were?"

"Saurians. They said *we* were the aliens."

When he spoke, it was almost a whisper. "Good Lord, they are subtle, very subtle."

"You telling me that's not true?"

He smiled in a way you could call apologetic and said, "It's absolute balderdash, Murdoch. It is nothing so elaborate. It is much more — if you'll excuse the pun — down to earth. We know very little about them, but we do know that they are alien and that their intention is to colonize Earth."

"What for?"

"Why did we colonize India and Africa? Wealth, power, economic imperatives. Trouble is that there are a lot of us and we are a very aggressive, dangerous species, as they have discovered to their cost on more than one occasion. But they are very subtle and very devious, and their technology is *very* advanced. They have managed to place hybrids under their control in the highest offices in the States, in the UK, in the United Nations, in the EU. And their greatest skill is the use of misinformation and manipulation, turning us against ourselves."

He was plausible. He was more than plausible. He was very believable and I *wanted* to believe him. But there was one big question that was bugging me like crazy. I wanted to know how come he didn't know Russell and Hook. It was too much of a coincidence. You couldn't have two setups like this side by side, not knowing each other.

But what was blowing my mind was that when I'd met with Russell and Hook, it had been at Russell's place or at a safe house. Right now, I was sitting with the Duke of Suffolkshire in the House of Lords at the Palace of Westminster — the heart of the British government.

But I also trusted Russell without question.

Do I? Then why am I sitting here making a deal with this guy?

I said, "So you want to test my DNA?"

He nodded. "Yes."

"Then you'll help me find Maria. And when I get her back, you want to test her DNA and the baby's?"

He nodded again.

"If we're all human, we go on our way. What if Maria or the baby are not? What if one or both of them are hybrids?"

He looked haggard. When he spoke, he addressed the fire, like he was thinking aloud. "We are not monsters, Murdoch. The whole point is that we are human. We don't kill creatures just because they are not human. And therefore, that is *not* the crucial question. The crucial question is, are *you* a threat? Is *she*? Are *they* a threat? If you can persuade us that you do not mean to aid or abet the invaders, as far as I am concerned, you can go on your way."

"How do I know you will honor that?"

He turned to face me. "I offer you the same answer you gave me a little while ago. You can't. It seems for the moment we have shared aims. It may be that with time, if we cooperate, we may find we have more than that. We may become allies. We are both taking a risk."

I thought, then said, "Is there another organization like yours? Is there anybody else fighting this invasion?"

He nodded. "Yes. The people you work for, whoever they are." Then he raised his eyebrows and fixed me with a look. "That is, assuming what you have told me is true. What I am wondering, Murdoch, is what has made you fall out with them, and why they have abducted Maria."

Yeah. I'm wondering that, too.

Chapter Eleven

He'd had a guy come and swab my mouth for my DNA sample then we'd agreed he would put his people to work trying to trace where they'd taken Maria. He'd given me a phone and told me when they found her, he'd contact me and we'd work out some plan for me to get her. He'd wanted her cell number and the numbers of the other people with her. I'd given him Maria's, but I told him no dice with the others. "They are good people and they are my friends. Don't ask me to betray them."

I could still hear the words in my ears. *'They are good people and they are my friends. Don't ask me to betray them.'*

He'd raised an eyebrow at me and said, "I hope they are as loyal to you as you are to them."

Me, too.

He'd had a car drive me home.

I stood on the sidewalk and watched it drive away through the dark rain. *The AE...who are they? Who is the Duke of Suffolkshire – another player in the game, another contender for absolute power?* I felt a twist of fear. Who did I turn to for guidance? Until now, I had always had Russell – timeless, wise and cool. He had seemed indestructible, immutable in his ancient Tudor house, always ten steps ahead of the game, knowing exactly what moves to make. But now I no longer had him to guide me. I was on my own, enemies on every side and just one dim light to guide me, my determination to find Maria and make her safe.

I stood in the doorway, fished out a Camel, lit up then leaned against the wall and watched the silver drops make ripples on the mercury blacktop. I needed time. I needed stillness — to get a grip on the chaos around me.

Around me and inside me.

Why had Russell and Hook betrayed me? Why had they not confided in me? Why had they kept me out of the loop? What did Sinead and Catherine want with Maria and the baby? Why were they so interested in her, and why were they trying to separate us? And, was it true, what Suffolkshire had said? That the Brotherhood were not Saurians but aliens?

I inhaled deep and held the smoke, trying to slow down my mind. If they were aliens, then the modem I had left in Gdansk might have a much bigger significance. It could be the precursor to a wholesale invasion. And that got me thinking about Agostinho and the two 'things' that had killed him. Why hadn't they shown yet? Were they still trying to track me down? Or were Sinead, Catherine, The Brotherhood and the HEAT corporation all in bed together?

Why? Why? Why?

What was it Russell had always said to me? Never ask 'why'? It is too open and there is no answer to it. Ask who? Where? What? How? These were questions you could answer, questions that led you somewhere. I looked at the glowing tip of my cigarette. Heat. I was asking the wrong questions, but what were the right ones? I felt the heat of the tip on my fingers and flicked the butt out into the rain. I heard it hiss in a puddle, turned and climbed the stairs to my apartment.

As I climbed, understanding — or at least the first dim rays of it — began to dawn in my mind. I was groping, but the first shadowy shapes of meaning began to emerge. One thing was certain, pretty soon the 'things' from Sao Paulo were going to find me, and when they did, I had to be ready for them.

I had my key in my hand and I was reaching to put it in the lock. Something, a perception just below the level of consciousness, made me freeze. There was a sound that was more like a feeling in the air. Somebody was moving in my apartment. I pulled the Sig from my waistband and slipped the key very softly into the lock.

I was quiet — I know how to be quiet — but she must have been right by the door, waiting. She wrenched it open and stood staring at me, dressed in old clothes of Maria's.

"Thank God you're back."

"Maggie? What the hell?"

She grabbed me and pulled me in, slammed the door behind me. She grabbed my lapels with both hands, looking into my face with wide eyes. "They were here. They were here at the door, asking for you."

"*Who* were? Calm down, Maggie. Take it easy. Who was here?"

"Them! The..." — she stared about, searching for words, waving her right hand — "the...*things!*"

"Things?"

She stared into my face. She was pale. "They were like people, Murdoch, but they weren't. They were like —"

I said, "Robots?"

She froze, nodded. Her voice was little more than a whisper. "Yes."

"What did they say?"

Tears sprang into her eyes and her lip curled as she bit back a sob. "They asked if you were in. Murdoch, they weren't *human!*"

"I know. Try to keep a grip. What did you tell them?"

Tears were spilling from her eyes and running down her cheeks. She said, "I told them you were away. I said I was minding your apartment and didn't know when you'd be back. What the hell *are* they?"

She was gripping my jacket tight. I said, "Good girl. You did good." She came to me and buried her face in my chest. I put my arms around her. I said again, "You did good."

I moved her in to the drawing room. I said, "Let me get you a drink. How long ago were they here?"

They must have seen me arrive. Why didn't they take me when I was smoking downstairs?

She said, "Maybe fifteen, twenty minutes. I've been so scared."

I poured her a generous measure and handed it to her. "What did they say when you said I wasn't here?"

She took the drink. "They said, you were to stay here and wait for them. They needed to talk to you. Not to leave."

I moved fast to my bedroom. Over my shoulder, I snapped, "Get ready. We are going. *Now.*"

"Where?"

"Don't ask questions. Do it!"

I opened the wardrobe and wrenched open the box where I keep my guns. I pulled out my Smith & Wesson, pocketing a box of magnum .44s as I did so. I froze. A kind of sixth sense kicked in. In slow motion, I saw my hand pushing the key into the lock. I saw the door being wrenched open and Maggie looking up at me in fear. I saw her grab my lapels, pulling me in and I saw the door closing behind me.

The key is still in the door.

Then everything happened at the same time. I shouted, "Maggie, the key!" and ran. But as I ran, I heard her scream. I burst into the drawing room. They were there, with their white moon faces and their black sunglasses. One was blocking the way to the front door. The other had a hold of Maggie's neck and was staring into her face. I threw myself at him. He turned his head to face me and let Maggie drop. I heard him say, "Don't fight," as I swung a right hook at his belly. He caught my wrist and threw me across the room. I crashed into a table and smashed a lamp.

He was striding at me as I struggled to get up. He bent at the waist and his right hand closed on my throat. His left grabbed my wrist as I swung at him. He said again, "Don't fight." He lifted me and rammed me against the wall. His big, black glasses were inches from my face. I kicked wildly at his legs and kneed him in the groin. He said, "Stop. I feel no pain. You cannot damage me. *Stop.*"

I pounded his white oval face with my fists. It was like ceramic and I saw smears of my own blood on it. I grabbed his sunglasses and yanked with both hands. They didn't budge. He slapped me across the face with his left hand then threw me across the room again. I hit the dining table and sent two chairs crashing. The pain in my back was crippling. I tried to move but my chest muscles were in spasm and my head was spinning from the slap. He was watching me, waiting.

As I clawed my way to my hands and knees, I noticed the other one. It had Maggie by the throat. She was struggling and kicking, but it was ignoring her, watching me. They looked like they were waiting to see what I was going to do next. I knew how they felt. My head was reeling and my mind was racing, but I couldn't see a way out.

They both spoke at the same time. "Are you spent?"

In my peripheral vision, I was aware of one of my chairs, splintered and broken by my side. I said, "Yeah, I'm spent."

The one who'd thrown me said, "Where is the case you took from Agostinho?"

I pointed at his pal who was holding Maggie. She was staring at me with wild eyes. I said, "I shoved it up your pal's ass."

As I said it, I grabbed the chair leg with both hands and charged, roaring like a demented berserker. I rammed the sharp, splintered end into his belly, putting all my two hundred and ten pounds behind it. He staggered back two steps and back-handed me like a ping-pong ball. The blow lifted me off my feet and I landed flat on my back. I could hear my breath wheezing in my throat and needles of electric pain pierced my lungs.

"Stop fighting."

I rolled on my side and tried to sit. I tried to breathe. My lungs sounded like a massed Welsh choir with collective bronchitis. The one who had Maggie said, "I will tear off her arm."

I said, "*No!*" and as I said it, Maggie screamed. It was the highest-pitched sound I had ever heard in my life. It was like a silver needle piercing through my brain. Then there was another noise added to it, like iron teeth being dragged across a blackboard, amplified to a thousand decibels. I covered my ears with my hands and realized I had my eyes screwed up. A voice in my head told me, "*Now! Now! Now!*"

I staggered to my feet. The one who'd thrown me was walking in circles, taking very small steps. There was a smell of burning—electrical burning. I took a step toward Maggie, still covering my ears. She seemed to have a hold of the thing's armpit. Both its arms were stuck out, as if it was crucified. They were shaking and there was smoke coming out of its head.

I didn't think. I saw my Smith & Wesson on the floor. I grabbed it and moved, shouting, "Let's go! Go! Now!"

She let go of the thing, grabbed her backpack and moved to the door. I saw she was holding something. It looked like an electric razor. She pulled open the door and we stepped out. The key was in the lock. I locked the door, pocketed the key and we ran down the stairs.

We hit the sidewalk at a run. She turned to me, the rain already matting her hair to her face. "Where are we going?"

I hesitated.

Do they know my car? One stupid decision will cost you both your lives.

I grabbed her hand and said, "Run!"

We ran down Church Street toward High Street Kensington, shouldering in among the crowds and the jostling umbrellas, losing ourselves in the press of damp humanity. We ran, ducking, stumbling, colliding with wet, angry people, down in the direction of Hyde Park. The gates were supposed to be locked after eight p.m., but since they'd started using the park as a refugee camp, they'd also started leaving the gates open at night. We dodged into the Broad Walk then slipped in, away from the light that spilled in from the High Street, among the shadows and the black, amorphous forms of the tents and the bivouacs. Voices, rasping and guttural, filtered into the damp night air, among the hiss of propane lamps and cookers and the smell of makeshift cooking. Here and there the blackness was split by the amber glow of an open flap, showing tangled families in second-hand woolens staring out at the mud and the rain of an alien world with hostile, calculating eyes.

We picked our way through mud and mire, among guy ropes and nylon sheets, heading north to Bayswater Road. I still held her hand. I looked back, wiping the rain from my eyes, and said, "What did you do to him back there? What was that?"

She ran two steps to get abreast of me. "It's a stun gun. One million volts. My dad gave it to me. I panicked and stuck it under his arm. I just wanted him to let go. I had no idea it would have that effect."

I glanced at her. "What was that noise?"

She shook her head. "I think I screamed. But when I stuck him, he started letting out this weird screeching noise. Then smoke started coming out of his head." We trudged on in silence for a while with the rain soaking through our clothes. Eventually, the tents and bivouacs thinned out and we were under the cover of the trees. She said, "What the hell are those things? What are you involved in?"

I glanced at her. "It's a long story. You're better off not knowing."

"Are they anything to do with your wife's kidnappers?"

"Not exactly. I told you, you're better off not knowing, Maggie."

We came out of the park at the gate opposite Queensway, and I turned left toward Notting Hill Gate. She stopped dead in her tracks and pulled me back. "What are you doing? You're heading back?"

I faced her. The rain was growing heavier. There was no point wiping it out of my eyes anymore, but I tried anyway. I said, "It's the last thing they'd expect me to do. I'll leave you in a café or a pub. I'll slip back and get my car."

"Your car? What for? Where are we going?"

I took a step closer to her. "To the airport. You are getting on that plane and you are going home."

She didn't answer. She just stared hard at me and there was real resentment and anger in her eyes.

I said, "Come on," and I turned and started walking again. I glanced back. She was a couple of paces behind me. She was half stomping, staring at the pavement. She was bedraggled, soaking from head to foot and her hair was hanging down in sodden rat's tails. I slowed a bit for her to catch up but she shouldered past me and marched on ahead. I drew level with her and we walked in silence until we came to the Gate then we turned down into the top of Church Street. There was a café there on the left and we pushed in.

The lights were bright and they had plate-glass windows looking out onto the street, so we went and found a table at the back that was more-or-less secluded. I said, "You want to go to the toilet and dry off a bit? I'll order some food and coffee. What do you want?"

She ignored me and brushed past me again, headed for the toilets. I went to the counter and ordered toasted cheese and ham sandwiches and two large cups of coffee. I sat with my back to the window, and after five minutes, Maggie returned with her hair and her face looking a bit drier. I said, "Sit next to me. Don't face the street." She slumped into the chair next to mine and bit into a sandwich. I said, "You're sulking. What's wrong with you?"

"Nothing."

"Good. Eat up and drink your coffee. I'm going to get the car. I'll pick you up outside in ten minutes."

She shrugged. "Whatever."

I didn't feel like arguing so I got up and left.

I dodged through the traffic, hunching into my shoulders, then made my way through the press of wet bodies toward my block. It felt like it had been raining forever. Everything was sodden. Even the headlamps of the cars and the buses looked wet, like they'd been painted in watercolors. I scanned the dodging, scurrying bodies as I walked. I must have stood out like a sore thumb with no coat and no umbrella but I didn't spot anyone following me.

I came to the gates that gave on to the parking lot at the back of my block. I stepped in and pressed into the shadows. My Daemon was parked at the front, opposite the main door, but I used the cover of the gates to observe the crowds to see if my car was being watched. After five minutes, I was satisfied it wasn't. I stepped out and crossed the sidewalk, reaching in my saturated pocket for my key. Then I froze. A body pressed up close behind me and said, "Don't do it, Murdoch."

Chapter Twelve

She was standing close, looking up into my face, blinking away the water that was running into her eyes. She may have been crying. It was impossible to tell in that rain. We stood a long time like that. Then she said, "Please, don't send me back. Maybe I can help you." She smiled and wiped her eyes with the back of her hand. "I did okay upstairs, didn't I?" She gave a small laugh and I realized she was crying. "I did better than you."

I started to say, "I can't put your life at risk, Maggie," but she cut across me.

"Listen, Murdoch. You need a friend right now. And frankly, I would rather die being that friend than go back to what I left behind at home."

I shook my head, frowning, struggling to make sense of it. "Why?"

She shrugged. Wiped her wet face with her wet sleeve. She sounded as desperate as I felt. "I don't *know*, Murdoch! Does it *matter*?"

My shirt was sticking to me. Hers was becoming transparent and I could see she had no bra. The chances of our being seen were growing by the second. She said, "Look. The airport is a risk, anyway. If they are as powerful as they seem to be, they'll be watching all the exits from the country — ports, airports, stations. I know a place where we can go, get out of the rain, be safe for a bit and dry off. Then we can think what we do next."

I hesitated, cursed myself for hesitating and said, "Goddamn it, Maggie! Get in the car!" I got in, and as she climbed in next to me, I said, "Where is this place?"

She sniffed and wiped her face with her soaking sleeve again. "Willesden. Villiers Road. One of my dad's firms has a warehouse there. It's not in use now, so we can break in and drop off the radar." I glanced at her and frowned. She caught my look and shrugged. "I've learned to survive in the last year."

I nodded and gunned the engine.

Willesden is a ghetto. It's mean and ugly in a way you can only be mean and ugly when you have no soul left. Villiers Road was just as mean and ugly and soulless as the rest of Willesden, only a little more so. It ran in a long curve, southeast to northwest. A handful of depressed lampposts cast ungenerous pools of dull light that dragged everything around them into gloom. Most of the street was a terrace of small houses with small front gardens spilling trash. The few that gave any sign of life looked like squats. They'd had blankets nailed over their windows, either by refugees or emaciated people with hollow eyes, who didn't want the world to see them burn away what was left of their souls in small, tinfoil twists.

At the apex of the curve, the mean, terraced boxes gave way to a big cast-iron gate that enclosed a broad courtyard wide enough for a handful of cars and a couple of trucks. Right now, it was empty and the windows were boarded up. In the glow of my headlamps, I could see a heavy chain and a big, rusty padlock that said the gate had been locked a long time.

Maggie looked at me. "Can you pick it?"

I studied her face in the light of the dash. She smiled. I said, "What makes you think I can?"

She shrugged. "You're that kind of guy." I was about to get out when she said, "Would you like me better if *I* could pick it?"

I shook my head. "No. I already know you can."

Picking locks is one of my professional skills and this lock was nothing special. It gave up after fifteen seconds.

I climbed back in the Daemon and we drove in. I parked in the shadows out of sight while Maggie closed and padlocked the gate behind us. The door to reception gave me about as much trouble as the padlock, and we stepped at last into dry shelter out of the rain.

It was real dark. I pulled out my pen torch and played the narrow beam around the room. Maggie closed the door. There was a desk with an empty swivel chair behind it and an old phone. The circle of yellow light moved on, parting the shadows, allowing them to close in behind it. The walls were a nasty color between beige and gray. There were nails but no pictures. Double doors loomed. They were open and cast black shapes deep into a passage with stairs on the left and big, push-bar fire doors on the right.

I illuminated Maggie's face and found that she was staring at me. She looked kind of eerie in amber, surrounded by darkness. I said, "You know the place. Where to?"

I followed her. She shoved the push-bar and we stepped through the double doors into a cavernous warehouse with a dirty concrete floor. You could tell it was cavernous by the sound, but it was too dark to see the ceiling or the far walls. I played the beam around and found a cluster of small shipping containers, maybe fifteen foot by ten. They were open and seemed to be empty.

"What did they use this place for?"

She didn't answer and I directed the beam at her. She shielded her eyes a moment, then shrugged. "I don't know. I was never interested in his business. Let's find some wooden pallets. We can break them up and make a fire."

It wasn't hard to do. There were plenty of them and pretty soon we had enough planks and kindling to get a decent fire burning. It gave us light and warmth. I squatted in front of it, feeling the heat on my hands and face. It might be muggy outside, but in there, the high ceilings and the dark and wet made it chilly. Maggie was still standing. I glanced at her and saw that she was shivering. She said, "You know what? I know my dad used to stay over sometimes when

110

he had a lot of work. He kept a bed or something upstairs. Give me your flashlight and I'll see if there are any blankets up there."

I frowned. "Seriously?"

She nodded and held out her hand. She was shaking and stamping her feet like she was freezing. I handed her the light and she half-ran for the big doors. That was the turning point. That was when things began to slot into place.

She came back ten minutes later with a couple of towels and rough blankets. She threw me one of each and started to strip off her wet clothes. Her teeth were chattering, and even in the poor light, I could see she had goosebumps. She had no bra, and when she pulled off her jeans, she had a skimpy pair of lace pants that showed the dark triangle of her bush. I'd seen her naked before, in Gdansk, but by firelight with wet skin, I had to admit she looked good — too good. And cold and shivering like that, she seemed vulnerable, too. I had a sudden impulse to hold her in my arms, to keep her warm. I turned away and stared hard into the flames and the smoldering wood.

I was aware of her peeling off her panties and I struggled to ignore her. I thought of Maria instead. Where was she? What were they doing to her? How far would Russell and Hook go in their alliance with Sinead? How far had Sinead bewitched them? I knew only too well what she was capable of.

Maggie spoke through chattering teeth. "You should take your clothes off and dry them. You'll catch pneumonia"

I glanced up. She was wrapped in the blanket and draping her clothes on packing crates by the flames. I knew she was right but said, "I'm okay."

She stopped what she was doing and stared at me. "Oh, *come on*, Murdoch! We're pals. I'm not going to rape you. Get over it and dry your clothes. I won't look."

I felt embarrassed, made some kind of grunt and began to strip off, but left my pants on. I toweled my hair and pushed it back off my face with my fingers. Then I stripped off my trousers, dried and wrapped myself in the blanket. It was rough and coarse — not the kind of thing you'd expect a millionaire businessman to use — but it was warm and felt a damn site better than the wet clothes. I sat cross-legged in front of the crackling flames and she edged over close to me. She still gave the odd shudder, but her teeth had stopped chattering.

I said, "You really feel the cold, huh?"

She shrugged. "I guess." We sat in silence for a while, watching our clothes steam gently as they dried. After a time, Maggie spoke again and her voice was startling in the silence. "I guess you really are in love with your woman, aren't you?"

The question was unexpected and made me stare at her a while. She met my gaze. After a bit, I smiled and looked back into the fire, glad I'd resisted temptation. I said, "Yeah, I really am."

We were quiet again. Then she asked, "What's it like, being in love?"

The wood crackled and spat and shot a shower of sparks into the darkness. I gave another grunt, staring into the incandescent heart of the flames. I shook my head and sighed. "You're asking the wrong guy. I'm not eloquent. It's..." I let the words trail away, searching the darkness inside me for some way to describe what it was like to love Maria.

Maggie said, "Sure, I know, not even Shakespeare could explain it, and he could sum up just about everything. But" — she picked up a splinter of wood from the floor, examined it then tossed it into the flames — "if I wanted to feel what you feel for Maria, what would I have to feel inside me?"

I laughed. It was a good question and it made me think. "Okay... Well, it's not always a nice feeling. Sometimes it hurts. It hurts a lot. And sometimes it's like being really happy, only off-the-chart happy." She was watching me carefully, paying attention. I thought a moment longer and said, "It changes. It's not always the same feeling. It's more like a weaving of feelings, all of them strong and intense, and sometimes one feeling is on top and sometimes it's another."

She was frowning, almost squinting, like she was trying to see what I was saying. "What *kind* of feelings?"

"The closest thing I could compare it to, Maggie, would be hunger. Like being really, *really* hungry for a person."

Her face seemed to clear. "Hungry?"

I nodded. "Sure. Imagine you are really hungry for sirloin steak or a roast leg of lamb—whatever your favorite food is—and it's right there on the table and you can have as much of it as you like. You feel happy, safe, fulfilled and you have all those sensual pleasures that go with it. Now, imagine you have that same hunger, but there is no food on the table or even in the house, and you have no money to buy any."

"I know *that* one!"

"You feel empty, craving, depressed, anxiety…" I let the words trail away, aware of all those feelings intensified in me right then. I sighed, "But it's much more than that, too. Because as well as all those feelings, you also have a powerful, imperative drive to make that person safe and happy, even if it means sacrificing your own happiness, wellbeing or life to do it."

I knew she was listening, but I had drifted away, back to the burning heart of the fire. I had a longing to see Maria, to be with her, hear her voice and feel her skin on mine. Above all, I had a need to know she was safe. Maggie's voice brought me back. "For a guy who isn't eloquent, you sure put it across."

I smiled. "I'm sure you'll feel it someday, Maggie."

She went quiet. I glanced at her. She was staring down at her fingers, fiddling with another splinter of wood. She spoke in a small voice. "I think I have already started to." It was the last thing I expected her to say, and it was the last thing I needed to hear right then. I didn't know how to answer, but before I could say anything, she continued talking. "Everything you described, everything you said, I feel for you." She raised her face and stared me straight in the eye. "Maybe not as intensely as your describing it — you're a really intense guy — but that's exactly how I feel."

I shook my head. "No, Maggie."

"Why? Why not?"

I spread my hands, searching for a convincing reason why not. "For one thing, you've only known me a few hours."

"Yeah? Tell me something." She threw the piece of wood into the fire and picked another off the concrete floor. "How long had you known Maria before you knew you were in love with her?"

I drew breath to answer, faltered and sighed. "About twenty-four hours."

She didn't say anything for a moment, just kept fiddling with her new splinter of wood. "So, it can happen pretty much instantly."

"I guess. Maggie —"

"Don't patronize me, Murdoch."

I shut my mouth.

She said, "I've read that most times it happens right away. You don't *grow* to be in love with someone." She glanced up at me. "You know? It doesn't happen over time. First six seconds, pow! Or not at all."

"I don't know what to say, Maggie. I don't know. It just happened to me. I wasn't looking for it." I laughed without a lot of humor. "God knows, I wasn't looking for it."

She turned back to her splinter. "Do you think that if you hadn't met Maria, if you'd met me and things had been different…"

I gazed at her a long time before answering. She didn't look up. She just sat, staring down at the small piece of wood, turning it over and over in her fingers. I studied the amber firelight on her cheek, the small flames reflected in her eyes, the warm glow on her hair. She seemed small and helpless under her feisty exterior. I knew she was trouble.

I'd known from the start that she would always be trouble. She was a lost soul searching for a path, searching for a mate, searching for love. We weren't so different.

I said, "Maybe, Maggie. Maybe if things had been different."

She gave a small laugh. "It's a blessing, anyway, right? Better to have loved and lost than never to have loved at all. I guess not many of us ever get to love. Not really love, the way you described it. Right?"

I nodded. "Yeah, I guess not."

Chapter Thirteen

The call came at six a.m. For a moment, I was confused. I stared at the cell Suffolkshire had given me. I could hear the ringing but the phone was dead. Then I realized it was my cell. I fumbled for it and saw it was George Chang from Gdansk. I stared at the screen, my mind racing, then I answered.

"Yeah."

"We need to talk."

"That's going to be difficult." He was silent, like he was confused. I said, "Has anybody spoken to you?"

"No. Is there a problem?"

My mind was speeding. "I had to leave."

"Where are you?"

I smiled to myself with not much humor. "Back where I started." I heard him swear under his breath. He hesitated, then said, "I haven't heard from anyone. There is total silence."

I said, "Can you come here?"

"Where is here? Did you go back home?"

I said, "We are timing out. Can you bring me the case to Luton Airport? Get an air taxi."

He didn't like it, but we'd been on too long already and the risk of being intercepted was growing with every second. He said, "I should talk to—"

I cut across him. "You're talking to me. Be there. This morning. Have me paged when you arrive. I'll be waiting."

I hung up.

I felt a movement beside me and realized that Maggie had curled up against me for warmth during the night. Her blanket had slipped off and in the half-light, I could see her skin and her breast tinged a smoldering red by the glow of the embers. I stood and went over to feel my clothes. They were dry. I dropped the blanket and began to pull on my pants. I sensed a movement and looked over at her. Her eyes were drowsy and her lips were slightly swollen from sleep. She stretched and arched her body, then smiled. "I wish you would come over here and fuck my brains out, Murdoch."

I pulled on my shirt and started to button it. "I wish you wouldn't talk like that, Maggie."

"Don't you feel even a little tempted? Don't you like my body?"

I grabbed her clothes and threw them at her. She started to laugh but I cut her short. "Loyalty is a big deal with me, Maggie. You talked a lot about love last night. Well, being faithful and loyal is part of that. Your body is beautiful and desirable. But the fact that you keep trying to seduce me, knowing I love my wife? That's ugly, so stop it. Get dressed. We're moving."

* * * *

We ate breakfast at a greasy spoon on Willesden High Street. It was called The Green House and everything was painted green. The coffee was dirty water served in mugs the size of fishbowls by a big Italian mamma who looked and sounded like she should have known better. But I was starving and the eggs, bacon and sausages were exactly what I needed, so I didn't complain. Maggie ate with the same voracious appetite she seemed to have for anything edible. I wondered if she was like that in bed but put the thought out of my mind.

By eight a.m. the fog and the rain had cleared, but the sky was a menacing, turbulent charcoal washed with dark blue-black. The air was as dense and humid as a sauna. When we stepped out of the Green House, the street was thick with

117

morning people milling on their way to their allocated jobs. I remembered the Kallisti Corporations facility in Algeria and wondered how many of these milling drones had been conditioned in a similar facility. I stopped and pulled my Camels from my pocket. I fished one out and lit up. Maggie had stopped just ahead of me and watched me watching the crowds. I paused and noticed her eyes. They looked like they could see something in me. She said, "Did you ever read John Mack?"

I shook my head and snapped the Zippo closed. "No."

She turned away, observing the milling stream of humanity, then turned back to me. "He was a highly respected professor of psychology at Harvard University. He got drawn into studying alien abductions. He thought at first it was a kind of psychosis but ended up convinced it was real. He said he reckoned maybe as many as forty million people have been abducted on a regular basis."

I frowned. "How did you know what I was thinking?"

She sighed. "I'm not just a stupid kid, Murdoch. I listen and I pay attention. It was written all over your face what you were thinking."

I gave the kind of smile you could call rueful and started to walk back, headed for Villiers Road. "Forty million, huh?"

"But worldwide, he thought the figure could be a lot higher. Harvard tried to discredit him, but they couldn't. In the end, he was murdered."

I glanced at her. "Who by?"

She shrugged. "They made it look like an accident. An immigrant in an illegal minicab. But it was probably the CIA or MI5 or the SIS or the AE."

I stopped dead. "The AE?"

She turned to face me. "Sure, the so called 'government within the government'. Why?"

"How do you know about them?"

She laughed. "Come on, Murdoch! I'm curious about conspiracy theories. It's all over the Net. I read the blogs.

118

Maybe you should, too."

"Maybe I should at that."

We got the car and headed north under dark, angry skies. As we moved out of London along the M1 freeway, everywhere we looked — in some field or parkland — there was another holding camp for refugees. A few seconds of mental arithmetic made a mockery of the official figures you heard on TV and the radio. Some were too far away and all you could see were the tents and the bivouacs. Others were closer and you could see the steel and wire fences and the haunted, haunting figures of the people staring out.

I remembered Russell talking about humanity. He'd said that we talked about it as though it was a state, some kind of moral standard, when all it really was was a biological accident. I hadn't agreed then and I didn't agree now. It had to be more. It had to be the moral standard that we aspired to and aimed for, even if we never achieved it. It was what had made him rescue me, and it was why I had stuck with him. He'd stared at me a long time when I'd told him that. Then he'd said, "Maybe I'm getting too cynical in my old age."

Is that what happened to you, Russell? You grew cynical and lost your faith in humanity?

Maggie startled me. "Who is the enemy?"

I glanced at her.

She was staring ahead through the windshield at the endless, gray concrete road hurtling toward us.

"What are you talking about?"

"Look around you. This road, the buildings, the seven-and-a-half-billion people, the filthy air, the CO_2, deserts, on land and in the sea, the mass extinction of species, the melting icecaps, the wars, the terror, the refugees." She studied my face a few seconds, then went on. "This is humanity — a species so obsessed with its own individuality, its own ego, that it will destroy the world it depends on and its own people, just to say it was the conqueror."

We drove on in silence a while. I said, "Are you reading

my mind?"

She laughed. "What?"

"Twice this morning you have voiced my thoughts as I was thinking them."

She beamed. "Seriously? That's so cool. They say that's a sign of people falling in love."

I sighed. "I am *not* in love with you, Maggie. I am in love with my wife."

"Would you know? If you were falling in love with me, would you know?" The humor had left her voice. She was serious.

We were approaching the exit from the freeway and I didn't answer for a while, as we came off and I negotiated the roundabout. The airport was a white gleam on the horizon, across an expanse of green fields. Somehow, against the dark, sagging clouds, it looked ominous, like a symbol of an approaching apocalypse. I glanced at Maggie. I felt irritated. I said, "What do you mean?"

She spread her hands. She sounded irritated, too. "Okay, maybe you feel nothing for me. But even if you did, would you know? You are so fixated, so obsessed, that there is no room in your mind for anything that you have not decided. It's your way or no way."

I shrugged. "What's wrong with that?"

"Breaking news, big guy! You are not God. You did not make the universe. Sometimes things happen that you cannot control or dictate. Tell me something…"

We were approaching the airport parking lot. She was waiting for me to answer, so I said, "What?"

"Were you planning on falling in love with Maria? Was that part of your life plan? Or did it come like a bolt from the blue and completely fuck up everything you had figured out?"

I didn't answer. I didn't answer because she was right and she knew it. As we pulled in to the parking lot, she said, "Sometimes good things come out of left field. And sometimes the things you have planned for yourself are not what's best for you. I'm just sayin'."

I killed the engine. Before I'd pulled the handbrake, she was out and slamming the door.

* * * *

The call came over the public-address system at twelve noon. He was at the café with the case. As I approached, he stared at Maggie and said, "What the hell is going on? Who is she? Where is...?" He hesitated. He didn't want to use names.

I said, "He couldn't make it. Let's go out to the parking lot."

I took his arm and hustled him out. A couple of times he tried to free his arm from my hand but I wouldn't let go. He was beginning to look sick. He said a couple of times, "Who is she? Why is she here?"

Maggie said, "I have a name. My name is Maggie."

He stared at her like she was crazy. I said, "It's a long story, George. Just keep walking."

We pushed through the crowds. A couple of people glanced at us with detached curiosity, but nobody was going to get involved. If we were hustling George, that was George's problem, not theirs. We got outside and moved through the cars toward the TVR. When we got there, I stopped and scanned the area. We were alone. I said, "Is the modem in the case?"

"Of course. But I'm not handing it over till I know what the hell is going on, Murdoch."

My options flashed through my mind. I could kill him and take the case. Maybe twenty-four hours earlier, I would have done that. But there was something sincere in his eyes. I almost believed he gave a damn. I was aware of Maggie watching me. There was something intense in her stare that unsettled and troubled me.

My other option was to put his lights out and take the case. But he was a hybrid and there was no telling what would happen to him if he was mad or in pain. From what I'd seen in the past, they could turn real nasty. Instead, I played it by ear and said, "I don't know what's going on. Russell and Hook have disappeared."

He went pale and I thought I saw his skin ripple. "*What?*"

I raised an eyebrow at him. I wondered if shape-shifting hybrids made better actors than normal ones. Catherine and Joanna had both been consummate actresses. I said, "You didn't know?"

He frowned. "Of course not."

"Your friend Sinead took them."

"My —" He looked at Maggie then back at me. Then he shook his head. "Sinead is not my friend. She inspired me to defect. That's as far as our connection goes."

I shrugged. "In any case, they were supposed to send a replacement to Poland for me, and obviously they didn't do that. I don't know where they are or what's happened to them. So, it's down to us. We take it from here."

He shook his head. "It's beyond my authority."

"Screw that! Was it within your authority to defect? I'll assume authority and you can pass the buck to me if it makes you feel better. I'm the last person you reported to, so keep reporting to me. You said we needed to talk."

He still appeared worried but he seemed to relax a little. Maybe he was glad he had someone to pass the buck to. Maybe that was his human side. Or maybe it wasn't only humans who like to pass the buck.

"The modem is more — much more — than Russell thought it was." He shook his head like he couldn't believe his own thoughts. "We would need to do a lot more research, *years* of research to even come close to understanding how this works."

"Give me some idea what we're talking about."

"It seems to operate using a thing called quantum potential. It's really hard to explain, but it's like a universal network of information that is everywhere at the same time, and electrons — all particles — follow paths dictated by this quantum potential."

I shook my head. "George, I have no idea what you are talking about. Tell me in English."

He spread his hands. He looked genuinely exasperated. "How can I begin to explain when I hardly understand myself?"

"Bottom line."

"Bottom line is it would be like a giant hologram enfolding the planet, only instead of light it would be information. Information that would be in every part of the planet at the same instant, instructing the brain of every human on earth to shut down and obey. Using quantum potential, they can reduce *every single brain on the planet* to absolute subservience in a nanosecond." He stared at me, waiting for me to register what he had just told me. "There will be no top table, Murdoch, no princes, no elite. There will be no salvation of any sort for your species. There will be the Naga, sitting as gods. There will be the Seraphs, hybrids, sitting as princes and administrators, and there will be a human population of slaves—if you survive at all. This will be the New Order."

"What do you mean, 'if we survive at all'?"

He looked down at the case. "If I am right, this technology that they have developed may well have another function. Numbers have frequencies. Frequencies are numbers. The whole quantum world that makes up reality is composed of frequencies. Each frequency has an effect in our material world. You humans have the ability to feel very intensely. You have powerful passions and drives that we can only imagine."

I nodded. I was getting impatient. "I heard. Cut to the chase, George."

"Just *listen*, Murdoch. It is our highest aspiration, as Seraphs—and the Naga themselves—to feel the way you do. The way you lust after money, power and sex? We *crave* feelings like that."

"I know, George. What is your point?"

"You *feel* that way because of the frequencies that make up your bodies and your brains."

"*What?*"

He sighed, walked away, stared at the heavy thunderheads overhead, came back and sat on the hood of the Daemon. "Imagine," he said, "that you throw a handful of pebbles into a pond. You will get a whole load of ripples spreading out. Where the ripples collide, you will get an interference pattern of bumps and troughs." He gestured at my body, then at Maggie's and his own. "This is basically what all of us are made of, the interference patterns of quantum waves forming into atoms, molecules and ultimately matter. The frequencies of the waves dictate the nature of the peaks and troughs — the objects. You are hot-blooded animals who can feel and think with profound intensity, because of the frequencies that make you human."

I was beginning to see, and I was beginning to see the implications. I said, "This modem could alter the frequencies of the Naga and the Seraphs..."

He shrugged. "It's possible. It would be like taking a drug, smoking a joint." He shrugged again and shook his head, struggling with the implications. "The way your mystics take hallucinogens to expand your consciousness, they could use these frequencies to experience feelings with the intensity that you do. It would open the doors of perception for them... For us." He turned to face me. "We could experience love, compassion, empathy. These are just mystical concepts to us, the way enlightenment and nirvana are for you."

My skin had gone cold and I felt true dread for the first time in my life. "If they have that available to them, even if it's just available to the elite, they will no longer have any need for the genetic hybrid program or for us."

He nodded, watching my face. He lifted the case. "With this, they could blow all of your brains out in a nanosecond."

I held out my hand. "Give me the case, George. I have to destroy that modem."

He handed it to me, but he was shaking his head as he did it. "It's not that easy and it's not enough, Murdoch. The modem is practically indestructible, and besides, you'd have to destroy the research and the brain that conceived it, too."

"Where? Who?"

He stared at the ground a long while. "I've been thinking about that. There is only one of us capable of developing something like this." He gave me a strange look. "My mentor Stephen Cohen at Stanford. He's a good man. He has never had a cruel intention in his life. He probably had no idea his research was being developed to this end."

I frowned. "Is he a hybrid, like you?"

He gave a small, humorless laugh. "Would that make a difference? You say it as though the simple fact of our species made us cruel monsters, and thus, expendable." He gestured at me with an open hand, smiling. "You are yourselves hybrids. Created by nature, but you are still hybrids. And God knows, you take cruelty and sadism to heights we are incapable of. We are cold and pragmatic, Murdoch. You are willfully sadistic, with your burning passions and appetites." He shrugged. "Yes, he is a hybrid. Though he didn't know it, he was probably created for the purpose of developing this project."

I moved and stood in front of him. I was aware of Maggie watching me carefully. I said, "Are you telling me I will have to assassinate this…man?"

He met my gaze. "You will have to destroy him and all his research. I can't think of another way, can you?"

I stared down at the case in my hands.

We become our enemy.

Maggie said, "Who is the enemy, Murdoch?"

The voice was quiet, the way a snake's hiss is quiet. It said, "Right now, I am. Just everybody stay real still."

I looked up. I knew who they were. There were four of them holding Sigs. They were like clones of each other. They were in dark suits with dark glasses and they all had crew cuts. They had Secret Service written all over them, only these were AE—the Secret Service within the Secret Service. Maybe they were the Men in Black. Who knew?

The one who'd spoken was a bit older. His hair was graying and he had that Colonel-Man-of-Action appearance. He and another had their weapons trained on me, the other two on George. George didn't look at them. He was watching me. He seemed sad. He said, "Did you do this? Did you set me up?"

I shook my head.

Colonel Action Man gestured toward George. "Who are you?" He was American, Mid-West.

I said, "Fuck you, Action Man. Who are *you*?"

He studied me a second, sizing me up. Then he said, "Colonel McGuire of the AE."

I said, "No shit, McGuire. Thanks for introducing yourself. Now, get lost before I shove your Sig up your ass and blow your brains out with it."

I saw his jaw bunch as he bit back his anger. He said, "Take it easy, Murdoch. We're on the same side. Now, I told you who I am. Who's your friend?"

George spoke before I could answer. He stared me straight in the eye and said, "You know what you have to do." Then he turned to McGuire and said, "My name is George Chang. I am a hybrid."

It happened in a fraction of a second. McGuire's Sig cracked and spat and George's head whiplashed as a plume of blood and gore erupted from his temple. He slumped and crumpled and McGuire turned to me. "You are coming with us."

Chapter Fourteen

There was a horrible scream. McGuire spun around and his gun wavered. The second guy who'd had his piece trained on me tried to turn, but he was too late. Maggie moved with the agility of a viper. She was all over him like termites on speed. She was on his back, clinging with her thighs while she grabbed his right wrist with one hand and clawed at his face with the other. All the while she was screaming a high-pitched, piercing screech. I didn't waste time.

The two guys who'd been covering George didn't know what to do. I solved the problem for them. I took one big stride and rammed my instep between the nearest one's legs. I felt his testicles crunch. As he wheezed and went down, I gave a little hop and as I landed, I smashed the back of my fist into the other guy's ear. He staggered, so for good measure, I grabbed his head in both hands and rammed it onto my knee.

McGuire shouted, "Freeze!"

At that instant, I heard a shot. We both looked. Maggie had levered the guy's automatic into his chest and pulled the trigger. I reacted first. I laid into McGuire's floating ribs with both fists at the same time. I grabbed the barrel of his gun and wrenched it from his fingers. As he doubled up, I gave him a right cross that might have broken his jaw. He gaped and his eyes rolled. He slid to the ground. I knelt next to him and grabbed his collar. I slapped him twice to bring him around. Maggie was saying, "Shit! *Shit!* What the *fuck?* We have to go. Murdoch! We *have* to get out of here!"

McGuire's eyes tried to focus. I said, "You are going to

take a message to Suffolkshire for me. Do you understand? Do you *understand?*"

He nodded. I said, "Don't *ever* try a stunt like that on me again! *Never!* You are lucky to get out of this alive. Do you *understand* me?"

He rasped, "Yes."

"I am going to deal with the modem then I'll be back for Maria like we agreed. If he double-crosses me, I'll tear his heart out and eat it."

I watched his face till he acknowledged me.

I threw the case in the car, Maggie jumped in and we moved out. I kept the speed down and my eyes fixed on the rearview mirror. Nobody followed us. It would take those guys a while before they could walk again.

Three. Only three will walk again. One is dead.

I glanced at Maggie. She was staring straight ahead. She was pale and trembling. I said, "You okay?"

She whispered, "I *killed* him."

I didn't say anything more until we joined the freeway headed south. I settled into the slow lane at a steady seventy then looked at her. She'd stopped shaking but she was very pale. I said, "Where did that come from? You went berserk, but what you did with the gun? That was pro."

She stared at me a while without answering. Then she stared at the road. She said, "I don't know. I was so mad that he'd just killed that poor man for no reason — because he said he was a hybrid. He just shot him in the head." Her lip curled and she started crying. "He..." She shrugged and tried several times to speak, but that just made her cry harder.

I said, "It's okay. Let it out. You're in shock."

"He seemed to be a nice guy." The tears flooded down her cheeks and she covered her face with her hands, sobbing in short convulsions. She was trying to stop because she really wanted to say what she was trying to say, but every time she tried to talk, it brought on another convulsion. She said, "He—" three times then finally burst out, "He didn't deserve to be shot like that—like an animal—just because he was different."

I didn't answer. I couldn't answer. We drove on in silence, a silence broken only by the rhythmic sound of the traffic and Maggie's sobbing. Eventually, her sobs subsided and she seemed to slip into an uneasy sleep. Shock will do that sometimes, as though your mind shuts down because it can't cope with what has happened.

I noticed the tail twenty minutes out of Luton Airport. I pulled into the fast lane and began to accelerate. I was thinking fast. I still had my passport in my jacket from my trip to Poland. Maggie must still have hers in her bag. I snapped, "Maggie, wake up!"

She turned and stared at me. Her eyes were hollow and uncomprehending. I handed her my cell. "Go online. Book us two tickets on the next available flight to San Francisco." I fished my wallet out of my jacket and tossed it on her lap. "Make it first class if you have to, whatever it costs. We need to be out of here today."

My tail was staying with me, closing a bit. I thought maybe we had a second one behind him. It was too far to see, but I was prepared to bet it was McGuire. Two got you twenty he'd called for back-up to replace the corpse and the castrato. There was an exit coming up ahead and I began to slow a bit to let him close the gap. I wanted him as close as possible in the fast lane.

Maggie spoke. Her voice was dull and lifeless. "I have a United Airlines flight out of Heathrow. The only seats available are in first class. It's expensive. It's going to cost eight grand each, one way."

"Book them...now. Check in and get the boarding passes sent to my cell and yours."

We were almost on the exit. I swerved violently, hit the gas hard and heard the big V12 roar as we lurched and danced through the traffic to a cacophony of horns and screaming brakes. We made the exit with inches to spare and I braked violently as we came to the roundabout. I went around it at fifty and took an exit at random. Maggie was saying, "What the fuck are you doing, Murdoch?"

I said, "Shut up and book the tickets."

I had one eye on the mirror and I was pretty sure I'd lost the tail. He couldn't have reacted in time, but pretty sure wasn't enough. I kept driving fast, taking random turns with the only criterion that they should take us away from the freeway and into the remote countryside, headed roughly west. I planned to get as lost as I possibly could. If I didn't know where I was, it was a pretty safe bet McGuire wouldn't know, either.

After ten minutes, I killed the speed and settled at a steady twenty-five to thirty miles per hour. I doubled back on myself a few times and finally pulled into a pub parking lot in a small village. There I sat and waited for a quarter of an hour. Nothing happened. After a while, two email notifications pinged on my cell and hers. I said, "Did you do it?"

She held up the two cells. "We have the boarding passes."

"Okay." I switched on the GPS and punched in 'Heathrow Airport'. As I pulled out, I glanced at her. She looked rough. Real rough. She was just a kid, out for a bit of adventure, rebelling against her dad the way you're supposed to, and in a few stupid seconds, she had killed a man. She seemed like she was going through some kind of internal hell, but I needed her sharp and alert.

I said, "Stay with me, Maggie. I need you to focus. When we get to the airport, there's a chance McGuire and his men will be there waiting for us."

She nodded. "I know."

"We'll dump the car then we'll go in separately."

She started talking with a dead, dull voice, like she was sinking into a deep depression. "We need to get you a hat, some shades and a different jacket. We should split up and head through to departures at the last minute. But don't leave it too late. You don't want them calling your name over the public address." She turned toward me. "They won't know what flight we're on, will they? They can't even be sure what airport. We'll hook up again on the plane."

We drove to Uxbridge, left the car in a long-term parking lot, found a mall called The Chimes and bought a change of clothes at Marks and Spencer, a chain store that specialized in a neutral, anonymous style of dress. We changed in the toilets and left separately to get taxis. I let Maggie go first, gave her ten minutes, then walked down High Street in the opposite direction to hail a cab of my own.

I arrived at departures with an hour to spare before boarding. I didn't go through. I bought a *Telegraph* newspaper at WH Smith and sat with the attaché case by my side, observing the area from behind the open paper. I couldn't see Maggie anywhere, but one of McGuire's guys was hovering around outside passport control. I wondered if Maggie had tried to get in and they'd grabbed her already. There was no way of knowing.

I waited another twenty minutes. A steady stream of people went through and the guy in the suit and the shades watched every one of them—so did I. I didn't recognize Maggie. All the while, I was wondering how I was going to get through myself. Then it dawned on me—one of Russell's favorite plays. *Hide in plain sight.* I was going to walk right through VIP. That's what I'd paid eight thousand bucks first class for. I pulled out my cell and called Maggie. Her phone was switched off. I swore under my breath and cursed myself for not having planned ahead properly. If they had her, there was no telling how quickly she would fold under interrogation and how much damage she could do.

I found the United information desk. The girl was regulation pretty and I gave her my best boyish millionaire grin. "I made a last minute Upper Class booking on your next flight to San Francisco. It's a bit of an emergency. I need to get to your Private Security Channel and the Clubhouse right away. I think you're about to start boarding."

She smiled in a way that suggested that solving my

problems was all that she had ever dreamed about doing. As she picked up her internal phone, she said, "That is no problem at all. I'll just call the concierge for you."

A concierge in an airport. Who knew?

He showed up two minutes later. He had the soul of a Victorian nanny in the body of a young man. He tutted at me and said, "Have we strayed from the herd?"

"It was a last-minute emergency."

He didn't plan to let me stop him talking. He turned and walked away. I followed. He was saying, "Not to worry. We shan't tell the captain. We shan't be sitting in the naughty corner on this flight." He eyed me sidelong. "And we *shall* be getting our glass of complimentary champagne. No luggage?"

"Ah, no, just my attaché case. Like I said, it was a last-minute—"

"Then *plenty* of time for a drink in the Clubhouse if we should feel like something to steady the nerves." He held out his hand as he walked. "Have we at least checked in? Passport?"

I handed him my phone and my passport and he led me over a plush purple carpet through a lounge that looked as if it had been borrowed from the set of Star Trek. There, he deposited me at the bar. I ordered a stiff Martini. I just had time to dunk the olive three times when Nanny was back. I drained the glass and he led me down a short passage and into the nose of the aircraft. There he handed me over to a regulation-cute stewardess. He told me her name was Cindy and she would see to all my needs. Cindy took me to my seat. Maggie had booked two cubicles next to each other in the central isle, and there, in the seat beside mine, was Maggie. She still looked haggard and hollow-eyed, but she managed a smile.

I slid into my seat and said, "How did you manage to get past McGuire?"

She held my eye a long while before answering. She seemed real sad. In the end, she sighed, smiled again and said, "It seems I'm really easy to overlook. Not even the people hunting for me notice me."

I leaned over, took her hand and squeezed it. "Hey, you got my attention."

As the engines roared and we surged up into the clouds, above the green fields of England, I thought about McGuire down below. What would he be doing right now? Did he have another team at Gatwick? How many exits from the country had he been able to cover in a few hours? I thought of the Duke of Suffolkshire, with his offices at the Palace of Westminster, and wondered about the AE's resources and their mission. Did they know we'd gotten through their net? Would they be waiting for us at San Francisco? Which led me to another question. How much did McGuire know? How much of my conversation with George Chang had he heard? Whatever he'd heard, he hadn't given the impression of understanding much of it.

I turned and studied Maggie. She was already asleep. I found myself worrying about her. It was like *Alice in Wonderland*. Nothing made much sense.

Chapter Fifteen

We landed at San Francisco International Airport almost eleven hours later, though by local time it was just seven hours later, on the same day. That's what you get for living on a big ball. I rented a Ford from Hertz, slung the case in the trunk and we drove north toward the city and Fisherman's Warf.

There was no mist that day. I hadn't been to San Francisco for a few years. There were people in California who wanted to see me a damned sight more than I wanted to see them, and it was because of them that I had moved to London. But I had always liked this town. It was one of the places in the States I really missed. I drove at a sedate pace, enjoying the sunshine and the broad, leafy roads. It was good to kid myself for a short while that it had all been a crazy nightmare, and I was back in the normal, sane, real world. Though even here, while landing and leaving the airport, I had caught glimpses of refugee camps in Marina Vista Park and Lions Park

I followed the Camino Real as far as Brisbane, then took Mission Street and Chavez to the Third Street Docks. After that, we followed the seafront to the Wharf. We parked at the Embarcadero and sat in the sun outside the Franciscan, smelling the sea and watching anonymous people pass, carrying their anonymous lives with them. It was good for a while to be uninvolved, detached, isolated.

I realized we hadn't spoken since we'd gotten off the plane. I couldn't think of anything intelligent to say, so I asked her, "How are you bearing up?"

She shrugged. "Are you going to kill him?"

I sighed. All of a sudden, I felt exhausted. It was like her question had pulled a plug and drained the life out of me. I looked away, across the crowds at the sun winking off the sea. What had started a couple of years back as being the bag man for Catherine Howard had grown to a size and madness that was impossible to comprehend. Professor Stephen Cohen wasn't even human. But if I sacrificed him for the sake of humanity, I knew I'd be sacrificing my own humanity along with him. Did the end justify the means? Did it ever?

Who is *the enemy?*

The doors opened and a bright, young waitress came out. She smiled and told us her name. Her voice and her face told me that her life was full of hope and fun and generally good stuff — hope and good stuff that she took for granted, like it was a normal part of existence, something you were entitled to expect. I smiled at her. I wanted breakfast, but I realized it was mid-afternoon, so I ordered two Martinis, real dry.

She pushed back inside and the door swung closed behind her. Maggie was watching me. I said, "I don't know, Maggie. What happens if I don't? There are nearly eight billion people on this planet. They could all be reduced to" — I shrugged, spread my hands, searching for the right word — "some kind of sub-human organisms...or exterminated, in a fraction of a second." I stared back at the sea and shook my head. "I don't know which is worse."

She turned her gaze to the table top and spoke almost as though to herself. "Is it a quantitative thing or a qualitative thing?"

"*What?*"

"Is killing eight billion people eight billion times worse than killing one?"

"Come on, Maggie. This isn't high school philosophy. We are talking about the extermination of the entire race. I can't just allow that to happen on some abstract point of philosophy."

She gazed out at the sea. The sun was bright on the water, but beyond the gleam, there was a thick mist obscuring the horizon. She nodded once. For a moment, she looked older than her twenty-four years. "I'm not asking you to. I'm just saying there is a real moral issue if you murder an innocent man simply because of what he knows."

An innocent man. Was he even a man?

She spoke before I could. "And please don't give me any bullshit about him not being human. To murder any creature that intelligent, simply because of what he knows, is a crime. It's immoral!" She sat forward and stared hard into my eyes. "If you kill him, Murdoch, what do *you* become? If you kill him, which one of you, in the end, is human?" She flopped back in her chair, still staring hard into my eyes. "Should we have killed Einstein to prevent the atom bomb?"

The girl came out with our drinks on a tray and a big smile on her face. She put them down with a kind of special care that was just for us. She thanked us and left, and the door banged closed behind her, leaving an odd stillness in her wake.

I said, "I am not a monster, Maggie. And whatever I become, whatever the moral or philosophical implications, I am not going to stand by and allow nearly eight billion souls to be exterminated so that those creatures can rule supreme. It's not going to happen."

She nodded and I noticed a tear spill from her right eye. It was the only sign she was crying. It reminded me of a day that seemed long ago, at Victoria Station in London, when another woman had cried in just the same way. The tear rolled down her cheek and stopped at the corner of her mouth. She said, "I know. And you're right. It just feels so wrong."

I said, "Maybe it's time for you to go home."

She turned her head to face me. "Is that why you brought me here? To get rid of me?"

"No."

"Haven't I helped you? Didn't I disable those freak robots? Didn't I take us to the warehouse? Didn't I nail that guy at Luton Airport?"

"Yes, but Maggie—"

"And now you want to get rid of me?"

"No. That's not what I'm saying. The risks are huge from here on in. You could get killed. Hell, you could get arrested for murder!"

"Bullshit!"

"Not only that, Maggie. You yourself said that from here on in it gets dark. You are not clear about what I have to do next. Hell! I'm not clear myself, but I know that if it has to be done, I will do it, if only for my wife and child. That's a choice I've got to make, but you haven't. I can't ask you to carry that moral burden for the rest of your life."

"But you can? Carry it?"

I thought about it then nodded. "I have a wife. I have a child on the way."

She nodded. "Yeah."

We were quiet for a bit. I sipped my drink and said, "Phone your parents. I'll give you some money and put you on a train."

"No."

I frowned. "What?"

She shook her head and made a twist of her mouth that might have been a smile. "No. What if you get into trouble again? Who's going to pull your sorry ass out? Besides…"

She let the words trail away and I said, "Besides, what?"

"I don't trust you to make the right choice." She looked me in the eye and something told me to take her seriously. "You might decide to let him live when the right thing is to kill him." She shrugged with her shoulders and her eyebrows at the same time. "Or you might decide to kill him when the right choice is to let him live. You have too much at stake—a wife and a child. You won't be objective. Don't worry. I won't stop you from doing what you have to do, but I'll be your conscience and I'll keep you human. I'm in it for the duration."

I sighed. "Maggie—"

"It's not your choice, Murdoch. I'm coming whether you like it or not. And there's another thing. I know where he lives and you don't."

I think I might have gaped. "You know where he *lives?*"

She smiled properly for the first time in what seemed like years. "While you were pissing around reading newspapers at Heathrow, I was doing something useful."

"You *saw* me?"

She winked. "My dad has a lot of resources. I got his attorneys to make a couple of calls for me. Professor Stephen Cohen is ex-directory, as you'd expect, but they were able to get his address from his publishers. He lives on Santa Ynez Close, just outside Stanford. I even have his phone number."

* * * *

I phoned the Ritz-Carlton and booked a double room. I left the Ford at the Embarcadero, took the attaché case from the trunk and we climbed Powell, watching the cable cars clank past us, up and down the hill. Maggie took my arm and I couldn't help smiling as we walked. You could still feel the ghosts of '68 and '69 watching over the city from behind their beards and shades, like very dubious guardian angels. They shouted from the great university campuses. They spoke up from the gardens and parks where they'd sat cross-legged and stoned, playing their guitars. They sang out from the cool, groovy bars where Dylan had droned his monotonous warning about rain. It was a strange heritage for this great city, perched on the sea astride the San Andreas fault—a heritage that called out to humanity to embrace peace and love, while all about it the silicon children of Silicon Valley reared up, wielding the mighty chip, and prepared to enslave and murder the entire race.

At the top of the hill we turned left into California Street and arrived at the Ritz.

The room was blue and white, with two queen-sized beds and an Italian marble bathroom. We took turns to shower. I went first, then her. When she came out wrapped in a bath towel and drying her hair, I stepped over to her and took her by the shoulders. She frowned up at me. I said, "Wait for me here, Maggie. You've done enough. You've been through more than enough. You look tired. You look drained. I'll be back before dawn and it will all be over."

She studied my face with slow eyes and a small smile. "Careful, big guy. I might start to think you care."

I tried to smile back, but I wasn't feeling it. I said, "I do care, Maggie. I care a lot. This is an ugly business. It's not for you."

She placed her hands on my chest. They were small and gentle. She said, "And it is for you?"

"I've done a lot of ugly things, Maggie. I'm already tainted. You don't need this baggage for the rest of your life." I hesitated. "What you wanted was to be free. This won't make you free."

She gave a small laugh — more like a sniff — and stepped a little closer, so she could rest her head on my chest. She spoke in a small voice. "Boy, you do care."

My heart was pounding. I was feeling like I was crossing a line that I didn't want to cross. But I stroked her hair and said, "Yes, I do care."

She turned her face, so she was leaning on me with her forehead. She ran her hands up to my shoulders. "It's strictly *Moon River* for me, Mr. Murdoch." She raised her face to look into my eyes, and our mouths were barely inches away. She said, "I'm going wherever you're going." She grinned on one side of her face. "Now, you had better take your hands off me before you do something you'll regret."

I nodded and went to the window. I stared at the lights of the darkening city reflecting off the still waters of the bay. Behind me, I could hear Maggie dressing. If I turned now, she would be naked. Her skin would be smooth and silken. If I went to her, she would surrender to me. But inside I felt a deep ache, a hollow pain that nothing could fill and nothing could quench except Maria.

I saw my wife looking up at me in the rain by the Round Pond, knowing me inside out, loving me easy and gentle, the way only she knew how. It was her, always her. It had to be her or no one.

We grabbed something to eat at the Parallel 37, the hotel restaurant, then stepped out into the night. I had the case with me. We started walking back in the direction of Powell. I pulled my cell out of my pocket and punched in Cohen's number. After a couple of rings, a male voice answered. I said, "Oh, hi, Steve. Listen, you going to be home later this evening?"

There was a moment's hesitation and he said, "Yeah, sure, but who is this?"

I said, "Bob, Bob Griswold..." I trailed off like I was waiting for him to recognize me.

He said, "I'm sorry, I don't know any Bob Griswold."

I sounded confused, even frowned like he could see me. "But, this is Steve, right? Steve Cruze?"

He laughed politely. "No, I'm afraid you have the wrong number. This is Dr. Stephen Cohen."

I apologized profusely and hung up. I said, "He'll be in all evening."

We dodged across the traffic and began to walk down Powell headed for the Embarcadero, where I'd left the car. Maggie said, "Have you thought about how we're going to get there?"

I was surprised and said so with my face. "We'll drive."

"If anything goes wrong, the car will be traced directly to you."

"What do you suggest?"

She grinned. "Use a different car, of course."

We'd parked the rental Ford in a public parking lot opposite the pier 43 Ferry Arch. There was some light from a few old street lamps and from the parade of shops across the road, but the lot itself was mainly in shadow. We approached from the east, through a small area set with benches and a few plane trees. Maggie spoke under her breath, talking fast. "I haven't seen any cameras, but keep your head down. Go to the rental. Don't use your keys. When I call you, follow my lead."

And she was off. I stared after her and I think I might have gaped. She skipped ahead, and I made my way at a slower pace. She stopped three cars past the Ford, just as I was arriving. She'd picked what appeared to be a Dodge Charger. I smiled. *Nice car*. She leaned over the driver's door a moment while I made like I was searching for my keys. I heard a bleep and saw a flash of lights, then heard her voice. "Let's take mine!"

I looked over. She had the door open and was climbing in. I stood, thinking, then went over and opened the passenger side. As I did, the engine roared into life. I climbed in and slammed the door. She was grinning a big grin. "I told you I was useful."

"You going to tell me how you did that?"

She winked and headed to the exit. "You're not the only one who's been tainted by life, big guy."

We took Beach Street and North Point to Van Ness then headed south into the city. San Francisco is part of an urban sprawl that engulfs the bay and has almost eight million inhabitants. But when you drive through it, apart from the financial district, it feels like a small town, with broad streets and old-world buildings that rarely rise above four stories. Each one is different, each one feels like home to somebody. We cruised south with the windows down, feeling the warm evening air. The rhythmic hiss of the traffic and the slow pulse of the street lights was hypnotic and peaceful. It was hard to remember we were on a mission of death and that the lives of these eight million people, the future of their world, would be decided that night, at the quiet, suburban mansion of a college professor.

We cruised down Market Street onto Guerrero and San Jose, then we were on the Camino del Rey. Soon after that, we were passing the airport on our left and it felt like we were in the suburbs with low, two-story houses, pretty lawns and massive eucalyptus trees rising into the broad evening skies, whispering among faint stars above the streetlamps. After Redwood and Lloyden Park with the superabundance of trees, you could even kid yourself you were in the deep countryside. Ten minutes after that we passed through Menlo Park and we were at Stanford. Maggie slowed and turned right into Sand Hill Road and I felt a sudden pellet of heat in my gut. We were here, and we were going to do it.

Within seconds, the landscape had changed. All about us were trees and parking lots. I knew there were buildings out there, probably the facilities and installations for the university, but you couldn't see them among the greenery. All you could see was a proliferation of trees and the desolate spaces of the lots, with their yellow pools of light showing only emptiness.

We followed Sand Hill around onto Santa Cruz then left again onto Juniper Serra Boulevard. We climbed gently through dense woodland. The trees loomed and leaned down at us, like crooked demons roused from sleep by the sudden light of the headlamps. I felt Maggie accelerate, like she was becoming impatient — or excited. A sick pit opened in my belly and I wanted to tell her to stop, pull over let me think through what we were going to do. But there was nothing to think about. There were no options.

She slowed again and turned left into Santa Maria. It was a narrow alley between tall hedgerows and we crawled to the end, turned left and a couple more bends among narrow, leafy roads brought us to Santa Ynez Close. Maggie pulled over, killed the engine and the lights then turned to stare at me.

"We're here."

I was aware of the weight of the Smith & Wesson under

my arm, aware that within minutes I would be using it to kill a man who had not wronged me in any way. I was going to kill him simply because of the knowledge he had in his mind. I said, "You want to wait here?"

She shook her head. In the darkness, I could see a strange gleam in her eyes where the light from the streetlamps reflected on them. "No, if you are going to kill him, I want to be there. You'll need a witness."

I frowned. "What the hell do you mean?"

"Your conscience. In the future. You will want a witness who saw what you did, to tell you that you did the right thing."

I opened the door and climbed out. The doors closing were like two gunshots in the night. Our footsteps were loud, almost shocking in the darkness as we approached his gate. We turned into his driveway between two tall cypress trees, and saw the warm light spilling from his front door onto his patio. There was the sawing of frogs on the sultry air and the gentle lap of the water in his pool.

Chapter Sixteen

We stood a long while, listening, reluctant to take the next step. His front door was open—a vortex of molten amber, a gateway to hell.

To kill a man for what he knows.

I stepped forward and climbed the steps to the porch. Through the doorway, I could see a parquet floor, a wooden hat-stand, a table with a drawer and a mirror. I stopped. Under the table was a toy car. On the table in front of the mirror was a baseball glove, and by the table on the floor was an old pair of trainers encrusted with dry mud. In a strange, lucid moment all the pieces came together and told a story. They were not just random objects in space, but pieces of a life. Each piece had a unique meaning and together they signified the life of a family, with their hopes and dreams and loves and possibilities.

I flashed back. I was a boy of ten or twelve in Watts, in LA. My mother was drunk again and screaming, and my dad, also drunk, was beating her back-handed till she fell on the ground. I was screaming, too, punching him, pushing him, dragging him away as he tried to kick her.

We'd never played ball. He'd never bought me a toy car.

I walked up to the door and crossed the threshold. There was a short passage to the right, where it seemed to open out into a broad living space. I could see a large palm in a pot. I called out.

"Dr. Cohen?"

A voice, deep, cultured, called back, "In here."

I moved to the end of the passage and stood looking. I saw a large room with cream walls. A dark wood, open-plan staircase led to a mezzanine floor that was obviously a work area. Everything was minimalist but comfortable. There were rugs scattered on the parquet floor. A heavy oak dining table looked used. It had a newspaper scattered over one end, where it had been studied over a mug of coffee. There was a set of French doors that stood open and a basketball sat on the floor beside them. Beyond the table, there was a large sofa and two armchairs gathered around an open fireplace. *The New Yorker* lay on the rug. A glass of wine stood by an open bottle on a coffee table. In one of the armchairs, a big man sat staring at the floor. I said again, "Dr. Cohen?"

He looked up at me, chewing his lip, and nodded. "Yeah, come on in."

I felt Maggie close behind me. I crossed the room and stood over him. He watched me all the way. His eyes were knowing. You could almost feel the intelligence radiating out from them, like a palpable thing. He said, "Will you sit down? Can I offer you a drink?"

I shook my head. "Where is your family?"

His eyes lost focus. He looked past me at Maggie and frowned. They stared at each other a while, then he turned back to me. "I sent them away after you phoned. Who is your friend?"

I said, "After I phoned?"

He leaned back in his chair and sighed. "You are not from the AE. That is obvious from your companion, from your dress, from the troubled expression on your face and from the fact that, if you were, I would already be bundled up in the back of a van on my way to an interrogation center.

"You are not from the Brotherhood. We are still on good terms and they bear me no ill will. That leaves only one option. You are Liam Murdoch. I have, as the cliché goes, been expecting you."

I looked around, listening to every minute sound. I could still hear the frogs on the still, warm air. I could just make out the lapping of the pool. Aside from that, there was nothing.

The house was empty. I said, "You sent your family away, but you haven't called in the cavalry to protect you?"

"That is correct, Mr. Murdoch."

"What stopped you?"

"Because I know why you have come here, and I agree with you. I believe it is the only thing to do – and the right thing to do."

I stared at him and felt sick. "I've come here to kill you, Dr. Cohen."

"I know. And, I imagine, to destroy all my research."

I nodded.

He went on, "It's the only option that makes sense."

I ran my hand through my hair. "Great." I turned and saw Maggie biting her lip. There were tears running down her cheeks. She stared at me and I looked away. Cohen started laughing but more with sad irony than mirth. "Sit down, Mr. Murdoch. We haven't got very long, but we have time for a quick drink and a talk. We need to talk."

Maggie stepped past me and sat on the sofa with her hands pressed between her knees. She was having real trouble controlling her crying. I sighed and sat in the chair opposite him, with the case by my feet.

"What do you mean, we haven't got very long?"

He shrugged. "It's a fair bet the AE has been tracking you."

I glanced at Maggie. I said, "I don't think so."

He smiled. "In any case, let's be brief. When I was commissioned by the HEAT Corporation to work on the frequencies for the modem, I had no idea what use they would be put to." He hesitated then took a deep breath. "You have to understand. With del Roble gone, there was a different mood in the Brotherhood. Sinead's defection and the slew of defections that followed made a lot of hybrids and Seraphs pause and think. There was talk in the Brotherhood – albeit whispered talk – of peaceful integration, even of halting climate change..." His words trailed away and he shook his head. "The last thing on

146

earth I could have imagined was that the stone would be used for this."

Maggie gave a small gasp, but I paid no attention. My mind had fastened on one word. I narrowed my eyes at him. "The stone? What are you talking about?

He studied me with curious eyes. He said, "The frequencies to be programmed into the modem."

"But you said 'the stone'."

Amusement—real amusement this time—suffused his face and he began to laugh. "Oh! You don't know?"

"Know *what*, Cohen? The frequencies are encoded in chips in a modem."

His laughter subsided, but he was still smiling, shaking his head. "No, Mr. Murdoch. The 'modem' is a nano-particle programmer. The technology to program it has been missing for fifteen thousand years or more. The research I did was to unlock the programmer and develop a method for feeding the frequency codes into it."

A nano-particle programmer.

I had gone cold inside. I had heard that term before, a couple of years back, when I'd come back from Spain with Maria. I said, "This"—I held up the case—"this contains the Ael Rune? What del Roble called the Çabra Stone?"

He nodded. "Yes."

"The stone was lost. I was there."

"It was found. You can't lose something like the Ael Rune. It finds its way back."

"Bullshit!"

He threw back his head and laughed. "You are priceless, Mr. Murdoch! That you can be *so* emphatic about something which you know *fuck all* about!"

Maggie spoke up through her sobs. "For once, Murdoch—just for once—you could shut the *fuck* up and listen!"

The intensity with which she said it made me turn and stare at her. Before I could answer, Cohen said, "You'd do well to listen to your young friend, Mr. Murdoch."

I scowled at him. "Okay, I'm listening!"

He got up, moved to a dresser and poured two tumblers of whiskey. He handed one to Maggie and smiled at her. Then he handed the other to me, minus the smile. He sat, picked up his glass of wine and sat swirling it and watching the liquid go around. "Sinead, among others, was listening for the stone. Del Roble thought it had fallen into the Thames. She wasn't so sure."

"What do you mean they were 'listening' for it?"

"Advanced Seraphs—and Sinead is a *very* advanced Seraph—have senses that are unknown to humans—at least most humans. We are able to perceive in ways that you would not understand. You would call it intuition, ESP or a 'sixth sense'. But for us, it is much clearer than that. The closest comparison for you would be hearing—perception at a distance. It is related to what Professor David Bohm called the quantum potential. We are aware of the correlation of particles—"

"Forget it. You're losing me."

He shrugged and spread his hands. "What can I tell you? Cats see frequencies that you can't. It's a bit like that. Seraph hybrids have senses you haven't. So, del Roble and Sinead were 'listening' for the stone. It emits frequencies that they were trying to pick up. It was eventually found in the possession of a homeless guy in Chiswick, in London."

I smiled at the memory of the bum's look of wonder, sitting there in the empty building site, as he poured his bottle of water into the hollow stone. "Who found it? What happened to the bum?"

He watched me, the amusement crawling up the side of his face. He glanced at Maggie, then back at me. "You see? That's what makes you human. You are as interested in the bum as you are in the stone, maybe more so."

I said, "More so."

He nodded. "One of Del Roble's listeners got there a couple of hours before Sinead and…her friend."

"Catherine?"

"It doesn't matter. The bum, as you call him, had joined

a Buddhist *vihara*. He had been living in a shelter, had recently gotten a job at a whole-food shop and was saving to move into a small flat. He was meditating regularly and was applying for a place on a degree course in Oriental Studies at the University of London, at the London School of Economics."

I burst out laughing. "Are you kidding me?"

"The Ael Rune can do surprising things."

I felt a wave of sick depression and asked, "What did del Roble's man do to him? Eat his liver?"

"No, we are not all monsters, Mr. Murdoch, just as you are not. They paid him ten thousand pounds sterling, provided him with a small apartment and covered his fees at the university — all of which will be of more use to him than the stone."

I raised an eyebrow. We were silent for a bit. I sipped my whiskey and felt a seed of anger burning in my gut. I said, "That's a nice story, professor. There is only one small problem with it." He began nodding, but I plowed on, anyway, "It just so happens that that bum will have his brain fried along with the rest of humanity if this rock gets back into the hands of whoever has taken over from del Roble."

He was still nodding. "Exactly. And that is why I am here talking to you, and why I haven't alerted them that you were coming. But let me point out, Mr. Murdoch, that humanity will not fare much better, nor will the hybrids, if the AE get a hold of the stone and my research instead of the Naga."

I thought about it and had to agree. "Okay, so neither of us has a high horse to sit on. What are you suggesting?"

"My research has to be destroyed. The work I did at the LYRE facility in Alaska has been erased. There is only what I have here at the house now. It has to be destroyed, and so has the Ael Rune — the Çabra Stone. And me? He sighed heavily. "I would rather not die, but it is hard to see an alternative."

Maggie said, "Can't we erase your memory?"

He nodded like she'd said something perfectly sensible. "Yes, but then what is to stop me from doing the research all over again?"

She said, "That is simple. The stone will be destroyed and you join with Sinead and the renegades, with Murdoch's friends. They will keep you from developing the research."

He smiled at her. "It's a nice idea."

I said, "I hate to put a damper on this, but I am not so sure my friends are my friends anymore. I am pretty sure the great Sinead is a double-dealing opportunist who has poisoned the minds of my so-called friends."

Maggie flushed and stared at the floor. Cohen was shaking his head. "No, Mr. Murdoch, you are wrong. The one virtue you might recognize in Sinead, if you knew her, is that she is actually incapable of lying. She is honesty itself. And I mean that pretty much literally. I can't hope to explain it and we are running out of time, but believe me, she is honest."

I erupted, "Then why the *fuck* has she abducted my wife!"

"Because, when she learned that the Brotherhood of the Goat had got hold of the Ael Rune and of the research they had commissioned from me, she realized, as I *should* have but didn't, that we were in desperate need of some means of saving humanity. We—the renegades—do not want to exterminate you, Mr. Murdoch. We want your help. We want to live in peace with you. You have so much to teach us, and we have so much to offer you."

I was barely listening. I cut across him, "Hold up, Professor. Spare me the electoral address. How the fuck is abducting my wife going to save humanity?"

He put down his glass and stood, staring hard at the French windows. He turned to face me. His voice had changed. Even his skin seemed to change. Maggie stood, staring hard at him. He held out his hand to me. "The AE gave you something. What? A cell phone so they could contact you? Give it to me. Go to your car and leave, now!"

"I said, what the hell are you talking about? Where is Maria? Do you know?"

"Give me the phone."

I stood and grabbed him by the scruff of his neck. "*Where is she?*"

Maggie grabbed my arm and screamed at me, "It has a *tracker*, you idiot! Stop being so fucking *obstinate!*"

I went cold. I reached in my pocket and handed him the phone. He said, "Take the stone to the HEAT reactor in Wales. Put it into the reactor core."

I shook my head. "How?"

"You'll get help. You are already running late. Go."

Maggie flung her arms around him and squeezed. She was crying again. He kissed her forehead and said, "*Go!*"

I said, "Tell me where Maria is or I swear to God..."

He stared hard at Maggie, as though trying to reach a decision. He blurted, "Shangri-La Clinic, Maine. Now *go!*"

Maggie grabbed my hand and we ran. As we made the kitchen door, I saw Cohen climbing his stairs to the mezzanine floor, where all his computers were. We stepped silently out into the dark and closed the door behind us. I took my hand out of Maggie's and pulled my Smith & Wesson from under my arm. I inched along the wall and peered down toward the front of the house. The pale light from the patio was reflecting on the turquoise water of the pool. The only sounds were still the frogs and the lapping of the water. I indicated to Maggie we should cross the lawn into the shadows by the hedge that separated Cohen's place from his neighbor's. She nodded and we sprinted across the grass. I told her to wait, and I crouch-walked a few steps till I could see the two tall cypresses and the gate. I heard footsteps and lay flat. Three men were coming into the garden. I was pretty sure one of them was McGuire.

Three. That leaves one in the car.

I let them climb the stairs then gestured to Maggie to run. We sprinted across the grass, keeping to the shadows and made the nearest cypress. There was no sign of them on the porch, but outside, maybe forty or fifty yards away, I could see a dark Audi four-by-four. Maggie had the keys to the Dodge. I urged, "Get in the car. Start the engine. I'll join you in fifteen seconds. Now!"

She slipped around the cypress like a pro and moved to the Charger. As she did, I sprinted across the blacktop toward the Audi.

Give him a minimum of four seconds to react.

On three, I stopped with my legs apart and my left leg slightly forward. I took half a second to level the revolver, held in both hands. I held my breath and aimed at where he had to be sitting. The cannon erupted twice in a double tap, just as he was deciding what to do. I sprinted the rest of the way to confirm the kill. What was left of his face was staring unseeing into the roof of the car. I ran back. the Charger was rolling with the passenger door hanging open. I climbed in, slammed the door and we took off. I turned and looked through the rear window. For a moment, I thought I saw McGuire run out into the road. Then Cohen's house exploded in a ball of red and orange fire. There was a silhouette in the road, black, covering its head against the blast of heat and flame. Then we were around the bend and accelerating.

Chapter Seventeen

We drove through the night.

We took the interstate to Santa Clara then turned north through Milpitas and Freemont, up into the Diablo Mountains as far as Dublin. There we turned east, through Pleasanton and Livermore. As we left Livermore behind us, she hit the gas and we started to climb toward a hundred miles per hour. I said, "Take it easy. It's dark. And besides, we don't want to get stopped."

She didn't look at me. She said, "I'm okay. We're okay."

I checked my watch. It was half past ten. I said, "We haven't talked about this. You want to tell me what you're doing?"

She spoke without inflection. "I'm driving to Maine."

"That's three thousand miles."

"It's okay. You can relieve me in a couple of hours."

I watched her profile for a bit, green in the light from the dash. "You know the way? No GPS? No map?"

She glanced at me and smiled. "I told you. I've been around. I'm not a good girl. I wasn't born yesterday."

I nodded. "I got that. What route are you taking?"

"I-80. Sacramento, Reno."

"I'll take over at Reno."

We were quiet for a bit. I fished out a couple of Camels, lit up and handed her one. She took it and sucked gratefully. She said, "They don't know where we're going, right?"

I thought about it. "I don't know." She glanced at me. I said, "They've been searching for Maria."

"Shit!" Then again, more forcefully, "*Shit!*"

"Maybe they think we're headed back to the UK. Maybe

they haven't found her but we can't assume that."

She looked in the mirror a few times. There was only blackness. She said, "Even if we drive nonstop, it's going to take three days to get there."

I ignored her. "How the hell do they think abducting Maria will save humanity?" She didn't answer. I said, "What do you think?"

She shrugged. "How the hell should I know? You said she's pregnant. Maybe it's something to do with the baby."

I remembered Russell. He said Sinead didn't understand the question, whether the baby was mine. But she said Maria had not slept with anybody else. The AE thought the baby was 'a weapon'. Nothing made sense unless —

The baby is a hybrid. It's not my *baby. It's* their *baby.*

I said out loud, "A last-ditch attempt to create a hybrid race that could survive the Ael Rune."

She smoked and drove like she hadn't heard me.

It grew real black outside. We were surrounded by translucent reflections in the dark glass of the windows and the windshield, like specters from other dimensions riding shotgun with us through the night. An occasional truck or car would pass us, going west, like a slow pulse. The light would appear in the distance up ahead, grow and swell, bathing Maggie's face with amber, then flood the cab for a second and vanish, leaving us alone again with our reflected ghosts.

Then a gas station or a scattering of low buildings would emerge from the blackness, motionless in the lifeless glow of tall, stooping lamps, like gravestones floating through the shades of time.

Maggie said, "You should get some sleep," and I realized I had nodded off. I leaned my head on the cool glass and closed my eyes. The motion of the car was hypnotic, and I drifted in and out of shallow dreams, not really sleeping. We dropped out of the hills, crossed through Tracy, Stockton and Sacramento, like sudden, brilliant snapshots of other peoples' lives in another universe. We were cocooned in our own safe haven, inside the Dodge, charging through small, shining worlds and on into the blackness. They were gone as suddenly as they appeared, and we were climbing again, into the mountains, through dense pinewoods that obscured the stars overhead.

A couple of miles outside Reno we came off at exit twenty-three and pulled onto some scrubland. We swapped over. She curled up on the seat without saying a word and went to sleep. I checked my watch. It was half past midnight. I drove on through desert scrub under vast skies for another two-and-a-half hours. Eventually, we came to a town called Winnemucca. It seemed to consist of warehouses, a McDonald's and a casino. They were all floodlit and they were all dead. I cruised past them and soon came to what I was searching for, a motel. I pulled into the parking lot and saw there was space behind the building, hidden from the road. I killed the lights and rolled around to the back. I checked my watch. It was three a.m. I shook Maggie gently and told her, "Come on. We'll get some sleep in a proper bed for a couple of hours."

She opened her eyes and stared at the dash for a moment, turned and stared at me. Then she blinked and climbed out of the car. Our doors slammed and our footsteps echoed as though they were muffled by the pall of sleep that lingered over the town among half-spent dreams. We pushed into the brightness of the reception, where stark light reflected off laminated chipboard. A kid, who looked like his day job was shooting down Thargozian battle cruisers for the Rebellion, stared at us in mild amazement. I said, "Give me a room for four hours. I need a call at seven."

He said, "You got some ID?"

I said, "Yeah, I left it between my .44 and my bad attitude. Do I need it?"

He absently fondled one of his zits and shook his head. "No, that'll be fine."

I paid, gave him a sawbuck to keep him happy and took the key. He tried a smile and told us we had a room by the pool. I told him to remember to call me at seven.

The room was functional and like every other motel room I'd ever seen. I locked the door and checked the window at the back. It overlooked the parking lot. I left it open and went into the bathroom. Maggie was naked in the shower. We had lost all self-consciousness with each other. I stripped and brushed my teeth. When she stepped out of the cubicle, I said, "Leave it running," and while she toweled herself, I stood under the hot water and lathered my body and my hair until I felt the tension easing away.

When I got back to the bedroom, she was sitting on the edge of the bed, still wrapped in her towel. I set my cell alarm to go off at six a.m. and said to her, "Sleep dressed, Maggie. We'll be leaving in a hurry."

We dressed and I lay on the bed. She curled up next to me with her head on my shoulder. There was nothing sexual or amorous in it. We needed each other's closeness and support, that was all. As she drifted off, she muttered to me, "Who's going to come for us? The AE or those freaks from the Brotherhood?"

I stroked her head. "I don't know. One of them or both. But we'll try to be gone before they arrive."

I don't know if I slept. I was semi-conscious and half dreaming. I was aware of dark shadows soaring high across a translucent night sky, blocking out the icy stars, scanning the desert, listening for us, smelling for us. I was aware of feral creatures running across the sand and the rocks, scurrying through the scrub, peering from the bushes, sniffing the air, searching. Then I was between dreams and wakefulness, and everything was heavy, oppressive darkness. I could feel shadows pressing in on me on all sides, black forms closing around me.

I opened my eyes. Maggie was weighing on my right arm. I slipped it from under her and sat up. I checked my watch. Five to six.

Get your head together, Murdoch. Time to move.

I thought it was the dawn light, a faint glow in the window

by the door. But the window was facing north. I stared at it a moment longer then shook Maggie's shoulder. "Wake up. Get up. *Now*."

She stirred. I rose and moved to the window. The slats of the blind were closed. I fingered a couple of them apart and peered out. It was hard to tell exactly what it was, but it looked like a large vehicle, maybe an SUV, parked facing our room. As I scrutinized it, a bank of spotlights on its roof snapped on. It was about fifty yard from the room, but the glare made it hard to judge the distance exactly. There were three, maybe four, vague silhouettes in the glare that seemed to warp and twist. I couldn't tell if they were standing motionless or walking toward us. Maggie's dark form came close beside me, still warm from sleep. I heard a sharp intake of breath and she hissed, "Shit! Run!"

Then she was grabbing her things, scrambling for the window. I didn't stop to question. I grabbed the case and did the same. Five seconds later, we were clambering out of the back window into the parking lot. She whispered, "Have you got the car keys?"

"Yes!"

"Give them to me!"

She gave a little skip and a hop and hurled them out onto the highway. I said, "What the *fuck*?" But she was sprinting past the Dodge, headed for an old red pick-up that was parked twenty yards farther down. I went after her. As I did, I heard a loud bang and a crackling like fireworks behind me. I looked back and saw the intermittent flashing of lights in our window. I kept running. Maggie had the door open and she was climbing in the driver's seat. As I caught up, she'd started the engine and was leaning across opening the passenger side for me. I jumped in and slammed the door as she reversed. I said, "What the *fuck* are you *doing*?"

She snapped, "Shut up!"

Then she was accelerating, not in the direction of the highway, but toward the side of the building. I shouted, "For fuck's sake, go left! *Left!*"

We fantailed around the corner and wound up next to the huge SUV with all its lights glaring at the door to our room, maybe forty yards away. There were two of the white porcelain freaks in the doorway looking back at us with their Stygian black shades. Maggie gunned the engine and slammed her bag on my lap. She snapped, "Stun gun!"

The wheels screamed as she let out the clutch and we charged. It took three or four seconds. We smashed into them before they could move. One went down under the left front wheel. The other smashed against the wall and slid to the ground. I already had the door open and was jumping out as she braked. The thing was struggling to its feet when I rammed the stun gun into its neck. There was a horrific screech and dense smoke erupted from its head.

The one under the wheel was flapping and struggling like an octopus on a spike, with two tons of truck sitting on its belly. Maggie vaulted over the hood and was by my side. Something moved inside the room and two goons with luminous white faces were moving at us out of the darkness. Maggie was reaching under my jacket. I said, "What?"

She said, "On my mark." I saw she had my Smith & Wesson in her hands. My head was reeling. They were coming through the door. They were eight feet away. She leveled the piece and it exploded twice with perfect control as she screamed, *"Now! Now! Now!"*

The magnum shells smashed into their heads and sent them staggering back. I sprang like a thing possessed, moved by desperation, suddenly understanding her thinking. I rammed the stun gun into the nearest one's face. The screech went up again among the acrid smell of burning circuits as she emptied the remaining rounds at the other droid. The last shot rang out and I moved and stuck the electrodes into the back of its head. Another scream. Another burned circuit.

She snapped, "Around back!" And she was running.

I followed. There were half a dozen cars. She stood for a

second, scanning them. She chose a Cherokee, did her magic and in a few seconds, we were in and crashing through a broad ditch and onto I-80, headed east. We crossed a bridge, and just outside town, she took exit one-seventy-eight and pulled into a patch of scrubland with scattered trees. Not for the first time that morning, I said, "What the *fuck* are you doing *now*?"

She grinned. She even gave a little laugh. "Come on."

She jumped out of the truck and I followed her. Not far from the where we'd parked, we came to a narrow alley that lead onto a road. To the right of the alley was a house and parked outside the house was a big red Chevy. She pulled a Swiss Army knife from her pocket, and with a speed and skill that should have surprised me but didn't, she began to remove the plates. Without looking at me, she muttered, "Get the front one, will you?"

I did as I was told, and in five minutes, we had the plates off. As I fitted them to the Jeep, she fitted the Jeep's plates to the truck.

Ten minutes after that we were back on I-80, doing a steady seventy. She was driving. She smiled at me. "By eight this morning, they are going to be searching for a Cherokee with those plates. They're not going to find it. It's anybody's guess how long it will take our guy to realize his plates have been changed. He might be a real Sherlock and spot it right away. Or he might be a dumb-ass and it might take him a week." She shrugged. "Either way, say he spots it in three hours. We'll be two hundred and ten miles away by then." I watched her a while but I didn't say anything. She said, "That was the Brotherhood. How did they find us?"

I shook my head. "Cohen said they could smell it."

She nodded. "Yeah."

By ten o'clock we were in the Great Salt Lake desert, and two hours after that, we were climbing out of the pretty, ordered suburbs of Salt Lake City up into the Wasatch Mountains. The heat was suffocating, even with the air conditioning turned on. Outside, everywhere you looked, the earth was a parched, dull gray, and where there should have been grass and woodland, there were scorched shrubs and dying trees. We hadn't had breakfast and we hadn't had lunch. Maggie appeared pale and drawn. She'd been going for six hours on no food and less than three hours' sleep. I was impressed. I said, "Pull over at the next service station. We'll eat and I'll take over."

She glanced at me and nodded. She was perspiring and her skin was pasty.

As it was, she kept going for another hour till we reached Evanston, just inside Wyoming. We took a left at the junction, leaving town and pulled in to the Pilot Travel Center. She parked out of sight behind the store, killed the engine and placed her forehead on her hands on the wheel. I noticed she was shaking and her breathing was unsteady. She seemed bad — real bad.

I said, "Lie down in the back. I'll bring you some food and drink. You're probably dehydrated. You think you need a doctor?"

She shook her head. "It's too risky. I'll be okay. Just give me a minute. You're probably right. It's dehydration and exhaustion." She turned her head slightly to smile at me. "I'm only small."

I went and bought a couple of changes of clothes, a small rucksack and supplies of water and food from the general store while she rested. I noticed the price of bread had gone up. Now a cheap, Chinese-made shirt cost what a loaf of bread used to cost, and a loaf of bread cost almost as much as a pair of jeans. As I paid, a guy on the TV behind the counter was saying that a piece of the western Antarctic ice shelf the size of California was threatening to break away, but that the US and the EU were putting together a panel of scientists to challenge the latest findings of the IPCC. They said there was growing evidence climate change was a natural phenomenon, not a man-made one — like that made a difference.

I got Maggie and we went in the diner next door. I had a couple of burgers with extra fries and a couple of gallons of what passes for coffee in the States. But Maggie had an eight-ounce steak, rare, which she ate ravenously with her hands and with total concentration.

When we'd finished, she began to look sleepy. I got her a coffee and refilled mine. She said, "They smelled us, right?"

I shrugged. "I guess."

"That's why it was the Brotherhood, not the AE. The AE need to use more conventional technology."

"I guess so."

She stared out of the window at the parking lot and the distant horizon beyond. She spoke like she was talking to herself. "We've killed six of their brand-new 'bots in just a few days. They'll be back, but it won't be so easy next time. They'll go and lick their wounds, and what they come back with will be harder to kill."

She glanced at me, seemed to study my face a minute then looked out the window again. "But the AE ain't going to be sitting on their hands, right? If the conspiracy theory sites are anything to go by, they may not have the kind of technology the Brotherhood has, but what they have is advanced. *Real* advanced!" I sipped my coffee. She chewed her lower lip. "They'll be using satellites — satellites and computers." She turned to face me. "They have access to all the government databases in the West. They'll have focused on car thefts in a radius of X miles from Stanford. I wonder if McGuire died in the blast."

I shook my head. "He saw us leave."

"*Shit!* Give these people data and they are unstoppable. They're like fucking *ants*." She was sweating again.

I said, "Take it easy," but she seemed not to hear.

"They'll have contacted the sheriff's departments in a radius of X, asking not only for stolen cars but abandoned Dodge Chargers. Once they hit the jackpot, everything falls into place. By now, they know we're on I-80. So, they are looking for a Cherokee doing a long haul headed east. They may even have the new registration."

I said, "What were you, a cop in your last life?"

She frowned. "I'm just using my brain."

I watched her. She looked real ill, but her brain was firing on all cylinders. I was thinking we needed to get to the clinic fast, not just to get Maria, but to see what the hell was wrong with Maggie. I said, "How do you feel? You look ill."

"I just need some rest. Quit worrying, Murdoch. There will be a chopper on our tail real soon. We need to decide what we are going to do."

And as her words trailed away and she stared into my eyes, I heard the distant thud of the rotors.

Chapter Eighteen

A few seconds later, the air was full of noise. There was the thud of a chopper gas turbine and the more distant wail of sirens. Pretty soon after that, I heard the screeching of tires as a stream of six cars from the county sheriff's department poured into the lot. Three of them fanned out in front of the building as the other three went around back. All the doors opened and the deputies climbed out and leaned on their vehicles, watching the diner. Then the chopper was landing behind them in a storm of air and dust. It was unmarked. The sheriff plastered his hat down on his head and ran, hunched down, toward the helicopter as McGuire climbed out. A seven-foot black giant in a *Men in Black* suit and shades climbed out behind him. He looked like he'd once had a thought and he was still confused about it.

McGuire and the sheriff walked back together, bent over and shouting to each other under the thudding blades. The sheriff pointed to the side of the building where we'd parked the Jeep. Maggie swore, got up and walked away to the toilets. She took her plate and her cup with her and dumped them on the counter as she went. I noticed everyone in the diner was watching us. We were as fucked as a six-dollar whore during shore leave.

I watched McGuire give the sheriff instructions then stride into the diner. He burst through the door and let it swing closed behind him. He scanned the room, saw me and walked over. He looked down at me then scanned the table. There was nothing of Maggie's left there. He said, "Where's your little tart? She get sick of sucking your dick?" I looked up at him. The waitress watched us. McGuire glanced at her and said, "Coffee – black – and a slice of blueberry pie."

He sat and studied me for a bit then removed his sunglasses. He had very pale blue eyes with really small pupils. The waitress brought him his coffee and pie. As she left, he said to me, "If you are really lucky, you'll go away for the rest of your life. In this country alone, I can pin five murders on you. But that's not what's going to happen." He dug into his pie with a fork and stuffed a large piece in his mouth. You could see he was a greedy man. He chewed, staring into my face, swallowed, licked his lips and drank some coffee.

He picked up a small paper napkin and wiped his mouth as he repeated, "That's not what's going to happen. I am going to take you away and I am going to interrogate you for a very long time. You will eventually die under interrogation. If past experience is anything to go by, you will weep and beg for your mommy. I'll enjoy that."

He spooned more pie into his mouth and sat, staring at me and chewing. After he'd swallowed, he picked up his cup and said, "Do you know why I'll enjoy that, Murdoch?"

I shrugged. "Probably because you're a sad, sick man. But, to be honest, McGuire, I don't give a rat's ass why you'd enjoy it."

He ignored me. "Because you humiliated me. You made me look bad in front of His Grace."

I laughed.

He didn't. He said, "You are going to come with me now to a secure facility where you will be" – he paused and smiled in a way I guess was intended to be menacing – "*debriefed*, about the case you picked up in Luton and about where your wife is. You'll hand over both. And if you cooperate, maybe – just maybe – we'll let your wife live. And her baby." He waved his finger over the table, taking in his coffee and his pie. "Pay up. We're going."

I watched him a bit, weighing in my mind whether to kill him then or save it for later. I said, "Fuck you, McGuire. Pay for your own damned pie." I threw a handful of money on the table, enough to pay for me and Maggie, and stood up. McGuire stood and smiled at the waitress. He said, "Mine's on the house. Ask the sheriff."

He pushed me out into the heat and the glaring sun. The sheriff stepped up, pulling his cuffs from his belt. He cuffed me, and McGuire shoved me in the direction of the Jeep. As we rounded the corner, I saw Maggie. She had the driver's door open and the engine running. She also had the back open. She looked like she'd gone crazy. She'd thrown the rucksack on the blacktop and my clothes were strewn over the ground. I stopped dead. I heard the sheriff say, "What in the name of — ?"

She slammed the back closed. She had the attaché case in her hand. She saw me and screamed, "You fucking son of a bitch! You call this *fun*? You call this showing me a good time? You fucking *asshole*!" She hurled the case on the ground, stomped to the open driver's door, climbed in and squealed away, out of the parking lot and onto I-80.

After a second, the sheriff reacted and turned to one of his deputies. "Get after her!"

McGuire snapped, "No!" The sheriff stared at him. He shook his head. "I know this son of a bitch. We stay with him until I say you can go. Understood?"

The sheriff shrugged. "You're the boss."

I snorted. "Yeah, but you're paying for his coffee and pie."

McGuire pushed me toward the case. "Shut up! Sheriff, have your men collect those things." To me, he said, "Is that the modem from Luton?"

I nodded. "Yeah."

As the sheriff's men collected my stuff, McGuire narrowed his eyes at me. "Did she know what they were?"

I looked at him like he was an amoeba asking amoeba questions. "What do you think, McGuire? Yeah, she knew, and I also told the girl who cleans for me and my Friday whore."

He snarled at me. "Okay, wiseass." Then to the sheriff, "Put the stuff in the chopper."

Three minutes later, we were rising above the gas station and I was peering down at half a dozen very confused lawmen who were staring up at me as though they were wondering what the hell had just happened. We nosed out over I-80 and started heading west. I scanned the highway for a Cherokee Jeep but couldn't see one. I had the giant on my left staring at the wall opposite like he was in a state of Zen bliss, enjoying the ecstasy of a totally empty mind. McGuire was watching me, so I asked him, "Where are we going?"

He grinned like he thought he was funny and said, "I am taking you to see my leader."

"Suffolkshire?"

"'His Grace' to you, pal."

"What is it I'm supposed to have done that's got you all pissing in your panties?"

He watched me a minute and I saw his cheeks color. "Shut up, Murdoch. You'll find out soon enough."

We flew for maybe forty or forty-five minutes, roughly following Interstate 80. James Town and Green River passed beneath us and we began to descend toward the craggy, stony face of the Quaking Asp Mountain. As we approached, I saw what seemed to be a mine or quarry with a couple of abandoned excavators and trucks. I looked at McGuire. "What is this place?"

He smirked. "A loan from a friend of the duke's." But that was all he'd say.

As we came down, I saw there was another chopper sitting a hundred yards from a large wooden shack that had probably once been the company site office. We settled and the turbine went into a descending whine as the rotors slowed. McGuire grabbed the case and he and Man Mountain McNeuron jumped down and came around to pull me out. They grabbed an arm each and dragged me across the white-gray dust to the shack. The heat was intense and the air was so thick with fine white dust that it dried out your nose and throat in seconds. McGuire opened the door and shoved me in. I stumbled as he and his pal stepped in behind me and dragged the door closed. After the glare outside, it took me a second to adjust to the gloom. There were only two small windows to let in shafts of dusty light that illuminated a desk at the far end of the room. I wasn't surprised to see Suffolkshire sitting there, watching me. It was what I had expected.

"We had a deal, Murdoch, a gentleman's agreement. You seem to have reneged on that. Perhaps you had better explain to me what you've been up to."

McGuire stepped forward and placed the case on the desk. Then he went back and leaned against the door. The giant dragged a wooden chair into the middle of the room and shoved me onto it. He cuffed each of my wrists to one of the back legs of the chair. Then he looked at Suffolkshire and said, "Should I hit him yet?"

"No, thank you, Brutus. That won't be necessary just yet. I *hope* it won't be necessary at all."

I looked at the big guy then at the Duke. I said, "Brutus?"

"A nickname."

I gave Brutus my best wiseass grin then turned back to the Duke. "What do you want, Suffolkshire? Why have you been hounding me since Luton?"

"You killed one of my men."

"Your men were pointing guns at me. People who point guns at me tend to wind up dead."

He smiled. "That's not unreasonable."

"Why were you following me in the first place? Our deal was, you find my wife and I get her back."

He stood and walked over to the window by the door. He put his hands behind his back and stared out at the stark, hot light. It bathed the planes of his face, making him look both ancient and vigorous, like an oak. I decided I liked him, which surprised me. After a while, he sighed and raised his eyebrows. "We are at war, Murdoch." He turned to me and his face went into darkness. "We have been at war for a very long time. Our enemy does not fight out in the open but in the shadows, poisoning our minds and our hearts." He walked back to his desk and placed his ass against the rim. He said, "I like you. I wish I could trust you. You are a formidable enemy, and you would be a formidable ally. But you are rogue and anarchic, and I am not at all sure I *can* trust you. You see" — he spread his hands — "you don't *know* who your enemy is."

I frowned. "Do you?"

He nodded. "Oh, yes. But you? You think *everybody* is your enemy. You think *I* am your enemy. My enemy, Murdoch, is them — the invaders...and anyone who is allied with them."

I felt a seeping unease. He was right. I did see everyone as an enemy. It was me and Maria against the world. There were no good guys. Every damn body had an interest, a reason to sacrifice somebody else, a reason to stab somebody else in the back. Even Russell and Hook, whom I had thought I trusted implicitly... Even they were the enemy now.

Suffolkshire was watching me. Maybe he was reading my face. He said, "There are no good guys. Is that it, Murdoch? Nobody is on the side of the angels? It's you and your wench against the world, *Murdoch et Maria contra mundum!*" He laughed. "That is a very lonely state to exist in. You could come home to us, you know. We would welcome you."

"Yeah? In exchange for what?"

He made an expression like it was obvious, like I was being obtuse. "In exchange, quite simply, for honoring the spirit of the agreement we had. We were going to help and support one another, Murdoch, in a common aim and a common cause. Instead, you went gallivanting off, doing shady deals behind my back."

"Agreeing to cooperate on one thing does not mean I work for you."

He pointed at the case. "What is this?"

"What it is, is none of your goddamn business."

His face went hard and cold. He stood and walked back to the window. He looked as though he genuinely didn't like what he was about to do. He spoke to the glass, to the sunlight outside.

"We have been the Dukes of Suffolkshire for nearly a thousand years. Other great families have come and gone, including a couple of royal dynasties. We have stuck it out, and instead of our power waning, it has grown." He glanced down at the windowsill. He seemed as though he regretted it was cheap wood instead of ancient English oak. "Our power is considerable. We have a large stake in the Federal Reserve." He turned to face me. "We are partial owners of the United States, you might say. When the king dines at my house, he is respectful, almost deferential. He knows where the power lies. We did not achieve this power by being soft, sensitive — or squeamish, Murdoch."

He gave Brutus a look and the big guy ambled away. As Suffolkshire started talking again, Brutus bent down, picked up a big toolkit and placed it on the desk, where he opened it and took out a pair of pliers.

The Duke was saying, "I believe passionately in our democratic, liberal way of life, Murdoch. My ancestors were active in bringing it into being and deeply committed to its architecture. I believe that this is the only possible way of life for humans. But in order for a society like ours to survive, we must have an army of men who are prepared to protect it, and those men must be, like me, utterly ruthless."

I said, "Slow down. You don't need to do this."

He shook his head. "I think I do. Until you realize exactly how far I am prepared to go, you will not cooperate. You are too obstinate and too arrogant."

McGuire was starting to laugh. Brutus showed the Duke the pliers and he nodded. "Now, Murdoch. I am going to remove, not one, not two, but three of your fingers. Even if you tell me what I want to know right now, I will still remove your fingers, because you need to understand that I mean business." He turned to McGuire. "Get the blowtorch. We'll need it to cauterize the wounds."

I said, "You're making a mistake."

"Perhaps, but I have to break your obstinacy to make you cooperate."

"You do this to me and I will never cooperate with you, even if you cut off every limb from my body."

He smiled. "I believe you, and I admire you." I heard the burst and the quiet roar of the blowtorch behind me. My mind was racing. I needed to get the stone to the reactor in Wales, and I needed to get to Maria. If this clown started taking bits off my body, I'd never do either. But if I handed the stone over to him, I'd just be swapping one fucking maniac for another.

I said, "You said these invaders are aliens. I understood they were here before us."

He knew I was playing for time and he smiled. McGuire approached and he and Brutus squatted down behind me. I could feel the heat from the torch on my hand. Brutus took hold of my right hand with surprisingly gentle fingers.

"We can chat while they chop, if you like. I've heard this story, too, but if you look at the timescales involved, it doesn't add up. Tens of millions of years go by when nothing happened. However long their lifespans are, Murdoch, it doesn't wash. They come from Proxima Centauri, from the planet we know as Proxima B."

Brutus spoke in a voice like a bassoon. "Which finger should I take off first, Your Grace?"

Suffolkshire gazed at me. All credit to the guy, he looked genuinely upset. He said, "This is going to hurt you a great deal. I'm sorry."

My heart was beating hard, high up in my chest. If it was going to happen, it was going to happen, but I'd be damned if I showed this son of a bitch I was scared. I said, "No shit, Sherlock. What or where is Proxima B?"

"It's a planet, similar to Earth, but in the Proxima Centauri system, about four point two light years away." He turned to Brutus. "Take the baby finger first. And, Brutus, do it by stages. We want this to hurt as much as possible."

McGuire gripped my wrist then Brutus forced open my

fist and stretched out the finger. I felt the cold, hard iron on my joint, and it began to bite.

Chapter Nineteen

I'm not sure what happened first. I screamed. It was a strange, deep, primal sound that erupted all on its own from my belly. It was a brutal certainty turned into noise — a certainty that no damned son of a bitch was going to take my fingers off. And as I screamed, I hurled the chair backward, crashing against McGuire and Brutus. They went sprawling and the blowtorch spun across the floor.

At the same time, there was a distant sound. I only caught it in my peripheral hearing and I paid no attention to it. It was the sound of a big truck firing up. I scrambled to a kneeling position, leaning forward so the chair legs were in the air. I strained to get the cuffs down to the bottom of the legs. I was almost there when the kick caught me in the side and sent me sprawling. I heard the duke shouting, "Don't kill him!"

I was on my side, skidding. McGuire and Brutus were coming after me. I came to a halt and strained down. My right hand was almost at the bottom of the leg. I saw McGuire's face twist with hatred as he lashed out again with his foot. I dodged but caught the full force with my shoulder and went crashing onto my back. The pain in my hands was excruciating. I ignored it and rolled. I needed badly to get on my feet. I scrambled back on my knees then on my feet, and I was looking up into Brutus' big, leering mug. He showed me the pliers and said, "Chop-chop." And that was when I knew I was going to kill him.

He slapped me and it was like being hit by a stone wall. I fell. He grabbed hold of the chair and carried me like a suitcase, slamming my face down on the table. I was immobilized. I could hear Brutus laughing. It was a weird, deep guttural sound. Out of the corner of my eye, I could see Suffolkshire staring at the window. He looked worried. He said, "Quiet!"

Then the wall imploded in an explosion of screaming, splintering timbers and gray dust. The roof groaned, whined and subsided. Brutus and McGuire staggered back, covering their heads with their arms. I couldn't see the duke. I could hardly see anything except dust, broken timbers and rubble, but I didn't waste time. I stood, squinting, trying to keep the fine gray powder out of my eyes. I turned my back to the table and hooked the legs on the edge, then I dropped and my hands came free as the chair clattered to the floor.

The dust was clearing and shafts of bright sunlight were filtering through. A big, yellow truck emerged where the wall should have been, and a very small person jumped down from the cab, half obscured by the billowing clouds. There was a scrambling on my left. McGuire had the duke by the arm and was pushing him toward the demolished wall. The duke's neck was swollen and his face was crimson. He was screaming at me, "You're a bloody fool, Murdoch! You need us! You *need* us!"

I screamed back, "I also need my fucking *fingers*, you asshole!"

Two shots rang out and I only realized in that moment that my Smith & Wesson was missing from under my arm. I saw Maggie, legs straddled, holding my piece in both hands, shooting at McGuire and the duke. She took off after them and I figured they were making for the chopper. Too late, I wondered where Brutus was. He hit me in the back like an express train and I went sprawling. He kicked me twice as I tried to roll. He had powerful legs and they were painful, paralyzing kicks.

I scrambled away from him and my hand found the pliers. Just past them was the blowtorch. It had gone out, but I could hear the gas spewing from the nozzle. I picked up the pliers and hurled them hard at his face. I'm an accurate shot and caught him between the eyes. He staggered and covered his face for a couple of seconds. It was all I needed.

I don't know if smoking is bad for your health or not and I don't much care. But one thing I do know is that my Zippo has saved my life on more than one occasion, and this was one of them. I grabbed the blowtorch with one hand and flipped the lighter with the other. The flame caught and I was on Brutus like a celebrity out of Betty Ford's on a gallon of gin.

He was coming at me, and maybe because of the dust or maybe because of the glare of light behind me, he didn't see the torch till it was too late. It was too late when I rammed the flame in his face. The scream was like nothing I have ever heard. It was inhuman, and for a second, I almost regretted it. Then I remembered his 'chop-chop' gag and hit him across the head with the cylinder. He dropped, writhing and clutching at his burning face. I reached in his jacket, pulled out his piece and blew his brains out. *Job done. Chop-chop.*

Then I went out to search for Maggie. She was walking back, headed for the wrecked office. I could see the chopper disappearing south. The other chopper was gone, too. The Jeep was parked a hundred yards from the shed, covered in gray dust. Maggie came up close and touched my face. She seemed real worried. Her skin was still pale and pasty and her eyes were hollow. She said, "Are you okay? Did they hurt you?"

I nodded. "I'm okay. How did you get here so fast?"

She laughed. "I drove like fuck! I know this area. I saw where they were headed and guessed it was here." She shrugged. "Educated guess." Then she frowned. "You happy to see me?"

I laughed. "You bet."

She smiled. It was a sad, grateful smile. Then her pupils dilated and her eyes began to cross. Her skin turned gray and her legs began to fold. I caught her and lifted her into my arms. I carried her across the baking dust to the

Jeep, opened up the back and laid her on the seat. She was beginning to shiver, like she was freezing. I got a bottle of water and splashed small amounts on her lips. I said, "I'm taking you to a hospital."

She shook her head. When she spoke, it was like a croak. "No. Just leave me the water and cover me. I'm freezing. Drive. Just drive, big guy, as long as you can keep going. We need to get that Rune to the reactor, right? If you don't do that, we're *all* fucked — not just me."

She did something that should have been a smile and spoke again, but her voice was almost inaudible. I leaned closer. She whispered, "I'll be okay. Just come a little closer."

I leaned close. Her eyes were just a couple of inches from mine. I felt a stab of emotion. Her eyes were flooded with what I can only describe as love and compassion. She reached out with a small, trembling hand and took hold of my chin. Then she leaned forward and very gently kissed me. She smiled and whispered, "Sorry, big guy. I may never get another chance. Now drive. Let me sleep. I'll be okay."

She pulled the cover up over her head and within seconds I heard her breathing slow right down. I jumped out, slammed the door and ran back the wrecked office. I grabbed the case and brought it back to the Jeep. Then I climbed in and fired up the engine. She was right about one thing. If I didn't get the stone to Wales and the reactor, we were all history.

I hit the track and headed back toward I-80. I checked my watch. It was two p.m. I had at least fourteen hours of solid driving ahead of me. No rest till four a.m. I glanced in the rearview mirror. I could see the bundle of jackets and shirts that was covering Maggie. She was motionless. I felt a stab of anxiety at what might happen to her.

I care, goddamn it! I can't afford to care!

As we rattled down the track, I tried to think. McGuire and Suffolkshire were not going to give up that easy. Faced with the shock and violence of Maggie's attack, they had withdrawn, but not for long. McGuire was a punk and a clown, but Suffolkshire was as tough as old boot leather and smart with it. While McGuire was licking his wounds, the duke would be planning his next move. They were in the air and knew exactly what they were searching for — a dirty, dust-covered Jeep Cherokee.

On an impulse, I turned right down a narrow track. As far as the eye could see, there were only rolling hills of dry earth, heather and gorse. North there was a low mountain range and I could just make out the buildings of Purple Sage. But ahead of me, east, it was almost desert. I followed the track for five or ten minutes and came to a broader dirt road that headed back south. I turned right onto that and accelerated, kicking up big pale gray clouds behind me. I followed the road for another five minutes or so, and pretty soon, I came to a fork. Without thinking, I turned left up a narrower track. I didn't know what I was hunting for exactly, but I knew I was hunting for it. And I knew that I'd know it when I saw it.

The track petered out as I crested the hill. The deeper I got, the more it was looking like desert and the more lost I began to feel. The clock was ticking and I was anxious about Maggie, too, but a voice in my head was telling me to keep going. I came to another broader track and turned left onto it. Fifteen minutes of flat, empty, near-desert later and I was approaching a small hamlet and I knew I had found what I was looking for.

A tarmacadam road intersected the track and there on my right was a pretty white house with a red roof and a few outbuildings. It appeared that it might be a small holding. One of the buildings was a garage. It stood open and I could see a Honda Accord coupe sitting next to a Chevy truck.

I bumped onto the road and turned into the yard. There was a wooden outbuilding, also painted white with a red roof, shaded by a tall chestnut. I pulled in under the tree and parked next to the outhouse, so the Jeep was pretty much invisible from the road and from the air. I jumped out and headed for the house.

As I approached, there was a guy in his fifties stepping down from the door, wiping his hands. He seemed like he wanted to be friendly but was real aware that we were strangers. He raised his chin and said, "Do for ya?"

I pointed back at the Jeep with my thumb and said, "We were driving through on I-80 and my niece began to feel ill. We turned off to find a motel or an inn where she could rest and get a drink, and we seem to have got lost. Could I trouble you for a glass of water for her and maybe you could point us — ?"

He was already waving his hand and saying "Bring the poor kid in. Sally will make her some tea and, if need be, will call the doc. Can you manage her on yer own?"

"That's real kind of you. I guess it was the heat."

I made my way back and he went indoors, calling Sally. I pulled open the rear door and removed the jacket Maggie had covering her head. She looked terrible. I took some water and bathed her lips and her face, and she began to stir. A little color returned to her cheeks. She turned and gave me a slow blink. "Where are we?"

"We need a change of vehicle. These people are going to help us. Come on. Let me help you. Can you make it inside?"

She nodded. "Yeah, I'll be all right." She sat up and slid over to me.

I said, "Don't say anything, okay? Follow my lead."

I put my arm around her to support her and led her toward the house. The guy and Sally, whom I took to be his wife, stepped out as we approached. Sally was one of those motherly, apple-pie types, with gray hair and a generous bosom. She appeared genuinely concerned when she saw Maggie and immediately took over, leading her inside, clucking like a hen, leaving her husband to talk to me. He offered me his hand and said, "Ken."

I took it and said, "Liam. Good to know you, Ken. I'm sorry to inconvenience you."

He ushered me inside. Sally had placed Maggie on the

sofa and was making tea in the open-plan kitchen. I noticed there were no French doors into the back garden. And the windows were double-glazed security windows — the type you need a tank to break through. I said, like I was apologizing, "I guess you don't get a lot of strangers through here."

He had that level, direct way of looking that you find in the American Mid-West. "We're pretty much alone out here. We got good, God-fearing neighbors and we take care of each other." He gave a nod in the general direction of a locked cabinet up against the wall. "And I've got my pump action and my old service Colt, if we need back up. But apart from the occasional brawl down at Buddha Bob's Bar in Rock Springs, people's good folk around here."

Sally came in with a pot of tea, poured a cup and gave it to Maggie. Maggie took it in feeble hands. She looked ill — really ill. I didn't know how much of it was an act, but if it was one, it was a damn good one. I genuinely feared I was losing her.

Losing her?

Sally was stroking her hair while she sipped her tea. Maggie gave her a sweet smile and thanked her in a voice that was practically inaudible. I glanced around the room. On the dresser, I saw a photograph of a graduation. It was a handsome boy with a slightly younger Frank and Sally. I smiled and pointed, real friendly. I said, "That your boy?"

Sally was feeling Maggie's forehead and muttering, "The poor child is freezing."

Frank gave a smile that managed to be sad. He said, "He's in Denver now. He's at a law firm. He's doin' good, but we don't get to see him much."

I seized the chance and smiled with as much compassion as I could. I hated myself as I did it, but if I had another choice, I couldn't see it. I said, "Don't you get lonely? You got other family nearby?"

He walked right in. They were trusting folk in a community that looked after its own. He shook his head and said, "No, it's just us now."

I nodded and stood with my back to the window so I could cover them both. I said, "Ken, Sally, you will probably never know how much I regret what I have to do now." I pulled the Smith & Wesson from under my arm. Maggie glanced up at me and I think her jaw actually dropped. Sally's face went pale as she probably remembered all the horror stories she'd seen on TV. Ken's face went hard and his eyes swiveled to his cabinet.

I said, "Don't do it, Ken. You are good people and I really don't want to hurt you. I can't explain why I have to do this, and even if I could, I couldn't expect you to understand or even believe me. I need your Honda, and I need at least a twelve-hour lead on the people who are chasing me. When I get to Canada, I'll mail you the money to cover your car and the inconvenience. You have my word. I'll also mail you the keys and the location of your car. Meantime, I need you to sit tight." I looked down at Maggie. "Get the phones, Sarah."

It must have been a huge effort, but she got up and scoured the house. She found two landlines, a laptop and two cell phones, plus a Wi-Fi router. Then she checked the bedrooms. As she came down the stairs, I said, "Put them in the Jeep."

She came back three minutes later. As she came in, I said, "Lock all the doors and windows." Then to Sally I said, "You got food and drink in here to keep you for twenty-four hours?"

Her lips were like a thin pencil line. She snapped, "Yes."

I said, "I'm going to need the keys to the cabinet."

Ken reached in his pocket and tossed me a set of keys. I gave them to Maggie and said, Get the guns and all the ammo. Put it all in the Jeep." Then I turned to Ken. "Give me the number of your local sheriff. I'll call him from Calgary and tell him to let you out. Meanwhile, I'm sorry. Take a day off, watch TV, do some crosswords. I don't like doing this, but…" I let the words trail off and shrugged.

Sally said, "Then why *are* you doing it?"

It was like she was biting the words in half as she said them. I stared at her. Her eyes didn't waver. She was a strong woman. Both of them were made of stern stuff. I was suddenly moved. I said, "Sally, I am a Godless man. I believe in people and I believe in survival. In recent years, for reasons I haven't time to explain, I have come to believe in goodness and compassion. But you, you believe in God."

She straightened and stiffened. "I do."

"Then maybe you will understand if I tell you that the Devil is chasing us. We are fighting pure evil. And if we fail…" I shook my head. "We can't fail. And that is why I am doing what I am doing."

Something changed in their expressions. I don't know if they believed me or not, but it made them think. I held out my left hand. "I'm going to need the keys to your Honda."

I gave them the keys to the Jeep and locked them in. I settled Maggie on the back seat under a blanket I'd borrowed from Ken and Sally, and we headed off through Rock Springs onto the Lincoln Highway, the I-80. We'd wasted an hour, maybe a little more. It would be five a.m. before I could think about getting some sleep. But the thought of seeing Maria put a fire in my belly that drove me on. My instinct was to floor the pedal, but I kept to a steady seventy. The last thing we needed was to get pulled over by the cops. If we were, it would cost us hours, maybe days. It could kill the operation altogether if we got tried and sentenced. That meant if we were pulled over, I'd have to shoot the cop and run, and something inside me was telling me I was already too close to becoming my enemy. When you do evil in the name of good, you become a monster.

Who is *the enemy?*

I stopped once at a desolate service station in Point of Rocks, bought gas and supplies and drove on through the endless semi-desert and desolation of Wyoming. Maybe it was my state of mind. Maybe what I was looking at through the windshield was my own, barren soul laid out before me.

But it seemed to me that all I could see was hopelessness, emptiness and desperate beings who were too dull and too conditioned by their masters to see their own despair.

Who is *the enemy?*

I get deep like that sometimes.

I peeled a pack of Camels, stuck a butt in my mouth and flipped my Zippo. Then I cracked a pint of Irish, one handed — that's a skill I've picked up over the years, along with lock picking and hotwiring cars — and took a long pull. It made me feel better. As long as there were Camels and Irish, there was hope. I smiled, but there wasn't a lot of humor in it.

I plunged on through the searing heat toward late afternoon.

Chapter Twenty

The terrain changed as evening fell, five or six hours later, about halfway across Nebraska. It became flatter and greener, though even here, everywhere you looked you saw the evidence of the lack of water, of crop failure, of the first terrifying signs that the earth was dying of thirst. It just wasn't producing enough food.

As we passed through Gothenburg, the lights began to flick on and the sky turned from pallid blue to violet. We left Gothenburg behind and night enfolded us. We drove on through the dark in a kind of timeless bubble, with only the occasional passing car or truck to remind me we were moving at all. I was beginning to feel fatigued. As we approached Lincoln, I spoke over my shoulder and asked Maggie if she was awake. She muttered something and I reached in the bag and threw a triangular plastic box of roast beef sandwiches at her, along with a tin of beer. After a couple of minutes, I heard her open the pack and eat. After that, I heard the hiss of the tin and I sensed her sit up and drink it. Then she lay down again, and there was silence.

We passed Lincoln and Omaha, and the night sky spread out above us like a small window onto infinity, speckled with tiny pieces of ice. The other traffic on the road faded out and disappeared, like a pulse growing slower until finally it stops and there is only darkness and silence. My eyes grew heavy. I was exhausted. I forced myself to think of Maria, waiting at the end of this road, over the next hill, around the next bend. But the road was straight and flat and endless, like the endless black space above my head.

I realized I'd slipped into sleep and snapped out of it. I

shook out another Camel and poked it into my mouth, and took another slug of whiskey. I spoke over my shoulder again. "You awake?"

She didn't answer. For a crazy moment, I wondered if she was dead, but in the silence, I could hear her soft breathing. It sounded rhythmic and steady.

We crossed Des Moines at a quarter after three a.m. Forty minutes after that, I almost drove us into a sign for a turnoff to Grinnell and knew it was time to stop. I came off the interstate, hung a left at a junction and six hundred yards down the road saw a Best Western Pioneer. I thought right then it was the most beautiful thing I had ever seen.

We checked in, and at four on the button, I collapsed on the bed next to Maggie, set the alarm for eight a.m., and as I drifted into sleep, I told myself that we had dodged them. I wondered if Ken and Sally had managed to rouse their neighbors or get hold of the sheriff, but before I could contemplate the answer, I had slipped into oblivion.

* * * *

It seemed I had no sooner closed my eyes than the alarm went off. My whole body ached and there was a hand shaking my shoulder. I sat up, reaching for my piece, but there were no choppers, no flashing lights, no androids. The sun was filtering through the blinds along with the gentle rumble of a truck, and Maggie was sitting next to me, appearing almost human. She smiled.

"How you doing, big guy?"

"Aside from being dead, I'm okay." She looked fresh-faced and her hair was wet. "You showered?"

She nodded. "Yeah. Can we get going? I'm starving."

I fell into the shower, and by nine, we were pulling out, having gorged ourselves on eggs and bacon and coffee. She sat up front, next to me. She was still weak, but she seemed a damned sight better than she had the night before.

The next eighteen hours were a kind of blur. First, early in the morning, were the endless flat green fields leading up to Lake Michigan, then the hot, crowded shuffle and grind driving through Chicago, then the interminable suburbs and traffic between Chicago and Lake Erie. Outside Euclid, I checked my watch and realized I'd been driving for five and a half hours. It was half past two and I was hungry. We pulled off, bought food and beer at a gas station and kept going. I used the pain and the exhaustion to give me tunnel vision. The hours dragged by in smog and stops and starts. Maggie drifted most of the time. Concentrating was hard and roundabout Cleveland, somebody had snuck up and buried a blunt hatchet in my skull.

We turned onto the I-90 at Wickiffe and picked up speed through green, tree-lined landscapes. But I was still exhausted and my back and my head were in constant pain. The hours rolled by with the miles. Nothing seemed to change. It was cars, roads, tarmacadam, trees and houses passing in a steady stream and Maggie by my side, sleeping, occasionally opening her eyes, looking around and closing them again. And all the while, there was the idea in my mind, the vision, the obsession of Maria waiting at the end of this road.

She was waiting for me. It was like she knew I was coming. *She is waiting for me.*

As we passed Buffalo, it was growing dark. The oncoming lights were blinding. I knew I should stop and rest. I'd been driving for about twelve hours on four hours' sleep but I couldn't stop. We were too close. Darkness enveloped us around the turn off for Rochester, and by Syracuse, I knew I couldn't keep going much longer. As it was, we made it to Glens Falls. We'd covered more than a thousand miles in just over fifteen hours. I was dead beat, starving and my head and back were killing me. But I knew we were close now, maybe four hours away. And I could feel her, like she was in the next room.

She's waiting for me.

We pulled in at the Landmark Patriot Motel at just after

midnight. It was cute, clean, well-kept and surrounded by dense woodland and pretty, suburban houses. We stumbled into reception and took a room at the back, opposite the crazy-golf course, facing the woods. Maggie opened the door and I fell onto the bed. I lay for maybe ten minutes, feeling like I was still moving, with the darkness flowing about me like a river. Then I sank into oblivion.

I don't know how long I had been asleep. I felt a gentle hand shaking my shoulder. I opened my eyes and saw Maggie leaning over me. There was a soft light filtering in behind her. She smiled at me and said, "Hey, big guy, there's somebody here to see you."

I frowned and levered myself up onto one elbow. My head was thick and my body still ached all over. She seemed to warp into shadow and recede into the light that was coming in through the door. I thought to myself it must be morning and I had overslept. The light was bright, like midday sun. Then there was another form, black and snake-like at first, twisting in the glare and moving to me. I shaded my eyes, but the door must have closed because the light was shut off and Maria was standing over me, smiling.

A thud of joy rocked me. I sat up, then stood. All the pain and exhaustion washed away from me. I said her name. Her face was radiant. She came close to me and we held each other. Tears welled in my eyes and I clung to her, whispering her name over and over, kissing her hair.

She pulled back gently and looked up into my face. She brushed the tears away from my cheeks and gazed at the wetness on her fingers in a kind of wonder. Her eyes were warm. There seemed to be a light about them that I could only describe as deep love. I began to ask if she was okay, if they were treating her right, but she silenced my lips with her finger and I tasted the salt of my own tears. She went up on tiptoes and softly kissed my lips.

Next, she was unbuttoning my shirt. Sweet pleasure washed through me and I began to undo her blouse. We stripped off our pants and stood naked in front of each other. I had never felt love so intensely as I did in that moment. It flowed through my body and my limbs like blood. But I felt it flowing out of her, too. There was an expression of amazement in her eyes and we both laughed. She whispered, "It is so strong…"

"I know."

"Touch me with your skin."

I drew her close so that our bodies were touching and our intense sensitivity was like a madness. We didn't kiss. We didn't bite or lick. We just stroked each other, and the more we caressed—not just with our hands, but with our whole bodies—the more sensitive we became.

She drew me down onto the bed and we enfolded each other. It was like my whole world had become her flesh sliding against mine. I caressed her hair and her neck with my cheek. She nuzzled my shoulder. The tender coolness of her breasts against my chest, our bellies pressed close together, our thighs entwined, my hands caressing the smoothness of her back, her small, cool hands on my skin… They were all part of an eternal, timeless place. The only reality—the only truth—was our skin and a limitless love that tied us together as we writhed in pleasure in each other's arms.

Then our faces brushed, our lips met and we kissed. And we could not stop kissing. We bit each other's lips tenderly, gently. We licked and sucked at each other's tongues. The closeness and the tenderness was like a slow, growing insanity. And as we kissed, she opened her legs. She slid her hands up my chest to hold my face. I held her tender cheeks in my hands and our mouths locked. I sank my tongue deep into her mouth as I sank deep inside her. She was moist, warm and tight.

I began to move, but her lips brushed my ear and she whispered, "Don't move. Stay motionless and kiss me. Love me. Never stop kissing me or loving me."

I kissed her. We kissed with our eyes open, staring deep into each other's souls. We kissed deep, and we exchanged a million tiny, pecking kisses. We licked and sucked and bit gently at each other's lips and mouths, and all the while, we stared into each other's eyes, and the love was a palpable thing, a solid mana that flowed between us. It grew and swelled until it was a kind of adoration and we were melting into each other.

Then she began to whimper and gasp. I felt a strange, pleasurable raw stinging in the tip of my penis. She gripped my face so our noses were almost touching. Her eyes were wide and her breathing was trembling. She half-whispered, half-gasped, "Oh, God…!"

The tingling sting began to spread to my loins and out into my body. But I could feel it spreading into her, too. My belly was burning. There was an insane excitement welling inside me. I could feel her body stiffen, pressing hard against me. My cock swelled inside her, getting harder. The stinging, tingling was turning electric. She was whispering and as she did, her lips brushed mine. "Wait, wait, wait…" Her cheeks and neck flushed red and she was suddenly screaming through gritted teeth. I exploded inside. I was gripping her to me, pounding into her and roaring into the pillow as she clawed at my back. Love, pain and pleasure seared together and she screamed and bit deep into my shoulder as I bit and sucked and screamed into her neck. It seemed to go on for an eternity until we collapsed, tangled and sweating, in each other's arms. I lay panting and drained, still deep inside her, kissing her face and her lips, stroking her hair, whispering her name.

Her skin was still my whole world—warm, moist with perspiration, pressed against my belly, her breasts against my chest, her face buried in my neck, her hair on my face. I was wrecked. I had never experienced anything so intense, let alone such intense pleasure. I heard her whisper, "I love you, Murdoch. Never, *ever* leave me. I couldn't bear it."

And I slipped again into blessed oblivion.

* * * *

The attack came at five a.m. I awoke with a blast of intense light through the window and Maggie screaming at me, "Murdoch! Wake up! Wake *up!*"

I fell out of bed, grabbing my pants and my shirt. I glanced at Maggie. She was climbing into her jeans. I could see her bare back. She was saying, "Who is it? Is it the AE or the Brotherhood?"

I snapped, "I don't know."

She was putting her sweatshirt on and I was pulling on my shoes when the door imploded. Blinding light flooded the room. Two black shadows surged in. One rushed at Maggie. The other rushed at where I had placed the case on the floor. I lunged for it and what seemed like a ton of bricks hit me in the face and sent me reeling across the room to crash into the wardrobe. I struggled to get to my feet, but my legs buckled under me.

I could see one of the china-faced androids. He had the case and was moving at sickening speed toward the door. Behind him, the other one had Maggie under his arm, like a roll of carpet. She was screaming and kicking, but she was helpless. I clawed at the bed and dragged myself to my feet. I could hear myself shouting, but my voice sounded weird, like a punch-drunk Stallone. They were out of the door. Somehow, I managed to run. I staggered out and saw they were heading for a huge SUV with spotlights trained on our room. I hurled myself in a flying tackle at the android that had Maggie. He back-handed me as Maggie screamed, "The case! The case!"

I struggled to my feet again, bellowing incoherently at myself to get up, and charged the thing with the case. He had a side door open in the truck and the other droid was throwing Maggie in like an old sack. I collided with the one with the case. He barely noticed. I ducked his back-hander, but he caught my shoulder and sent me sprawling on the ground. My body was racked with pain. My ears were ringing and I barely had the strength to move. I saw one of the droids slide the door closed and move around the other side of the van, while the other climbed into the driver's seat. The truck started to move.

I screamed something — I don't know what — and charged the van as it pulled away. I managed to grab the rim of the roof with my fingernails and it started to accelerate. I had no idea what I was going to do. I felt the blood ooze from my fingertips as I dragged myself up against the momentum of the accelerating SUV. I clambered onto the roof. I grasped for the lip along the side and pulled myself along toward the front, lying flat in a kind of eastern cross, moving forward one agonizing inch at a time.

Then it started to turn weird. At first, I thought it was the exhaustion playing tricks with my eyes. There was a faint green wash over everything. We were speeding through sparse woodland. It was real dark, but the harder I looked, the clearer it became. There was a luminous green haze developing around the SUV, and the ride was becoming smoother. The ride was becoming smoother because we were rising off the road. I shouted, "Oh, shit! Oh, shit! Oh, shit!" And that was when I felt the thud of the rotors.

They came in on both sides, keeping pace with us as we hurtled through the trees. They were black, unmarked and almost silent, except that you could feel the pulse of their powerful gas turbines on the air. Their side doors were open and I could make out what looked like M-134 Miniguns mounted in the openings — the sort of thing the Terminator would use to annihilate an entire police force. They both opened at the same time, spitting fire and raking the side of the van. I felt the bus shake and we dropped and hit the road with a bone-jarring crash. Then we started a series of violent swerves as luminous threads of lighting crackled and pierced the cloud of green haze. Next thing, my hair was standing on end and a billion electric ants were burrowing furiously into my skin. I must have screamed, but all I could hear was the thunder of the Miniguns and the agonized squeal of tortured metal where the bullets were ripping open the van,

Then there was another squeal. This time, it was the brakes as the SUV slowed to a halt. The chopper on my right stayed on it. The one on my left shot past, then banked and circled back. On my right, the bullets were still hammering the side at a rate of a hundred rounds a second. The cab door opened and the droid climbed out. He pulled a cannon from his belt and took aim before he was hit by a torrent of fire that crumpled him and hurled him against the side of the van. The hail of bullets stopped abruptly. I slid over to the left. The other droid was climbing out, letting loose with an automatic rifle. The chopper was banking away from the shots. Then it swung around and began firing. The hail of bullets smashed into the droid and he went down.

Then the chopper on my right started firing again. I scrambled over and saw the droid climbing to his feet. He took aim with both hands and his automatic spat fire. I thought I heard a scream and the chopper began to swing. I didn't waste time. I was thinking of Maggie inside, dreading she'd been torn to shreds by the hail of bullets. I slid over and jumped down.

The damned droid was also climbing to his feet again. I wrenched open the side door and leaned in. Maggie was curled up in the corner in the fetal position. I grabbed her by her waistband and dragged her to me. She lashed out with her foot. I dodged and shouted, "It's *me!*"

Then the Minigun opened up again. I dragged Maggie to the ground and pushed her under the SUV. She screamed at me, "The case!"

I nodded and leaned close to her. "*Run!* Run for the woods!" I gestured at the woodland that spread away from us about fifty yards away.

She looked, stared at me, nodded and repeated, "Get the case!" stabbing her finger up at the cab. I nodded and she scrambled out from under the van and took off. I slid toward the cab, behind the droid. I leaned in the cab and a bullet sang by my ear. I saw the case, grabbed it and hightailed after Maggie.

I tore across the field like all hell was breaking loose behind me. It was. Maggie was a few yards ahead and I was catching up to her. A high-pitched whine tore the night in half. There was an instant of silence followed by an intense flash of light then a massive explosion. A powerful blast of hot air hurled me to the ground. I covered my head with my hands then staggered to my feet and ran to where Maggie had fallen. She was climbing to her hands and knees, looking back over her shoulder. Her face was bathed in flaming orange light. I helped her up and turned.

One of the choppers had exploded. The other had swung around to the front of the truck. The two droids were standing shoulder to shoulder, hammering the copter with small arms fire, but the Minigun was unloading a barrage of lead into them and the SUV's engine. I shouted, *"Run!"* and as I did, the truck and the two droids were engulfed in a ball of flame.

We took off. Soon we were among the trees, racing blind, dodging among ferns, fallen trunks and pitted, uneven ground. Maggie fell. I helped her up. We ran three more steps and I sprawled over a fallen branch. I kept a grip on the case, struggled to my feet and we continued on. Then the sound of the chopper began to close on us, slow, steady and implacable.

Maggie stopped and looked up, scanning the inky canopy above us. She grabbed my hand and whispered, "This way!"

She dragged me, stumbling, down a slope overgrown with ivy and ferns. A stream coiled its way along the bottom, with a high bank on the other side. We scrambled along, following the slope. The chopper seemed to fade and she glanced at me. There was hope in her eyes, but it died as soon as it appeared. Within seconds, the thud of the rotors was growing again, and as we turned a bend in the stream, we saw them ahead of us—two tall, black silhouettes framed in the arch of the overhanging trees, backlit by the spotlight from the helicopter.

The droids were burned, their clothes shredded and one of them had lost one of his black lenses. But they were there and they were training their weapons on us. The weapons spat as I dragged Maggie to the ground. We dropped, splashed in the mud and I tried to cover her with my body. I saw what happened next as though it were in slow motion. They must have changed the ammo in the Minigun. A hail of explosive rounds hit the droids, and I guess they had taken about as much punishment as they could stand, because the shells ripped them apart. They literally erupted. I saw a small explosion on the ground, sixty yards away, where a shell had passed right through one of the disintegrating bodies and hit a rock. I saw the rock shatter and jump, and I saw one, small, incandescent shard swirl through space toward us. In the next instant, it had plunged right into Maggie's chest.

I heard the small gasp and cry. She was lying on her side and she half-turned to me. She looked astonished. She reached up with her hand and touched my face, and a hundred yards away the rotors of the chopper thudded like a slowing heartbeat.

Chapter Twenty-One

She said, "Listen to me."

Her voice was failing. I knew she was dying and all I could think to say was, "Oh, Maggie, no..." Tears flooded my eyes and streamed down my face. I kept shaking my head and repeating, "No, Maggie, no."

She stroked my face and there was a small, sad smile on her lips and in her eyes. She said, "Hush, we haven't much time. Listen to me."

I cradled her head and rocked back and forth, whispering, "Please, Maggie, no..."

She said, "You knew, didn't you?" I nodded. She went on, "Please, forgive me. I have always loved you, Liam. Always. But it took me time to realize."

I stroked her face. "Hush. We'll steal a car. We'll get you to the clinic. It's not far."

She placed her finger over my lips. "Stop. Listen for once—just listen. It's my time. And I am happy. You are a good man, Liam. You knew, but you were kind to me and steadfast in your love for Maria. I understand that now." Her smile flooded with love and she held my face in both hands. "Don't feel bad about last night. You were faithful at every moment. You truly believed it was her. But Liam"—a look of true wonder spread across her face—"I found *rupa!* You took me there with your love. I felt it and you carried me there. I felt the way *you* feel." She relaxed and sagged against me. Her eyes began to fade. Her voice was barely a whisper. "I knew," she said. "I always knew from the moment you walked into Noddy's Diner that I would learn to love with you."

I was biting my lip. I could taste my own blood. I was half blind with the tears, but I could see the chopper settling in the clearing, maybe sixty yards away. I looked down and wiped the tears from my eyes with the back of my hand. It wasn't Maggie anymore. It was — as I had suspected for a while — the beautiful, lethal, unpredictable Catherine Howard. She whispered, "Hold me close, Liam. Let me go in peace, having you close."

I bent down, held her and sobbed like a child, and as she died, I passed from consciousness.

* * * *

There was a white lace curtain. It was moving in sunlight under a soft breeze. It gave a small waft, then described a slow semicircle before coming to rest where it had started. It paused and wafted again. It had a pale-gray shadow that slid back and forth along the white windowsill. I don't know how long I stared at it. Time wasn't a part of things yet. There was a large oblong of light, warped like a Dali clock over the end of the red, blue and yellow patchwork quilt on my bed and across big, nut-brown wood of the floorboards. There was a rug. It looked old and expensive. A tissue of shadow from the lace curtain drifted back and forth across the floorboards and the rug. There were birds singing, but more than song, it was like a busy, melodious conversation. It made my smile. And there was someone clipping a hedge with old-fashioned shears, which meant there must be people.

And that thought brought back the darkness of the night and Maggie lying in my arms as her brilliant light went out. And that brought the question.

Where am I?

I moved my head. I was in a large, high-ceilinged room with heavy, exposed beams. There were white walls and a large, open fireplace with a vase of dried flowers in it. Across the room, opposite the window with the lace curtain, there was a big, oak door, and beside my bed there was an armchair. In the chair, Maria was sleeping.

I watched her for a long time. Her black hair was pulled back in a loose bun, a few strands over her forehead, her long, dark lashes and her dusting of faint freckles were all a soothing medicine. It may have been five minutes or it may have been half an hour, but eventually she stirred, her eyes fluttered and she focused on my face. We stayed like that a while, just smiling at each other.

After a bit, she stood and took off her sweatshirt and her jeans. She pulled back the covers and slid in next to me. I turned onto my side and we lay with our noses touching, stroking each other's face. There was no need to speak. We kissed — lots — long and slow. She took my hand, rolled onto her back and placed it on her belly. Somehow, in some weird way, I could feel the life inside her. I knew, in my bones, that I didn't give a damn if I wasn't the father. I kissed her eyes, her nose and each freckle in turn. I hadn't fathered them. I hadn't created them, but I couldn't love them any more than I did. This baby was a part of her and that was enough for me. I told her all this with my eyes — and with every kiss.

She stroked my face and said, "I knew, you know."

I smiled and kissed her again. "What did you know, baby?"

"That night, I knew we had conceived."

I kept the frown from my face and managed to smile instead. I said, "You did?"

She pulled closer and wrapped her leg around me. "Sure. And it wasn't just the sheet lightning or making it out in the storm like that." She stared up at the ceiling, smiling, like she was searching her mind. My mind was straining, reaching for something. She went on, "It was something in you. You were so..." She pressed up against me, growled and giggled and bit my neck. "You were such an *animal!*"

I started to laugh. I grabbed her and rolled her on top of me. We laughed and kissed again and I said, "Cornwall."

195

She looked slightly surprised. "Of course, Cornwall! I told you."

She had. She'd said five weeks. I hadn't remembered until she'd mentioned the storm and the sheet lightning. Something had blanked it from my memory. We'd been on the beach. We'd taken a cottage above Bedruthan Bay. It had been a beautiful evening and we'd been down to the sea, watching the sun set. The storm had boiled up out of the Atlantic without warning. There had been sheet lightning, turning the clouds purple and violet from the inside. We'd sat and watched, and for some reason, the wild, awesome nature of the storm had turned us on. We'd started to kiss then the electricity in the air and the thunder — like the sky was shattering over our heads — had driven us crazy. The more crazy she'd gotten, the more wild I'd become until, in the end, we'd stripped naked and made love like savage animals right there on the sand. Then we'd gone swimming naked, laughing and out of our minds, and made love again in the water and on the shore, with the waves caressing us. It had been a crazy night.

It was crazy that I could have forgotten it.

We'd walked back up the cliff then, laughing, stopping along the way to kiss like teenagers, holding each other close. I remember we'd fallen into the cottage like we were drunk. I'd made a fire and mixed some drinks while she'd started cooking. After that, I didn't remember anything.

The seed is mine. The baby is mine.

I said, "What happened after we got back to the cottage?"

She kissed me a few times, stroked the hair from my face. "You made a fire. I went to cook…"

"Then?"

She shook her head. "I can't remember. Why?"

"No reason. Maria?"

"Yes, Liam?"

She giggled. I kissed her. "How the hell did I get here?"

She went serious. "I don't know exactly. Sinead got a call. I think it was from your friend…" She let the words trail and searched my eyes.

I shook my head.

"Whatever you're thinking, baby, you're wrong."

"I'm not thinking anything."

"But you wondered." She shrugged.

I said, "Welcome to my world."

She laughed. "Point taken. Who — ?" She hesitated.

I said, "It's okay, baby. I know she's dead."

"Who was she?"

I sighed. She rolled off me and I pushed myself into a sitting position. "Catherine Howard. You remember? In Çalares, she turned up at your house asking for me. You thought she was my girlfriend."

She frowned. "She's the one who told you I was pregnant."

I nodded. "Yeah. She and Sinead were lovers for a while. They defected from the Brotherhood together because they were having a relationship and that wasn't allowed."

She stared at me a while, then muttered, "Shit. It sounds like a bad Mexican soap."

I laughed. "We're just scratching the surface, baby. Is Russell here?"

She nodded. "Don't be hard on him, Liam. He feels bad, and they have really cared for me and the baby. Sinead has been amazing." She hesitated, looking down at the sheet. "Liam. I know what you were thinking."

I studied her face. "Yeah?"

"You must have been through hell, and I didn't help with my tantrums."

"Forget it."

"You thought the baby wasn't yours. I hope you know now that this little baby is a bit of you, a bit of me and a whole lot its own self."

I nodded. "I do."

She got up on her knees next to me and we kissed again, for a long while. She said, "You feel up to seeing Russell and Reggie?"

"And Sinead?"

"And Sinead."

"Yeah, sure."

"You shower and get dressed. I'll go down and tell them you're awake. You've been out almost eighteen hours."

* * * *

They were sitting on a kind of Colonial veranda overlooking an expanse of lawn. At the foot of the lawn was a large lake. As I stepped out, Russell did his usual trick of continuing a conversation I didn't know we'd been having.

"You were right, of course. And I suppose I owe you an apology."

Before I could answer, Maria was on her feet giving me a kiss and Hook got up and stepped toward me with his hand outstretched. "Murdoch, I am very relieved to see you safe and sound." He frowned slightly. There is nothing the English dislike more than unnecessary emotion, so he was making a real effort. He said, "Sorry about, your, um… friend."

I shook his hand. I said, "Thanks," and meant it. Sinead was sitting in a porch swing watching me. I held her eye a moment and said, "Hi, Sinead. I'm sorry about Catherine."

She didn't react. She said, "Is it true she achieved *rupa*?"

I sat in a big wicker chair next to Maria and said, "Yeah." I peeled a fresh pack of Camels and put one in my mouth. I lit it, and as I let out the smoke and snapped the Zippo shut, I said, "That's what she said, and I believe her. Had she really gone rogue?"

"Yes. That's why I love her. There is one in many, many millions of the Seraphs who blazes a trail toward feeling as she did." An unexpected smile lit up her face. "And she did blaze a trail."

I snorted a small laugh. I felt a pang of sadness and realized I missed Maggie. I said, half to myself, "She did that."

"Ironically, Murdoch, you saw her for most of the time.

You knew her as a traitor and someone you could not trust. But if it had not been for her rebellious, uncontrollable nature, the Ael Rune would never have found its way to you. It was her idea to steal it in the first place, her idea that she and I should become lovers and escape, her idea to entrust it to you and, ultimately, her idea to pursue you in this mission."

I thought about that for a long while then I said, "I have to agree. In the end, there was a lot more to her than what showed on the surface."

She nodded once. "In her own wild way, she was the wisest of us all."

A guy stepped onto the veranda dressed as a waiter. He asked if he could get me anything and I told him he could get me a long Martini, extra dry.

He went away to get it and I asked Russell, "What is this place?"

He smiled. "It's registered as a clinic, but it's an extra-safe safe house."

I raised an eyebrow at Hook. "This belongs to the SAS?"

He and Russell both laughed. "Heavens no, old chap."

I frowned. "A safe house for who, then?"

Russell did something he very rarely did. He looked me square in the eye. "Liam, I have reached a decision and I have discussed it with Reggie, who has been at my side for many, many years. I have decided to tell you everything. You were quite right. I should have trusted you and confided in you. Frankly, you are a violent, explosive, unpredictable man and I was worried about how you would react to our alliance with Sinead and what she had done to your baby. And I was right to worry." He turned to Hook then to Sinead. "But when we start putting worries of that sort above people and friends, we lose our humanity. And, actually, Catherine knew that on some level." He turned back to face me. "And you knew that, too. However, please humor me, and let me reveal the truth to you in my own way."

I nodded. "Okay."

Sinead said, "Liam, as a matter of personal interest, when did you realize that she was Catherine?"

The waiter came out with my Martini. I took it and sipped it before answering. "She had me completely fooled as an annoying kid called Maggie. But when she followed me to London, tracked me to my apartment and killed one of those china-faced droids, I began to realize there was something odd about her. She was obviously more than the naïve kid she claimed to be. Then she took me to a warehouse in North London to hide out. It was a hot, muggy night. We both got real wet, but she was shivering like it was minus two. I was pretty sure then she was a hybrid. I suspected she was a renegade, because she'd killed one of the droids and helped me escape, but I wanted to play along to see what she was after. It seemed her main interest was in our personal relationship, and that's when I started to wonder if she was Catherine.

"Then, in San Francisco, a couple of things happened. She refused to go back to her parents, despite her life being in real danger, which suggested there were no real parents. She knew where Professor Cohen lived. When we met him, he hid it well, but I could see he recognized her. I realized then the same thing had happened with George Chang at Luton airport. They both seemed to recognize her but kept silent about it."

Sinead nodded. "Yes, they would have seen who she was beneath the morph. It must have been exhausting for her. How long did she keep it up?"

"Days." I sucked on the cigarette and looked at the burning tip, remembering her during the long drive. "How do you do that?"

She was watching me with that strange, direct stare. "We don't, not all of us. It depends on our genetic root. I can't do it, but Catherine was very skilled."

I said, "Is that what you call a Golika?"

She nodded. "Yes, that's a Golika. They have chameleon

qualities and they can alter the configuration of their skin and their muscles to a greater or lesser extent, to take on a different appearance."

"Like Maggie — or Mary-Jane Carter."

In as much as she was able to show emotion, she appeared sad. When she spoke, her Irish brogue was soft. "But it is tiring to sustain for any length of time. To hold it for days..." She shook her head and gazed out at the grass and the lake beyond.

I watched her. I was curious. I kept telling myself she wasn't human, but it was hard to assimilate.

I said, "She became quite ill. She turned very gray. In the end, she asked to be laid on the back seat and covered up. That kind of clinched it. I guessed what was happening, and it tied in with Catherine going rogue and showing up at the hotel in Sao Paulo."

Sinead nodded and turned to face me again. "She became obsessed with you. She believed you could make her feel."

Maria gave me a very direct look. "And did you?"

I met her gaze, and I was grateful to Catherine for her dying words. I had promised myself long ago that I would never lie to Maria, and Catherine had understood before dying how important that was to me. I said, "Yes. She learned to feel on that long journey. She shifted from obsession to being in love. She was in love with me, and in her dying words, she told me she admired the fact that I had stayed faithful to you every step of the way."

She grinned. She even seemed smug.

I turned to Hook then to Russell. "So, what happens now?"

Russell said, "Well, I imagine you are famished, so I fancy some luncheon is in order — and perhaps some debriefing over lunch. Then we can put together a plan over some rather fine Bushmills I have here."

I smiled. That's the thing with Russell. He's so damned civilized.

They stood but I stayed sitting. So did Sinead. She was

watching me. I turned to Russell. "Give us ten minutes, would you?"

They went inside. I crushed out my cigarette and said, "What did you do to Maria?"

She was about as expressionless as it's possible to be while remaining organic. "When Professor Cohen told us that he had been working on the Ael Rune and he had realized how the Naga intended to use it, we knew that we only had two chances of saving humanity – to steal and destroy the stone and to try to create two human children who had the capability of surviving what the Naga were planning to do."

"I know this much already."

A flicker of something that might have been amusement lightened her eyes. I was surprised. "Patience is not your strength, is it, Liam? You are similar to Catherine in that. Allow me to continue and we will get there sooner. Then you will understand our motivation, as well."

"I am not really interested in your motivation."

"Well, you should be, because the welfare of your wife and your child depend on our motivation."

"Please, go on."

"On the night that you and Maria went down to the beach at Bedruthan Bay, we generated an electrical storm over the Atlantic."

"You can do that?"

She almost smiled. "It isn't difficult. Even you could do it if you put your mind to it. We used the energy from the storm to affect your hormone levels. You probably felt very much like animals. Your mental limitations and inhibitions began to fall away – "

I was getting uncomfortable and I interrupted, "Yeah, I know. I was there."

This time, she actually smiled, though it was an odd, secret smile. "That, in turn, allowed us to neutralize the contraceptive pill she was taking, so she became pregnant."

"So, the baby *is* mine."

She got that odd expression that people who think they know everything get when they don't understand something. "I keep hearing this phrase. Russell kept asking me — and Reggie, too. It is not *anybody's* child, Liam. You, of all people, should understand that.

"You're playing word games!"

"No, *you* are being imprecise. If what you are asking me is whether the child is growing from your sperm and whether it carries your DNA, then the answer is yes."

I shook my head. "So, why is this kid — ?"

"Because we have altered your DNA. We carry many genes, Liam. Most of them lie dormant and are never activated. We activated genes in this child that will allow its sensory perception to develop in such a way that it can process the frequencies generated by the stone and many others besides."

I thought about this a long while. The birds were still having their strident conversation. They had no idea what was going down here. I said, "You said there were two children."

"There is another child."

"Who?"

"It's best you don't know."

"Why?"

She smiled and shook her head. "Because it's none of your business, Murdoch. What *is* your business, on the other hand, is your wife, and your lunch."

I studied her face a while. I decided there was humor in her eyes — and compassion. I wondered how you could have compassion without emotion but could find no answer. I decided in that moment that I liked her, and for the first time since I had met her, I smiled at her then we stood and went in to lunch together.

Chapter Twenty-Two

Over lunch, I gave them a rundown of everything that had happened since I had last seen them at the hospital. Russell and Hook became real interested when I told them about the AE.

Russell said, "We've known about them for some time. They've been around in one shape or another since 1776. They don't know about us, of course. Not really."

I stared at him. "The Declaration of Independence?"

He kind of nodded and shrugged at the same time. "And the founding of the Bavarian Illuminati by Adam."

"Adam?"

"Weishaupt. He founded it pretty much at the same time as George—George Washington—was declaring the independence of the United States."

I put a smile firmly on one side of my face. "You are on first-name terms with these people, naturally."

He snorted. "Anyway, the AE made its first appearance that year. Weishaupt could see Napoleon coming and founded the AE as a preparatory measure."

I sighed. Usually this kind of thing would have amused and interested me in Russell, but Maggie's death and my exhaustion were still raw, and I just found it irritating. I was about to talk, but Maria surprised me by speaking first. "Russell, I am sure this is really interesting, but I confess that I, for one, am getting lost. I don't see what Napoleon and the Bavarian Illuminati have to do with the AE wanting our baby and trying to steal the Çabra Stone, or the Ael Rune or whatever it's called."

He smiled at her. It was a real, warm smile, and for the

first time, I realized how much affection he had for her.

"Forgive me, Maria. My head is a bit like an ancient library. I have lived in there for many years and I know my way around it quite well, but sometimes, I forget that other people don't."

I burst out laughing and held Maria's hand. "That's a first, kid. Savor it. I have never seen Russell explain himself to anybody until just now."

He raised an eyebrow at me, but apart from that, he ignored me. "The thing is, the Allied Executive—the AE— believe that the Naga—the Brotherhood of the Goat, if you prefer—are a race of aliens. And, in many ways, they are right. Now, the Brotherhood have been at war with humanity for many centuries, and at times, they have used certain unique individuals as their puppets in those wars."

Sinead spoke. "We have created certain world leaders to further our project. We created Napoleon, just as we created Hitler exactly one hundred and twenty years later. They were hybrids whom we used to engineer world wars. The Allied Executive—and their masters the Illuminati— believed, and continue to believe, that they are our sworn enemies. For them, the issue is very clear. We are evil aliens and they are good, because they are fighting for humanity."

I said, a little more aggressively than I'd intended, "And what's wrong with that?"

She smiled...almost. "There is nothing *wrong* with it in the sense that you mean it, Liam. But they are as much puppets of the Naga as the people they are fighting against. And not only that, but the acts of cruelty they perpetrate in the name of humanity render the term 'good' pretty much meaningless."

I nodded. "Okay. I agree."

Hook broke in. "Anyway, to get back to the subject at hand, the latest incarnation of the AE dates back to the end of World War II and the Roswell Incident. A government-within-the-government was established in Washington with the aim of preparing for and resisting an invasion by the aliens."

I said, "Wait a minute. I keep hearing about these aliens, suddenly. I thought the whole point was that *they* were the natural, native inhabitants of Earth and *we* were the aliens from Mars, and that's why we behave like a damned virus on this planet."

Maria was watching me and nodding. Sinead said, "It is confusing because it was intended from the beginning to be confusing. Now is not the time to explain the whole thing, but let me say this. We are both—both our species—originally alien. But we have both been here so long now—especially the Seraphs, what you call the hybrids, like me and Catherine—that we can all also call ourselves natives of Earth. The one big difference is that the Naga, the original reptilian race—the Saurians that you have heard about, Liam—they retain their home planet in Proxima Centauri. It takes them about seventeen years to make the round trip, and each trip causes severe distortion for them in relative time. Let's leave it at that for now. The point is that the AE believe there will be an invasion from Proxima Centauri and they must prepare for that invasion. It is what we have led them to believe."

I said, "And is it true? Will there be an invasion?"

She nodded. "Yes, but it will not be as they expect it."

A wave of exhaustion washed over me and I was overcome by a longing to end this conversation and go down by the lake with Maria to talk about our baby—to pretend this nightmare was nothing but science fiction. I said, "I'm sorry, guys. It's been a tough few days and I am dead beat. I need a break. Can we cut to the chase? What concerns me now is how to get the stone to Wales, put it in the reactor and start making plans for the birth of our child. So, without the history lessons and lectures on morality and ethics, what now? Where do we go from here?"

Hook glanced at Russell. Russell looked at me. He said, "Washington D.C."

"What?"

"Tomorrow or the day after, you and I go to Washington D.C. to meet with the heads of the Allied Executive. Once we've had that meeting, you go back to Wales to dispose of the stone."

Hook said, "In the meantime, I have some errands to run. No doubt I'll see you in Wales, Murdoch. I suggest you use the next day or so to rest and build yourself up a bit. You're going to need it."

* * * *

The next two days were a kind of bliss. Hook had gone to do his 'errands', whatever they were, and Russell and Sinead discreetly disappeared a lot. We pretty much saw them at lunch and dinner, but aside from that, Maria and I spent a lot of time in bed. When we weren't making love, we were walking by the lake or just lying on the grass in each other's arms, dreaming of a day when all the madness would be behind us and we could live as a normal, happy couple with our child. In retrospect, it was a measure of the madness of the times, that living a normal life should have seemed to us a crazy dream.

Thursday came, two days after I had awoken at the Shangri-La Clinic, and at eight a.m., I kissed Maria goodbye, and Russell and I climbed into his Bentley and we drove down to Portland to take an air taxi to D.C.

On the way, I stopped and posted Ken a parcel with his keys and directions on where to find his car, plus a very generous payment. I hoped they would understand that we'd had no real choice. I had a hunch they would.

The flight was just short of two hours and we touched down at Reagan National Airport thirty minutes after noon. There was an official limo waiting for us. I was surprised to see a USAAF lieutenant at the wheel. We took the George Washington Memorial across the bridge into Virginia, and in just over five minutes, we were in the Pentagon parking lot. I stared at Russell. He looked bland. I said, "Jesus,

Russell. This is big league."

"What did you expect? It always was, dear boy. You just didn't realize it until now." He smiled. "You may have a few more surprises today."

We pulled into a lot in the North Parking. Our driver stepped out and opened the door for Russell. I had to get out on my own. He took us to the Corridor 8 entrance, where we were met by a USAAF Major who saluted smartly and gave us authorization badges. Then he led us through rings E, D and C to Ring B. From there, he took us up a couple of floors to a room whose number I cannot disclose. There he knocked and we were admitted to a large office, twenty or twenty-five-foot square. There was a flag against the wall and a portrait of the President. There was a large, mahogany desk to the left of the door, and opposite, there was a window overlooking an internal garden.

There was nobody behind the desk, but three men stood from where they were sitting around a large coffee table in the center of the room. One of them was the Duke of Suffolkshire, another was McGuire. The third man I didn't know, but he had an expensive Italian suit and steel-gray hair and eyes. He was tall and slim, the way a reed is tall and slim.

He stepped toward us, holding out his right hand to Russell, with a smile on his face you could only describe as urbane. He said, "You are Professor Whittering?" Russell muttered something and the man turned to me. "And you must be Liam Murdoch. I have heard a lot about you." We shook and he went on. "I am John Palermo, advisor to the President on issues of air defense and national security. These gentlemen are His Grace the Duke of Suffolkshire and Colonel McGuire, both of whom I believe you have met." This last was directed at me. He gestured at a couple of chairs and said, "Won't you sit?"

We sat. I said "Sure, we've met. How are you, Your Grace? I hope you managed to get the dust out of your pants." I showed him my hands, with all my fingers splayed. "I'm

208

still intact. Sorry about your boy, Brutus. He ended up getting a little hot under the collar."

Suffolkshire gazed at me as though I were transparent, then turned and stared hard at Russell, who was doing his usual bumbling, absent-minded professor act. McGuire studiously ignored me, which suited me fine. Palermo offered us drinks. We declined and he sat and looked at Russell. He said, "So, Professor, you said you had some important business to discuss with us."

Russell glanced at him like he was surprised that they expected something from him. "Yes, quite important, yes. You, of course, Mr. Palermo, have not been aware of us until now. We, on the other hand, have been aware of you since your foundation in 1776, and we have been following your progress with some interest."

The three of them exchanged a look. Palermo said, "Really?"

"In the summer of 1947, you established the so-called 'government within the government', to organize the fight against the invaders from Proxima B, and you are satisfied that you have been moderately successful so far. You believe you have brought down several of their ships since Roswell and that you are on the verge of developing a level of technology that will enable you to repulse the beachheads they have established on Earth — and, who knows? Perhaps even chase them back to Proxima Centauri and colonize *them*." They didn't react, but they were serious enough to show that he had made an impression. Now he said, "I am here to disabuse you of that belief and to offer you a deal."

Palermo made several movements of his head and his hands in that way Italians have and finally said, "I am neither going to confirm nor deny what you are saying, Professor, but as you have come all this way, and you *are* a professor of mathematics at the University of London, I am happy to hear what else you have to say."

I had never in all the years I had known Russell ever heard him swear. Now he turned to Suffolkshire and said, "Do we really have to go through this bullshit, Suffolkshire? Will you be good enough to tell this man that I am serious, that I am not here to waste my time and to cut the ridiculous song and dance routine?"

The duke's eyebrows rose halfway up his forehead and he gave a small cough. Where he came from, that was an emotional reaction. He turned to Palermo, who was struggling not to gape, and said, "I think we can cut to the chase, John." He coughed again and frowned at Russell. "I thought I recognized you. You were at Oxford when I was. I have to say, you are…" He hesitated a long time, as though searching for the right words. Finally, he said, "I have to say you're keeping very well."

Russell blinked and said, "Yes, how unfortunate. And perhaps it would be best if that was all you said."

Palermo was beginning to seem antsy. He glanced at McGuire, who shrugged. Then he turned back to Russell. "Look. Before we go any further, Professor, I would like to know just exactly who you are."

Russell gave him a once over and I almost burst out laughing. "Yes, I'm sure you would. Let me tell you then. *We* are the people who have the Ael Rune and the baby, and you and the Brotherhood are the people who haven't. *We* are the people who have been watching you for over two and a half centuries and you are the people who didn't know we existed. *We* are the people who are going to send the Naga running with their tails between their legs, and, if you get in our way, *we* are the people with the power to completely obliterate you. Have you some idea now, Mr. Palermo, just exactly who *we* are?"

Palermo and McGuire were beginning to stand. Palermo was saying, "Hey now, just one goddamn minute!"

But the duke was waving him back, saying, "John, John… keep your hair on, John. We need to listen to this man."

Palermo stopped, eased himself back down and stared hard at Suffolkshire. Suffolkshire made a face like 'watcha gonna do?' and said, "I think he's right. I think he's telling the truth."

Palermo turned on his frown. It had become an incredulous frown. "Who the fuck *are* you?"

"I think we've just covered that. Now, there are some things you need to know." He leaned back in his chair and the look he gave Palermo was almost frightening in its arrogance. This was a side to Russell I had never seen, a side I had never even suspected existed. "For almost three hundred years you have been engaged in a war against an attempted alien invasion. However misguided you may have been at times, you have fought bravely and with commitment, and you have won some significant *military* victories. Every single battle Sir Arthur, the Duke of Wellington, fought against Napoleon he won. In the early twentieth century, you shone somewhat more dimly, but still there were significant victories, in North Africa, Normandy…"

He paused and studied first McGuire, then the duke, then Palermo in turn. I was aware that when we had entered, Palermo had commanded the room. Now, he was just part of an audience, and the room was totally dominated by the huge presence of this small, skinny old man. When he spoke again, his voice was low and deep.

"But every military victory you have had has been part of a tactical rout. For almost three hundred years, you have been playing directly into their hands. Because their purpose has always been twofold and you have served both of those purposes faithfully."

McGuire spluttered, "What the hell are you talking about?"

Russell turned to him. "I am talking about industrialization, and I am talking about standardization. Every war they have engineered in the guise of imperial expansion, with one of their hybrid puppets at the helm, you have seen as a first move in an invasion. And you have responded with ever greater armies, developing your military technology, beefing up the military industrial complex until it was an empire in its own right—*especially* since Roswell. During the Cold War, the military industrial complex of NATO and the USSR achieved proportions that beggared belief. And *this...this...*was the purpose of the Naga. Their *true* purpose, since they had Tarquinius Superbus unite the Latin armies in Rome two thousand five hundred years ago, has been to have us create an industry capable of burning fossil fuels and standardizing our society."

Palermo rolled his eyes. "Is this some kind of Bilderberger shit?"

Russell snapped, "Don't be foolish! As a Director of the Cavendish Foundation and one of the architects of Bilderberg, you don't need me to tell you that your Bilderberg group is concerned with acquiring and retaining power, not transforming the environment."

There was a very heavy silence. Palermo, Suffolkshire and McGuire stared at each other. The duke was the first to speak. "What are you saying?"

"I am saying that you have been used — manipulated — by the Naga, since the dawn of the Industrial Revolution but especially since World War II and Roswell, to create CO_2 factories, to pump billions of gallons of carbon dioxide into the atmosphere for the simple purpose of making the atmosphere habitable for Saurians. Think about it! Have you never wondered why there is zero political will to address this issue? Have you never wondered why the environmental movement is ridiculed and sidelined? Think! What kind of environment did the dinosaurs thrive in? The last time CO_2 was at this level was *precisely* when the dinosaurs walked Earth!"

Palermo stood and moved to the window, looking down into the pentagonal courtyard. Eventually, he muttered, "Sweet Jesus, everything we have done, every step we have taken, every battle we have fought" — he turned and stared at Russell — "every life we have lost, every sacrifice we have made, has been to strengthen the hand of our enemy and aid him against us."

Russell's voice was quiet. "Don't feel too bad, Palermo. You had no way of knowing, and your enemy is very subtle indeed."

But Palermo was frowning, spreading his hands, shaking his head. His whole body was evidence of his confusion and frustration. He said, "Why have you left it so late? Why are you only coming to us now?"

Russell's answer was like a slap in the face — to Palermo and to me.

"Who is the enemy, Palermo?"

The words rang out and lingered in the air. We all stared at him. He went on, "Is this a war of race? Are we fighting them because they are Saurian? Are we fighting them because they are hybrids? Are we fighting them because they come from another planet? Why are we fighting them, Palermo?"

Palermo was shrugging, spreading his hands again, turning to the duke for support. But Suffolkshire knew what Russell was getting at and he said, "It is a question of survival, Professor."

Russell snapped, "For whom?"

McGuire flashed, "For us!"

"And who, precisely, is 'us', Colonel? Humanity? Western humanity? *Democracy?*" His scorn was palpable. He plowed on. "America? White America? Black America? Republican or Democratic America? Or the WASPs? Ultimately, the military group that is engaged in the war? Who, precisely, is 'us', Colonel?" He looked back at Palermo and the Duke. "And more to the point, how far down the road of 'the end justifies the means' are you prepared to go? Because I, for one, am acutely aware that the means define *precisely* who 'us' is."

Suffolkshire said, "What do you mean?"

But he already knew what he meant. Russell didn't pull his punches. "I mean, Suffolkshire, that if you are prepared to go to the depths of torturing a good man in order to achieve your end, then you are less than a lizard. You are no 'us' that I would care to be identified with. You are not any kind of humanity that I consider worth saving." The Duke had the decency to color and stare at his knee. Russell said more quietly, "Unless we are careful, we become the enemy, Suffolkshire. I would have hoped that Oxford had taught you at least that much."

Palermo dropped back into his chair, threw his head back with his eyes closed and pinched the bridge of his nose. It was an eloquent gesture. He said, "I am guessing, Professor, that you didn't come here to give us a lecture on ethics."

Russell gazed at him with what can only be described as disdain and said, "I wouldn't waste my breath. Your morals and your humanity, as far as I can see, are beyond redemption. You are, however, an intelligent man, and I have come here to try to make you think."

Palermo's jaw muscles were jumping. He'd had about as much as he could swallow from Russell, but he had no choice. He had to suck it up. I may have been smiling.

Russell said, "If you will give it a few moments thought, you will find that the implications of what I have told you are quite far-reaching." Palermo breathed deep and thought. The Duke was nodding at his knee. He had gotten there a few minutes earlier. McGuire was puce, so I guess he had gotten there, too. I saw the realization dawn on Palermo's face through his anger.

Russell went on. "So, you will realize that the answer to my next question will have enormous consequences for the future of humanity and the whole planet." He waited. They all exchanged looks. Russell said, "Are we being watched and listened to by the Chief Executives of the Alliance?"

They all stared at him for a long time. The duke said, "Yes."

Russell said, "Switch them off."

The duke turned toward Palermo and nodded once. Palermo looked at McGuire and nodded once. McGuire got up and went to a cabinet. He opened it. There was a control panel with several switches. I got up and peered over his shoulder. It was a touch screen that governed four cameras and eight microphones, plus an amp and a bank of speakers. He killed them all. I turned to Russell and nodded. We sat and Russell reached in his breast pocket. He took out a piece of paper and slid it across the table to Palermo. Palermo picked it up, unfolded it and studied the list that was written there. He swore softly under his breath and handed the list to the duke, who examined it then closed his eyes. "Dear God!"

Russell said, "The five names in red."

Palermo said, "I get it."

Suffolkshire leaned forward and handed the list to McGuire. McGuire flushed. "How the hell do we know this is true? How the hell do we know he's not lying to us?"

The duke said, "No, Colonel. It makes perfect sense. You know it does. See to it. See to it *now*."

The colonel got up and left the room. The duke appeared drawn and unhappy. He turned to Russell. "What do you want in exchange for this information?"

"Nothing. It's a gesture of goodwill. We are approaching the end. CO2 levels are about right and they are preparing to make their final move. When that happens, we need to be united. We want you on our side. Once you've taken care of your house cleaning, we'll talk to your executive and we'll reach terms. Believe me, you want us on your side. In the meantime, we have an operation to carry out, and we would like one of your men on our team. If not as a show of mutual trust, at least as a show of a mutual intent to learn to trust."

I turned and stared at Russell. He ignored me. Palermo looked at Suffolkshire and shrugged. Suffolkshire nodded. "Agreed."

"Good. I would suggest your man Colonel McGuire. We'll be at the Mandarin Oriental. When you have taken care of your business, I suggest you contact us and Murdoch will fill you in on the details."

We stood and they stood with us and saw us to the door.

We shook, and as I stepped out after Russell, the Duke said, "Um, Murdoch?" I stopped and turned to face him. He seemed embarrassed and stared at his shoes. It was hard for him, but he said, "I, um... I apologize. Russell is right. I suppose we did rather lose our way."

I'm pretty good at reading people and to me, he sounded sincere, so I nodded. I said, "It happens in hot blood."

We kind of smiled, and Russell and I left.

Chapter Twenty-Three

We were offered a car but Russell refused. We took the Metro to New York Avenue and he led me to a lunch counter called Litteri, down a broad street that was more like an industrial estate than a road. The place was small and crowded and the shelves were spilling over with bottles of olive oil, jars of red peppers and cheese and just about anything Italian you could imagine. We bought a couple of cheese and ham rolls that would probably have fed a couple of Roman regiments and took them across Sixth Street to Brentwood Park, where we sat on the grass to eat.

We hadn't really spoken since we'd left the Pentagon, and now we ate in silence until I said, "You want to explain to me what just happened back there?"

He studied his roll like he could see what had just happened inside its filling and he was going to explain it to me. Then he said, "McGuire is probably a morally reprehensible man, but then, most people are. I think he is committed to the cause and he, and the AE, could be significant allies in the near future. And I assure you, we are going to need them."

I nodded. "His Grace the Duke of Suffolkshire said he recognized you from Oxford. You said that was unfortunate, and you then told him to shut up." I licked my fingers and added, "His Grace the Duke of Suffolkshire spoke to you with respect and deference. Correct me if I'm wrong, but dukes aren't supposed to do that."

I glanced at him and he looked smug. "Yes, that's true."

"But you're not going to explain."

"All in good time, dear boy."

"Were you friends?"

"I was one of his professors."

I glanced at him. "That would make you a hundred and ten, at least."

He grinned and I swear his eyes twinkled. I sighed. I knew better than to argue. I said, "What about this two-thousand-year-old war? How come you never told me about the AE before?"

He stuffed the last piece of his roll in his mouth, chewed for a bit then spoke with his mouth full. "Perhaps I should have. Frankly, at the time, I thought you had enough to take in as it was."

I made a 'hmm' sound that told him maybe he had a point, so he went on.

"If there is any truth in the old Martians versus Saurians story—and there may well be—then the AE represent the Martians, even if they don't remember it." He shook his head and looked at me like I'd asked him to explain Heisenberg's uncertainty principle in two words or less. "It is immensely complex, Liam. It goes back thousands of years and involves all sorts of groups who have become all mixed in with each other and confused." He sighed. "It's like a bowl of soluble spaghetti. The thing is, you can't avoid humans behaving like humans and they will always eventually make a mess of things. Then the whole thing comes crashing down, usually with the help of some natural or semi-natural disaster, and we start again."

He wiped his mouth with his paper napkin and looked at me. "The only way we stay sane is by focusing on the individual."

I swallowed the last piece of my roll and wiped my mouth with the back of my hand. I ignored the image of a bowl of soluble spaghetti crashing down and thought about staying sane by thinking of the individual, instead. I said, "Explain that," but it sounded like "Eshpane dah."

He raised an eyebrow at me and stood. We started to walk back toward Sixth Street. He said, "Never pick a fight you can't win. The essential nature of human beings is that they are confused, ambiguous, neurotic and conflicted. If you traumatize them, they become traumatized and if you don't, they have no empathy and no maturity, so they become monsters."

"What's your point?"

We stepped out into Sixth and headed toward Florida Avenue. He said, "Trying to save humanity, in a spiritual sense, is pointless. It's a fight you can never win. The most we can do is to try to maintain, as far as possible, the best conditions in which the individual can grow and flourish and develop toward..." The words trailed away and I could tell by his face that he was looking for the right ones for me to understand. In the end, he shrugged and said, "The ability to feel empathy, compassion — the ability to be kind. You see, Liam, we are all about the individual. The Naga, the Ael, the AE? They are all about grand designs, races, species, *rupa,* enlightenment and salvation — great concepts. But us? We are just about one individual at a time."

We walked in silence for a while. I was thinking about everything he had said. We turned south on to Third Street, walking toward Union Station. I was aware I was about to ask the very same question that Palermo had asked him and got no answer. But I asked, anyway, "Who is *'we'*, Russell?"

He was studying the houses and the chestnut trees as he walked. "I always feel," he said, "when I am in Washington, one could almost be in London."

I said, "Russell?"

"The design of the houses, the streets — "

"Stop, Russell." I stopped dead in my tracks. He sighed and looked down at his feet. "Enough with the bumbling evasive Oxford Don bullshit, Russell. Who is *'we'*?"

He turned to face me. "You want a name?"

"I want something, Russell."

He nodded. "Fair enough, dear boy. Then for now, let me tell you that we are a loose-knit group of very powerful people called the Deru, among other things. That is our

219

most ancient name. Our primary concern is, as I have just outlined to you, to ensure that human beings can evolve toward being compassionate, empathetic, kind creatures, but as individuals, not as a species. We leave that to others." He smiled and held my gaze. "And you are one of us."

"Deru?"

He ignored me. "There are no membership cards, no fees, no club HQ."

"Members?"

"A few. You and me, Reggie…a few more."

I nodded. "What does 'Deru' mean?"

He studied my face a while with another twinkle in his eye. Then he said, "It means 'tree'."

"In what language?"

"Proto Indo-European."

* * * *

The next day, McGuire turned up at my hotel room and we spent a couple of hours discussing the upcoming operation. I told him the minimum he needed to know. We were hitting a power station and we would have the help of a special ops group. I roughed out the floor plan and told him that we would go in together, but at some point, he and the special ops guys would hit the antenna while I disposed of the stone.

He was a pro and knew the value of team work and discipline. In the movies, you see highly trained military personnel behaving like hysterical girls because their unresolved issues about needing their dad's approval surface every time they get shot at. It isn't like that. Trained soldiers, especially special ops, know that their survival depends on clockwork efficiency and discipline. I didn't like McGuire, but I could see he was a real pro and he was there to get the job done. We developed a rapport and some kind of a mutual respect.

We arranged to meet at Heathrow Airport in four days.

I didn't tell him where we would go from there or what we would do. Like I said, the less he knew, the better. Meanwhile, Russell met with the duke and Palermo to discuss the possibility of future cooperation and what the terms of that cooperation would be.

After they'd left, I saw a small feature in the *Washington Post*. A light aircraft had crashed over Lake Michigan, crossing from Chicago into Canada. Five men had been killed. Two of them were prominent executives in the oil industry, one was an executive of the board of the HEAT corporation. The other two were Senators. There was no sign of the pilot. It was assumed he had drowned in the lake. There were signs of engine failure and foul play was not suspected.

That evening we took a cab to Dulles International. Russell hadn't told me he'd booked the tickets. He was playing his cards close to his chest and about as deadpan as you can get without actually becoming a dead pan. In the back of the cab, as we were approaching the weird, space-age pagoda of the airport, with the massive tower against the burnt orange and violet of the sunset, he said — as though he'd been reading my mind — "You understand, Liam, that not confiding in you is not a lack of trust."

I glanced at him. The dying day washed his skin with peculiar colors. I felt a sudden, inexplicable sense of foreboding.

He went on, "It's simply that, at the moment, the less information is moved about, the better. You understand?"

I nodded. "Sure." I added, "Where are we going?"

"London."

"What about — ?" I was going to ask, what about the Ael Rune, but he cut me short.

"Reggie has taken care of that. He sailed in his yacht a couple of days before we came here."

"The errands he was going to run?"

"That's right."

We boarded the plane through the VIP service with ten

minutes to spare. I smiled to myself. I derived a stupid satisfaction from knowing that Russell and I had a similar way of thinking. I would never tell him that, but I wouldn't need to. He already knew.

We took our seats, and shortly after that, we were thundering down the runway and rising into the enfolding darkness of night, headed east, away from the sun. The windows went black and a *pung* sound overhead told us we could unfasten our seatbelts. Russell looked at me over the divider and said, "Drink."

I nodded and we made our way to the bar. He ordered a double Bushmills straight up and I had a Martini, extra dry. He took a long pull, swallowed and sighed, "*Uisce beatha*." He made it sound like 'ishka-baha'. He added, "The water of life," in case I didn't know. I did and told him so.

He ignored me and took a deep breath. Then he peered deep into his drink and said, "I don't know if you keep up with CO2 levels, Liam. I do. They are the clock that tells us how long we have left."

I nodded. "Before what, exactly, Russell?"

"Before they invade. Once the levels reach a critical mass, two things will happen."

I frowned. "Go on."

"The Greenland ice cap will become unstable and start to collapse into the sea. This will cause tsunamis of truly unimaginable proportions that will have a devastating impact on coastal cities in the North Atlantic."

An icy tingling crept down through my skin. He was watching for my reaction. I shook my head and muttered, "Christ…"

He nodded and went on, "And when that happens, they will strike. We will be defenseless."

"But the Rune…"

"Oh, indeed. That is what they are relying on. Once the ice cap collapses, the temperature of the planet will soar and they won't need us anymore. Then they will use the stone. That is why it is imperative that you destroy it. But I want you to be aware, Liam, that destroying the stone and the antenna will not be enough. The fact that they have built the antenna, the fact that they had programmed the Rune with the frequencies, all point to one thing."

"That the CO2 levels are right."

He nodded. "That was the thrust of my conversation with Suffolkshire and Palermo. Very soon — it might be a week, it might be a year, it might be now — all hell is going to break loose."

I frowned. "Are we ready?"

He gave a strange little laugh and shrugged. "I have no idea." He looked me straight in the eye. "Nobody has ever seen them — not anyone living. Even high-ranking Seraphs have never seen them. They are the stuff of legend."

I was overcome by a feeling of unreality — more than that, a feeling of unreality becoming reality. There was a strange terror to it. I said, "The Ael, Rafael, Michael, Gabriel…"

He shook his head. "No, not really. I know they have been talked about as though they were one and the same thing, and I have kept my counsel. The confusion comes about because it all happened such a long time ago. So, we think of them collectively as 'them', the aliens, the gods — but the Ael were the original visitors from Mars. Ael was what they called their home. Ael and Eah were the two sister planets within the habitable zone of our sun, the name Eah, we have corrupted to Earth. Mars is the Latin name. The Greeks called it Ares, a corruption of the original Ael. They were seen as angels, again a corruption of the name, Aels." He snorted a small laugh. "There is a kind of beautiful irony in the fact that we turn to them for guidance and help, not realizing that we are, actually, them."

I drained my glass and ordered another. Russell muttered, "Good idea," and followed suit.

I frowned. "They were seen as angels… Who by?"

He held my eye a long time, like he didn't want to talk about it. "The original humans. A simple, gentle species. They were enslaved, partly extinct and partly assimilated.

We carry their genes."

I said, "Holy shit. So, the Naga?"

"The Naga, as far as we can tell, originate from Proxima B, in the Proxima Centauri system. It is a much older planet than ours. Their sun is a red dwarf and comparatively cold. This may be the reason for their interest in Earth. It seems they need heat. We don't know what speeds they are capable of, but if they are traveling close to the speed of light, every year they spend traveling to and from Proxima B is going to mean eight years on Earth. That is going to make planning very difficult, so we must assume a permanent command base of operations here with a very difficult communication system linking them back to their home planet."

I said, "That means that their initial invasion force will have to be home-grown hybrids and droids. That would explain their long-standing genetics program." I shrugged, thinking aloud. "The fact that the Rune is so important to them suggests that the home-grown force is not everything it could be."

He nodded. "It is dangerous to jump to conclusions, but it does seem they are very keen on a devastating knockout in round one. Maybe — *maybe* — that suggests they haven't a lot of staying power, because bringing reinforcements from home will take a long time." He smiled at his whiskey. "That's how we lost America, you know. It was taking three months to send reinforcements across the Atlantic."

I half-frowned, half-smiled. "Was that back when you were friends with George?" Something was nagging at my memory. "Joanna told me that they were never great military planners. That was why they were originally driven underground. The Martians were much more efficient at waging war."

"It's possible. This is why we need the AE. We need to organize and prepare."

I took a slug and poked a Camel into my mouth. I caught the stewardess' eye and said, "Don't worry. I'm not going to light it." To Russell, I said, "How can we prepare when we don't know what they are going to do once they've lost the Rune?"

He examined his whiskey, tipping it various ways. "There are some things we *do* know. We know we are going to lose the stock exchanges overnight. We know that the economy will collapse in a matter of a few hours. We know that mass manufacturing and distribution will become impossible. We know that London, New York, Brussels and Washington will be wiped off the face of the earth — all of this within just a few hours."

"Within a few hours..." I turned the words over in my mind. "Within a few hours, our whole world will crumble. Vanish."

"Yes. They'll be pretty confident this will be a knockout blow, similar to the one that sent them underground way back when. It won't wipe us out completely, as they would like, but it will give them the upper hand. Plus, the environment on the surface will be ideal for them, so we need to be ready to rise from the ashes and strike."

"Jesus."

"We know something else, Liam." I asked him the question with my face and he said, "We know that you and I have become people of extreme interest to them. We may yet become the first humans to meet the Naga face to face."

We stared at each other, then as of one mind, we ordered another drink.

Chapter Twenty-Four

As it turned out, it was Hook and not me who met McGuire at the airport. He was immediately whisked away in an unmarked Land Rover with tinted windows to some place in Warminster where he and a small squad of Hook's men were going to practice a theoretical attack on a power station. I was kind of glad. Even though I'd grown to respect the guy in some way, I still couldn't bring myself to like him.

Meanwhile, Maria and I moved to the safe house in Wiltshire. Sinead was there, and she and I spent a lot of time together, assembling a plan of the Lyn Celyn Reactor and how I was going to get the Ael Rune to the core. They were strange days. I had grown accustomed to the idea of hating Sinead, of seeing her as the enemy, the woman – the creature – who wanted to steal my wife and child from me. Now we were working together, as colleagues and allies, and she was easy to work with. Her mind was fast and clear, and she seemed to be completely free of all the ego issues that affect most people when they work together. Things like competitiveness and one-upmanship were completely alien to her. Sometimes she even displayed a sense of humor and that always surprised me. Where I found it almost impossible to like McGuire, I found myself really growing to like Sinead.

Sitting in the garden with Maria among the sweet-smelling roses, watching the long, English evening taking its sweet time moving toward night with the blackbirds engaged in their long, beautifully complicated conversations, I said, "It's a strange thing, Maria." She smiled at me and took my hand. I went on, "McGuire is a man, a human being. And Sinead is a Seraph, a hybrid with non-human DNA. Yet, I find myself disliking McGuire for his lack of humanity and liking Sinead, because underneath that cold, detached exterior, she has so much humanity."

Maria nodded, biting her bottom lip and gazing at the roses. "Yes, that is strange, but I know what you mean. It makes you wonder, doesn't it? Just what it means, to be human?"

Later that evening, Russell announced that a car would be coming the next morning to take me to Wales. Conversation over dinner was subdued, and apart from a few, very eloquent looks, Maria and I hardly exchanged a word. After the meal, Russell rose and went up to bed early. As he passed behind me, he placed a hand on my shoulder. "I'll see you in the morning, dear boy, for breakfast."

Maria rose too and I was about to get up as well, but Sinead said, "I'd like to discuss a few last details with you before you go up, Liam. Can I see you in the drawing room?"

"Sure."

I stood and she went next door. Maria came close and gave me a long, lingering kiss. "Don't be long. I'll be waiting."

She left and I went next door. There was a fire burning in the grate and Sinead was standing in front of it. I pulled a Camel from my pack as I stepped in and closed the door. I lit it and sat, facing her. It was an echo of the first time I'd met her, but I'd been standing by the cold fireplace, smoking, and she'd been sitting curled up in the chair, by candlelight. That was long ago.

I said, "What is it?"

"Russell has asked me to talk to you about the Naga."

"What about them?"

"It is very possible, Liam, that you might meet one of them."

I felt a hot pellet of fear in my gut. I said, "I'd guessed as much."

"You need to be prepared."

I smiled and shrugged. "How do you prepare for the unknown?"

"There are one or two things we do know that you need to know." She hesitated, then smiled. The smile was unexpected. It looked oddly compassionate. "Unfortunately, they are things that are very difficult for a human to understand."

I gave her a look that said I was tired of hearing that and said, "Try me."

She moved to the sofa and sat in the corner nearest me. She said, "Can you imagine what a two-dimensional world would be like?"

I sighed. "Not really, Sinead. I'm not good at all this abstract stuff. I guess it would be really flat."

She shook her head. "No, it wouldn't. That would just be a flat, three-dimensional world. For it to be two dimensional, you'd have to eliminate one of those dimensions completely. Can you imagine that?"

I thought about it and shook my head. "No, but what has this got to do with – ?"

"Bear with me, Liam. To have any understanding of the Naga, you need to understand a two-dimensional world. If you want to know what a two-dimensional world is like, just think of your dreams. That is what a world is like in only two dimensions, and that is what existence is like for the Naga. They are two-dimensional beings. It's like that for us – the Seraphs, too – but not as much as the Naga. The Naga live entirely in a world of mind."

"How is that possible?"

She laughed. "Why not? You live in a three-dimensional, material world, and with your mind, you have access to the two-dimensional world of mind, thought and dreams. Their existence is the mirror image of that. They live in a two-dimensional world of mind, with access to the three-dimensional world of matter."

I stared at her, struggling to grasp what she was trying to tell me. After a while, I said, "So what does this mean?"

"It means that he will attack your mind. You will go there prepared to battle him with fists and guns, and he will attack your *mind*. And he will have a distinct advantage over you. Your only hope of surviving his attack will be to keep reminding yourself that everything he throws at you is illusion."

She reached behind her neck with her hands and lifted a pendant on a leather thong over her head. It was a small stone encased in a silver spiral. It had a vaguely Nordic appearance to it. She knelt in front of me and looked deep into my eyes. The power of her mind was palpable. It was like a substance that flowed from her and enfolded me. She placed the pendant around my neck, took my hand and folded it over the stone. "If, at any time, you feel you are losing your grip, if you feel you do not know which way to go or what is real and what is illusion, take a hold of this stone and it will ground you. Do you understand?"

I nodded. "Yeah."

She returned to the sofa. I stared at her. "You said 'he'. You are expecting me to meet a particular..." I trailed off because I didn't know what to call them.

"Tor Sheh. Del Roble and I were the only two to come close to him. We were admitted to his antechamber. I sense he will be waiting for you. He is aware of you. He is aware of everything you have done. He is aware that you killed del Roble, Joanna and Golika"—she gave a small, surprising giggle—"whom you called Rinpoche. He is aware that you made it possible for Catherine and me to escape the Brotherhood. Above all, he is aware that you allowed Catherine to achieve *rupa*. Do you realize how dangerous this makes you? He *knows* how dangerous you are, and he is curious."

"How do you know?"

She narrowed her eyes at me. She looked like she was struggling to understand the fact that I didn't get it. "We *are* mind," she said. "We are two-dimensional beings, Liam. We are *made* of mind. I feel him. He *feels* you, as you feel the breeze or a change in temperature. He is active. He has become agitated. He is moving. He is moving toward Wales."

What I can only describe as a deep and terrible dread took hold of me inside. I wanted more than anything else on Earth for this not to be real. I wanted to wake up in the morning and discover it had all been a crazy dream—a wild nightmare—and my normal world was still populated by Noddy and Russian Pete, and Russell was just a nutty mathematician who thought he could mend my ways.

But this *was* real. This *was* reality. She reached out and took my hand. "Reality," she said, like she'd been reading my mind, "is Maria upstairs, your baby and the deep love you have for each other. That love is your truth, and it will make your mind clear and strong. Hold the stone when you falter, and remember Maria, the baby and the love you have for them in your heart. It will bring you victory. Believe me."

I thanked her and made my way up to bed.

Maria was still awake. I stripped and she held her arms out to me. I climbed in beside her and we held each other close and kissed tenderly, whispering to each other things that we already knew but we needed to hear, until we fell asleep in each other's arms.

* * * *

I was up and showered by six and made my way down to the kitchen. Russell was already there, frying eggs and bacon and brewing coffee. He didn't look up as I walked in. He just said, "You'll need to get through the doors, of course, and this time, you won't be able to take bits of the guard to fool the security system with, because they will almost certainly be expecting you."

"Good morning."

"So, we've put together a rather fun little toy. You'll find it on the table by your plate. Pour the coffee, would you?

There's a good chap."

I went to the cooker where the percolator was gurgling and took it to the table. As I was pouring, I saw what looked like a flashlight beside my plate. I set the pot down and picked it up. I said, "A flashlight?"

He was putting the eggs onto the toast beside the bacon and said, "No, and for heaven's sake, don't switch it on. It's an EMP-photon condenser."

I froze with my thumb on the button and smiled. He brought the plates over and we sat to eat. He said with his mouth full, "It has a dual—well, a triple function. In mode three, it's a hot laser, and in mode two, it sends out a powerful electromagnetic pulse."

I stuffed bacon and toast in my mouth and eyed it. "Seriously? How will that help with the doors?"

"Well, instead of cutting off people's hands and gouging out their eyes to present them to the security scanners, you hold the lamp over the panels then press the EMP button for two seconds. The electromagnetic pulse will burn out the locking mechanism and release the door."

He reached across the table and pointed at the second of three black buttons that sat in a row across the spine of the condenser. He said, "That one's the EMP. The one at the back is the laser. It will burn through two inches of steel without any difficulty."

"What's the one at the front?"

He looked at me as though I were insane. "A torch, of course."

"Of course."

He mopped up the remains of his egg with a hunk of toast and said, "You'll be dropped at a guest house near Lyn Celyn. Tonight, you'll drive to the power station and park on the roadside, fifty or sixty yards from the car park. You'll be met there by McGuire. Go the rest of the way on foot. Remain concealed until the strike on the antenna, which will happen at eleven-fifteen precisely. Is that clear so far?"

"Sure."

"When the strike happens, you and McGuire take out whatever guards there are and enter the power station as you did last time. From there on, I'm afraid it's down to you. McGuire will join the attack on the control room within the station. You proceed as you have arranged with Sinead and dispose of the Rune."

As he said it, he stood, and from the big French dresser up against the wall, he took a black linen bag. It had a heavy weight in it and I knew it was the Çabra Stone. He handed it to me and said, "It's wrapped in a metal-fiber mesh which, I am told, is resistant to most microwaves. We hope that will stop them from detecting it and tracking it until it's too late."

"What they call 'listening' for it?"

He nodded. I took it and he raised and cocked his head. I hadn't heard anything but he obviously had, because he said, "Ah, I believe that's Tom."

As I stepped out into the early morning, it had started to rain again. There was a big, black Land Rover with tinted windows idling in the driveway. I stopped and turned to face Russell. I smiled at him.

"Did I ever tell you you're a miserable, Anglo-Saxon iceberg?"

"You've implied it a few times."

I grinned. "I'm going to embarrass you by being very American now."

He looked down at his feet and said, "Oh, dear."

I'd been thinking about it all night and all morning. I knew I was probably never going to see him or Maria again. I had said my goodbyes to her and our child while she slept. Now I coughed to control my voice and said, "I love you, you crazy, genius son of a bitch."

I took him in my arms and gave him what was probably the first hug he'd ever had from a man in his life. Tears flooded my eyes. I gripped him hard for a second, then let him go and gently punched him on the shoulder. I saw he had tears in his eyes. A big knot in my throat wouldn't let me speak. He gripped my hand with both of his, gnarled and wrinkled as old tree roots, squeezed it, then turned and hurried inside, closing the door behind him.

I wiped my eyes with my sleeve and crossed the drive to the Land Rover. I wrenched open the door and saw Tom at the wheel, watching me. He smiled and shook his head. "Bloody Yanks, going around embarrassing everybody."

I shrugged and wiped my eyes again. "Miserable English bastard."

"Good to see you."

"Yeah, you, too."

We pulled out of the drive and headed for Wales.

Chapter Twenty-Five

It was almost three by the time we arrived. We were in deep countryside, surrounded by the kind of lush, rolling hills you only see in the British Isles. Only, that day they were shrouded in low cloud, drizzle and mist, so you couldn't see them anyway. Lyn Celyn, the lake itself, was half a mile down a rough, narrow road to the east.

We parked on the grassy, muddy verge outside a small, stone cottage. We sat in the Land Rover with the rain spattering the windshield, and Tom showed me the lay of the land on a map.

"Stay here till ten-forty-five. Then drive west, up along this road. At the end, you'll come to a junction with the A212. Turn right and follow the road back toward the lake. It'll bring you to the power station. Be there by eleven. McGuire will be waiting for you by the roadside about sixty yards from the car park. You need to get in position before eleven-fifteen."

"What happens at eleven-fifteen?"

"All hell breaks loose. You'll know when it happens. When it does, you and McGuire take out any guards that show up. When you've cleared the area, make for the same entrance you used last time you were there. A couple of the lads will rendezvous with you at that door. Then you and McGuire split up. He comes with us to take out the antenna control room. You go down to the reactor core and do your business. Got it?"

I nodded. "Yeah. How do I get there?"

He pulled the keys out of the ignition and showed them to me. He pointed in turn to an ignition key and a latch key.

"Defender, cottage."

He handed them to me. I took them and asked, "What do you do now?"

He gestured up the road with his head. "I have a lift."

There was a pale gray Ford Fiesta making its way down the road. It stopped next to us and Tom climbed out. He gave me a quick glance. "Take it easy, Murdoch." Then he slammed the door, climbed in the Fiesta and he was gone, leaving only the damp patter of the drizzle behind him. I looked at the shiny, wet stone cottage, with its gray-slate roof reflecting the limpid light from the wet, gray sky. Gray was the thing today.

I got out, loped unsteadily over the mud to the door and let myself in. The air was damp, but there were logs and kindling in a basket by an open fireplace. I built a fire, and as the flames started to lick and crackle on the wood, I found the kitchen and made some lunch. Then, as the room warmed up, I stretched out on the sofa and listened to the patter of the rain on the windows and the drip, drip from the guttering. I thought of the long journey I had taken from my birth into a slum in Watts, through a life of crime preying on the glitterati of Hollywood, to London's Notting Hill then to Russell's subtle, tolerant, guiding hand leading me toward a wider, richer world and leading me ultimately to Maria and our child. I thought of all the things I had learned — about life, people and about myself. Above all, I thought about how Maria had taught me to love. Perhaps that had been the whole point, and now, having learned that, it was time to die, to give my life for something worthwhile.

The journey was almost over. I knew with absolute certainty that I was going to die that night. I had made my farewells to the two people in the world that I'd learned to love, and now I knew it was time. I could feel death present, closing in, final.

My one determination was not to survive — I was reconciled to my death — but to destroy the Rune before Tor

Sheh destroyed me, and if possible, to take him down with me.

I drifted off among the crackles of the fire, and the wet drip and patter of the rain—and the dark, certain presence of death.

I awoke at just after eight with a crick in my neck. The fire had burned down and was just smoking, smoldering embers. I got up and stretched, found the bathroom and had a long, hot shower with the strange, unreal knowledge that it was the last shower I was ever going to have. It made me acutely aware of every moment and every action, as though by paying extra attention to it, I could somehow preserve it.

I wasn't hungry, but I forced myself to eat some scrambled eggs on toast. It is strange how when faced with death, we seek to give importance and meaning to every small event, and I sat wondering why my last meal should be scrambled eggs rather than anything else. A symbol, perhaps, to connect me to my life.

And suddenly it was twenty minutes to eleven. I felt a jolt and a pit in my stomach. I put on my rainproof leather jacket, took the keys to the Land Rover and stepped out into the rain. After that, focus was everything.

The headlights were two funnels that cast the whole world into darkness, making a narrow tube of light along which I raced toward death. I killed the thought and forced my mind to think of Maria, the peaceful joy I had seen in her face in the last couple of days, her sweet belly with the life growing inside it.

Tall hedgerows and trees leaned down at me like black claws reaching out of the heavy clouds. I came to the intersection and stopped. The wipers squawked on the windshield, casting globules of molten light aside. The engine thrummed, almost inaudible. Outside my cocoon, there was only dark and silence. I spun the wheel and turned right.

A minute later, the glow of the gigantic Lyn Celyn reactor

was illuminating the low clouds in the north. I passed the obsidian sheet of the lake on my right then I was climbing the tree-lined hill toward the power station. I saw a figure in a black mack standing on the grass verge up ahead. I killed the lights, pulled over, then killed the engine. When I climbed out in the reflected glow from the parking lot, I could just make out McGuire's face. He looked wet.

As I approached him, he said, "You armed?"

I nodded. "Yeah."

"Let's take up our positions."

We stayed close to the line of trees and bushes that formed the hedgerow. He crouched down on one knee and pulled an automatic rifle with a telescopic sight from under his raincoat. I crouched down behind him and looked over his shoulder. He had a direct line on the hut at the barrier, but with the rain, the guard was inside. I heard McGuire cuss. "Shit! I can't get a bead on him."

I checked my watch. It was three minutes after eleven. I said, "He's not going to come out in this weather."

He was silent. Then he said, "You should take up a position at the other side of the entrance. We need to catch them in a crossfire."

I searched across. He was right, though the position was exposed, and in any case, the guard was going to be stuck inside his cabin and he needed drawing out.

I said, "No."

He was a colonel and not used to people saying 'no' to him. He turned to me. "We need a crossfire. We need to create a killing field."

I said, "I know." I checked my watch again. "We will." I pulled Russell's torch from my pocket and said, "Stand by, Colonel."

I've lived in England a long time and I can do a passable English accent. I flipped on the torch and bellowed at the top of my voice, in my best imitation of Hugh Grant, "Rover! Here, boy! Rover!"

I aimed the beam of the torch right at the guard's booth

and heard McGuire splutter, "What the fuck?"

But I was already walking toward the hut. I shouted again, "Rover! Here, boy! Where are you, you bloody dog? Rover!"

It didn't take long. The guard stepped out with his thumbs in his belt. He looked mad. He was one of their six-foot-six Aryan types with real short hair and pale-blue eyes. He seemed like a nasty son of a bitch. I aimed the torch right in his face so he couldn't see anything. He frowned and raised his right hand to shield his eyes.

"This is a restricted area. You can't come here."

The accent was South African. He said 'thus' instead of 'this'. I spoke through my nose, keeping the light firmly on his eyes. "Oh, good evening, officer. Have you seen my dog? He's a golden retriever. He came bounding this way and won't answer. You know what dogs are like."

"Please turn off your torch, sir. I have to ask you to step back. This is a restricted area."

I talked right over him. "He's a dear chap, but you know what dogs are. Catch a whiff of a bunny and off they go, bounding over the hills like anybody's business. I keep telling the wife we should have got a terrier."

"Sir! Please back away, sir. Switch *off* your torch."

"But would she listen? Of course not! So, we got this — very lovable, I grant you —"

"*Sir!*"

He was reaching for his piece, squinting into the flashlight, raising his left hand to cover his eyes. That was when I heard the thud of the choppers. He heard it, too, growing louder fast. I said, "But you know what women are. They'll break your heart every time." I glanced at my watch. Eleven-fifteen on the nail. I pressed the last button in the line. In a nanosecond, the laser had burned a whole right through his brain and he just kind of crumpled in silence, like an empty suit of clothes.

I slipped the light in my pocket and pulled out my Smith & Wesson. I stepped over to the side of the hut and squatted down. Then, as promised, all hell broke loose. Two choppers erupted over the hedgerows just thirty feet above our heads. The noise was deafening and the downdraft from the rotors bowed and twisted the trees, making them dance like they were in a typhoon. Next thing, one of the helicopters opened up with a Minigun while the other fired a barrage of RPGs at the vast antenna on the roof. Half a dozen explosions rocked the roof in rapid succession while windows shattered and rounds ricocheted off the walls.

Through the mayhem, I saw a dozen guards racing from the side of the building toward the barrier where, behind me, the two choppers were pounding the antenna. I signaled McGuire 'twelve approaching'. I held my breath, waiting for their left flank to come into his line of fire. I counted three seconds and he turned loose with three short bursts, taking down the four guys nearest him. My .44 exploded and I took out the three guys farthest away. Seven down, five left. The noise of the rotors, the Miniguns and the RPGs was deafening and the guards couldn't tell where the fire was coming from. McGuire sprinted five steps, knelt and shot again. He took down three and I picked off the remaining two as they turned to run.

We vaulted the barrier and scanned the area. It was clear. McGuire signaled the chopper and four men slipped down on ropes. I ran toward the entrance I'd used last time I'd broken in. McGuire was close behind me. I stopped at the door and pulled out the light. I put the lamp over the screen and hit the EMP button. The door thrummed a second, glowed green and seemed to shake. I pushed and it swung open.

McGuire said, "What the hell is that?"

I said, "It was on offer at the DIY store."

"Cute."

One of the choppers had pulled away and I heard the tramp of running boots. We waited. Four men in black with balaclavas and night-vision goggles pushed in through the door ahead of us, aiming their automatic weapons as they went. The shout went up, "*Clear!*" and we stepped in.

One of the guys pointed at me. "You! Do your thing!" Then he pointed at McGuire. "You! With us!" And they moved down the passage toward the reception area. I ran for the entrance that led down into the bowels of the building, where I'd been before. Another blast of the light and that door swung open. I was at the top of the long, metal staircase that wound down into the shadows and the darkness. A chill crawled over my skin.

He's here.

I stepped in. The echo of my footfall rolled down into the blackness below. I knew he heard it. I knew he was aware of me. Gray dread seeped through my body, hollowing out my gut and draining away my courage. Every ounce of me was telling me to turn around and step back through the door. Instead, I took another step down. Another steel echo rolled into the void. I forced my feet, one after another, to descend the spiral staircase. As I sank deeper, I left the dull light behind me, pallid and dead on the concrete walls. Eventually, I stopped, half a dozen steps from the bottom. I stared.

In front of me was a lake of black water. It lapped at the steps with small, liquid slaps, its depth unknown. If I went in, I would sink into eternal darkness. There was a small island, the size of a large rock, maybe fifty yards away, maybe a hundred yards away. It was impossible to tell. Distance seemed to warp over the jet, liquid surface. On the island, there was a man. He was just an inky shape, ill-defined, watching me, sensing me.

He is here.

Chapter Twenty-Six

I stared at the impenetrable liquid. I knew the only way to the reactor core was across that water, but I also knew that if I once stepped into it, my very existence would be sucked out of me. It would burn me like acid, engulf me and extinguish me completely. I would become nothing.

I looked again at the figure on the rock. It was shrouded. Its features were invisible. It seemed to be seated in the lotus position. Its focus was unwavering. I could feel its mind heavy upon my own, pressing down like a living weight. I thought of Maria, of her loving eyes peering into mine, of the cute spray of faint freckles across her nose. And I knew that whatever happened to me, I had to cross that water. I took a step and watched my foot sink into the blackness. The liquid began to froth and hiss. Acrid vapors rose. A searing pain gripped my foot and stabbed up through my leg. I screamed. Every fiber in my body screamed, telling me to go back. But I held firm to the image of Maria's face, of her sweet belly and the life that was growing inside it. I roared and plunged my other foot into the pitch liquid. Agony like a thousand living knives tore through my legs, stabbing up into my belly and my back, tearing at my lungs and my heart, piercing my brain.

A whisper, Sinead's voice in my head. *'You will go there prepared to battle him with fists and guns, and he will attack your mind.'*

I took a step forward. I looked down at my feet and saw steaming, decomposing flesh dropping from my bones. I roared again and took another step, but my mind was spinning and I could feel consciousness slipping away from me.

'If at any time you feel you are losing your grasp, if you feel you do not know which way to go or what is real and what is illusion, take a hold of this stone and it will ground you.'

I fell to my knees and the scorching acid tore through my thighs and my muscles. In a spasm, I reached for the stone she had given me and gripped it in my hand.

I could hear my breath rasping in my throat. I was trembling. But there was no water, just hard concrete under my knees. My legs were intact. The dim, pallid light from the lamps high above filtered down like wan, dying moonlight. Thirty yards away he now stood watching me. It was as though the very light had been ripped apart and he were a thin window into the obsidian void. And now, along with the immense weight of his mind, I felt a depth of black hatred.

I forced myself back to my feet. He moved, not with steps and not gliding, but simply one moment he was there, fifteen paces away, and the next he was over by the wall. There was a door beside him. On the door, there was the international radiation hazard symbol. I moved toward it. I could feel my strength returning. He shifted, shimmered and was gone. I kept going, one step, then another. Then I started to run.

I burst through the door. I was in a long passage painted white. Bright strip lighting glared and hummed overhead. I followed the passage to a 'T' junction. I'd been over this with Sinead. I turned right then left down a flight of stairs. Another door. I kicked through it and there was a large room, like a locker room. Thirty feet across that room was another door. Above the door was a sign. It read *Reactor Core Access. Intense Radiation. Wear Radiation Suit at All Times.*

He was standing in front of it. True terror is a kind of emptiness. It's as though all your substance drains away from inside you, leaving you hollow. He was tall, but it was hard to say how tall. He may have been six-two—or eight foot or nine. The harder I tried to focus on him, the more vague and tenuous he became. He was big, like a thunder cloud. I couldn't make out any features because he was wearing some kind of hood. Sometimes it looked like a shroud, at others it was as though his head itself was hooded, like a reptile. But gazing at the space where his face should have been was terror itself. It was like looking at black glass in a window onto stygian emptiness. A voice, a hiss, a whisper crept into my brain like a vapor.

"You have done enough. Nobody could blame you for turning back now. No man has ever gotten this far. You are a hero. No human can be expected to endure this. Leave the Rune. Do you know what lies beyond death?"

It is impossible to describe the feeling of gazing into absolute emptiness, of facing the absolute vacuum, yet that was exactly the feeling, searching the void of his face and feeling his voice creeping like a fetid infection into my mind.

Something stroked my cheek. It was a sticky thread. I brushed it away and noticed he had gone. I glanced to the right and saw there was a rack of radiation suits. I stepped toward them. Several sticky threads brushed against my cheeks and across my eyes. I tried to brush them off and felt them smear on my skin. I wiped the back of my arm across my face, and saw that my sleeve was covered in a kind of white slime, like melting cheese.

I heard myself say, "What the hell?" and realized that I was walking through a kind of mesh. It was like a spider's web, only thicker and stickier. I tried to back away but realized then that it was behind me, too. I shouted. I turned left and tried to fight my way out. My heart was pounding. The more I struggled, the more I was wrapped and enfolded in the wispy, mucous strings. I shouted and pushed, dragging myself forward toward the rack of suits. But the more I pushed, the more threads there seemed to be, wrapping tighter about my chest, my arms and my legs until I was practically immobilized.

Then I saw the spider.

It was by the door where he had been standing. It was seven or eight foot across. Its body was fat and hairy. It darted with horrible speed, clambering through the threads toward me. I thrashed and struggled, but my arms were pinned to my sides and my legs were bound tight together. I tried to scream, but my mouth was stuck with cloying, acrid slime.

The spider was over me. I was suspended, half-lying in the matrix of glutinous mesh. Its soft belly was maybe two feet from my face, and seemed to be weeping a thick, milky liquid. There was a wild terror thrashing inside me, but my body was helpless, paralyzed within the viscous web. Then its jaws were snapping down at me, dripping saliva, and I knew that once it bit me, I would be truly paralyzed and its poison would be an acid that dissolved me from the inside out. I would cease to exist altogether.

Its front foot, like a curved blade, was cutting through the threads, reaching down toward my shoulder, where I had the bag with the Ael Rune.

His voice, like an insidious infection, was creeping through my mind, into my blood stream, permeating my muscles until there was nothing — nothing but his voice.

"Yield. Surrender. Hand over the Rune. Peace is in surrender. Surrender will make you free. You will not be blamed. You will be admired for making it this far. This much is enough. Surrender the Rune. Surrender."

Surrender. Surrender was like a pulse, the rhythm of life. All there was was surrender.

The spider's front leg was scratching at my shoulder, tugging at the string from the bag. I felt a strangled scream in my throat. But where it had cut away at the sticky web to get at the bag, it had also released my left arm. An instinct, a reflex, made me grab at the stone that Sinead had put around my neck.

There was a shriek that filled my mind and seemed to fill the whole universe. Then it was gone.

I was on my knees, retching in violent spasms, clutching at the stone. I collapsed on my side, trembling. My clothes were sodden with sweat and my teeth were chattering. I kept repeating, "I can't. I can't. I can't do this."

'It's more than any man can endure.'

The voice in my head was sobbing. *Oh, God! Oh, God, please have mercy! Oh, God, have pity. Pity...*

The word was like a germ. Pity. Self-pity, spreading like an infection.

I became aware of something cold and hard inside me — a steel core that I knew was me. I had never begged for mercy in my life, and I knew that voice was not mine. I felt my lip curl and I snarled, "Shut the fuck up!" Then I was shouting at myself, "Get on your fucking feet!"

I staggered, but I stood. And suddenly my belly was a knot of iron and I was bellowing like a demon possessed. It was incoherent. It was the sound of madness. But I knew what it meant and so did Tor Sheh. I took two steps toward the door, roaring like a stuck bull.

I stopped. I knew that if I went through the door as I was, the radiation would kill me. I was panting. I turned and returned to the rack of suits. I found one my size and climbed into it. I wound the pendant Sinead had given me around my hand so the stone was permanently in my palm. The suits had big side pockets with Velcro seals and I stuffed the bag with the Rune into my right one and the flashlight into the left.

Before I put the helmet on, I turned toward the doorway. I was on fire. I could see Maria in my mind, and I could see her tender belly with our baby inside, and a wild mixture of love and rage was burning within me. I snarled and roared.

"Tor Sheh! Can you hear me? I have beaten you twice, you son of a bitch! Now, I'm coming for you! And I am going to tear your fucking heart out and send you screaming back to Hell!"

The door was a security door with a pad. I used the flashlight and swung it open. I was in a long, white, brightly lit corridor with a metal floor. I tramped to the end where there was a hatch. This one was an airlock. I pushed the button by the side and it hissed open. I stepped into a chamber and the door hissed closed behind me. Then the one opposite hissed open and I stepped through. I was in the core.

The radiation levels must have been off the charts, and I felt the first inklings of panic. I suppressed them and looked around. It was a circular room, maybe forty or fifty feet across. The ceiling was high. There were twelve steel circles on the floor, arranged like the numbers of a clock. Each one was about five or six foot across. Beside each one was a stand like a steel lectern with a control panel on it. I knew what these were. Sinead had described them to me. Each metal plaque was the top of a cylinder that worked as a hydraulic lift—a kind of elevator used as a delivery system to feed fusionable matter into the reactor.

I scanned the room. I could hear my own breathing, loud within the suit. Tor Sheh was not there. I walked to the nearest cylinder and looked at the control panel. The screen was live. There was a button top right that said, 'Raise Cylinder'. I pressed it and the metal tube began to rise. It hissed to a stop after five seconds. It was about seven foot in height and seemed to be solid steel. I looked through my visor at the pad again. There was an 'Open' button. I pressed that and a hatch slid open on the cylinder, about four foot across and six high.

It was too easy. All I had to do now was place the Rune into the hatch and send it down. I searched around. He still wasn't there.

My hands were shaking. I reached in my pocket and pulled out the bag with the Ael Rune in it.

Why the strange combination of biblical and Norse? Why the Ael Rune? Why not the Naga Rune?

I pulled open the bag and slipped out the stone. It was still wrapped in the mesh cloth. A stab of curiosity pierced my gut. I unwrapped it. I had never really looked at it before. I had never really understood what it was until now.

Why Rune? Why the Ael Rune? Why not the Naga Rune?

It was smooth, like a big piece of obsidian. It had changed since the first time I had seen it. Then, it had been a dark gray, with faint symbols etched into its surface. Now it was an impenetrable black, and the symbols glowed with what I can only describe as a fierce, dark light. I examined the symbols, one after another, and they seemed to sear themselves into my consciousness, as though they were somehow becoming a part of my mind — a part of me.

Why Rune? Why the Ael Rune? Why not the Naga Rune?

The Ael, Russell had said, were us. The humans. The great warriors of the past. Sons of Ares, come to Earth as conquerors. We had driven the Naga underground with sword and fire and bloody war — we, the hot-blooded warriors of legend. Rune, this was the *Ael* Rune. Rune, as in the Viking script. The Vikings, the Norsemen, the greatest warriors of all time. And wasn't it the Druids who guided them? Wasn't it the Druids who used the runes?

Druid, dru wid, true seer.

This stone, then, this Ael Rune, belonged to us. It did not belong to the Naga. It was ours! Hadn't destiny placed it in my hands? Hadn't destiny chosen me to face and defeat Tor Sheh, whom no man had ever faced and defeated? Had I not just beaten him twice? Was it not then, my destiny to be the master of the Rune? This, then, was *my* Rune.

A flood of inconceivable power rushed through me. I was too great even for my own body. I seemed to expand into infinity and my body vanished. I was all mind, all consciousness. I was the Great Power of the Universe. I would take the stone. I would heal Earth. I would govern mankind with compassion and love. I could see endless the timescapes of my destiny. I could see the endless green fields where deserts had lain. Small streams, great rivers and oceans would flow clean. Life would abound, there would be no more war, no more hunger, no more disease. My endless love would feed the world. I would banish the Naga to the outer darkness, as Yahweh had banished Lucifer, and humanity would thrive. I had been transformed. I had died, as I had known I would, and been reborn. I was now Master of the Rune.

There can be no light without dark.

He was there, two feet from me. I was as big as he was. I was his equal. And so I understood. We were two halves of a whole. I realized that all my life had been leading up to this one moment of union. The light and the dark. Neither had meaning without the other – no pain without pleasure, no suffering without joy, no life without death, no existence without the obsidian void.

His voice was a part of me as my voice was a part of him. *"I am your brother."*

But it was more than that. It went far more than brotherhood.

"We are as one. I am you. You are I."

And both our voices joined as one.

"I am."

Then I lost the very concept of 'I'. A voice that was the size of the universe, a voice that *was* the universe spoke, and it said, *"Am!"* and I knew that Tor Sheh and Murdoch were forever one.

My power was limitless – and it was good.

Somewhere in the immensity of my being, I was aware of her face. It was and delicate. She was fragile, yet strong. Her eyes were dark, warm, kind and there was an infinite sadness in them as she looked up at me. A love that was immeasurable washed through me. I remembered her graceful fingers brushing my cheek. I looked down at the Rune in my hand. With this power, I could bring her infinite joy – infinite happiness.

I raised my eyes and looked at Tor Sheh standing before me. Under his hood, I could dimly make out his features now. His face was a black window into nothing, but reflected in its glass I could make out the features of my own face.

Who is the enemy?

We were suspended in time. I was aware that I was not Murdoch anymore. I was aware that Murdoch was gently being absorbed into something greater, something more cosmic and magnificent. I was aware that a vast, numinous change was about to enfold us — *us* — and the world as we knew it was about to change forever.

And it was good.

It is good.

There was a hiss.

My mind was deeply absorbed, because I was being absorbed. And because of that, I didn't see it until it was too late.

There was the tramp of running feet on the metal floor. I felt my mind released. I heard myself gasp. The loss was horrific. I had been the Universe. I had felt infinity. I had been a god. And now I was nothing, a shred of humanity. I clutched for the stone in my hand. My legs trembled. My mind clawed for the memory of Maria and our baby. I was aware I was folding, going to pieces, my soul draining out of me.

Then a black shape sprang at me like a panther out of the darkness. It screamed like a demon from hell and ripped the Rune from my hand. I screamed, "Nooo!" but it was too late. The shape was behind me. I staggered, encumbered by the clumsy suit. I reached out, suddenly agonizingly aware that Maria's life and our baby's life and the lives of all humanity depended on my not letting go of the Rune.

The black feline shape did something — a movement, a rapid, efficient gesture — then it was inside the hydraulic cylinder. I stared. McGuire stared back. He held the Rune in his hands. I realized he had hit and smashed the close button on the control pad and the cylinder was already shutting. Our eyes locked and a terrible grief took hold of me as he was lost to view, as it sank irrevocably into the core below. In five seconds, the cylinder would open again and he and the Ael Rune would be vaporized forever.

A terrible moaning started beside me, a wailing like stygian winds twisting in turmoil, howling in an eternal night. It was the sound of a tortured soul crying out against an eternity of pain. I looked at Tor Sheh and saw eyes and a distorted, gaping mouth that threatened to suck me in and crush me out of existence. I ran.

With awkward, clanking steps, I clattered to the airlock. I hit the button. The door opened, impossibly slow. As his baying and crying grew more wild and insane, I staggered through. The door closed behind me and hoses blasted water and foam at the suit, to wash away the radiation.

I hammered at the button to open the other side of the airlock. After an eternity, the jets stopped and it hissed open. I ran along the passage as more foaming, steaming water was hosed over me. The door at the far end opened and I fell through, panting and exhausted. I struggled out of the suit and ran again, out into the vast concrete area where I had seen the obsidian ocean and the island. I ran. I may have been screaming or shouting. I know I was gasping for air and sunlight. I clambered onto the steel stairs and up, with aching, trembling legs that threatened to give way under me. I felt my lungs going into spasm. Finally, I fell through the door at the top of the stairs and lay half-retching on the carpeted floor. The distant, sporadic stutter of gunfire came to me. It sounded almost listless.

I saw four men approaching from far off. The passage seemed impossibly long and I knew fatigue was setting in. Tom stood over me, reached down and helped me to my feet.

"Fuck," he said, "I didn't expect to see you again."

My voice was barely a whisper. "I need a chopper, Tom. I need to get to the house, fast. He's going for her. He's going for Maria and my child."

Chapter Twenty-Seven

We flew low and fast, skimming the trees and the hedge rows. I didn't know how it worked, but I remembered Maria going through a similar thing with Joanna, only in my case, it felt deeper. It didn't feel like communication. It felt like we were part of the same whole. I knew — *I knew* — what his intentions were. I knew what he was going to do.

We circled in over the house. I saw the light from the windows washing the driveway and the gardens. I slid back the door and jumped before we'd hit the ground. The front door was open and I burst in, shouting, *"Maria! Maria!"* But I already knew what I was going to find.

They were in the drawing room. Russell was standing by the fire, watching me. Hook was standing next to him. Sinead was in one of the armchairs, sleeping. Maria was on the sofa, staring at me, expressionless. I was sitting next to her.

I whispered, *"No..."*

Tom came running in behind me and stopped dead. "What the fuck?"

I looked at Russell and Hook then pointed at the other me on the sofa. My hand was trembling. I said, "That is not me. That is Tor Sheh."

They didn't answer. They just stared. I turned to Maria. "Maria, baby, stand up and walk away from that man. Come to me."

I held out my arms to her. She swallowed and blinked, but that was all she did.

Tor Sheh smiled. When he spoke, his voice was not like mine. It was like a whisper, only louder, as though he was breathing mind into each word. He said, "I am going to feed on your suffering, Liam Murdoch."

Tom behind me said, "What the fuck is going on?"

I still had Sinead's stone wrapped around my hand. I handed it to him and said, "You'll know."

I took a step toward Tor Sheh. "What have you done to them?"

"They can hear. They can understand. But they are paralyzed. Hell is immobility, Liam Murdoch. Hell is when you cannot move."

I took another step closer and held out my hands. "We were almost one. You know that. We were joining. We were almost joined. McGuire broke the spell. We can still make that happen."

He didn't laugh. Instead, his mouth creased into a thin smile, as though a snake had unfolded across his face. "You think I need you? We were not joining, Liam Murdoch. I was *eating* you! But now the Rune is gone and all I am left with is hatred. And it is my pleasure to cause you pain and feed on your agony."

I said, "Wait!"

"I will take you and place you in a vat of liquid where you shall neither live nor die. You will never again feel pleasure or pain in your body. You will live in numb agony as I do."

"Stop. Wait!"

"All your pain will be the pain of your mind and your heart. It will be the pain of knowledge."

"What are you talking about?"

The smile again, not like a snake this time, but like a long worm wriggling slowly on his face. "The knowledge, Liam Murdoch, that I am living as you with your wife and child. And she, her memory erased, believing me to be you, weeps and suffers every day, as her child does, wondering why you have changed, wondering why you have become a sadist, wondering why she hasn't the strength to leave you, despite the sadistic things you do to her and her child, every single day."

My heart was racing, pounding high in my chest. I shook my head. "No, wait. Wait!"

"And you shall know this, suspended, immobile, year after year, powerless to act, powerless to do anything but know the pain that they live in."

"I have the stone."

"A lie."

"I have a piece of the stone."

"Impossible."

"Think about it! *Think* about it!"

He could feel the conviction in me, and it troubled him. He frowned and his eyes explored me, searching for the truth. He did not understand what he found. I said again, "Think about it! How did I resist you when you created the obsidian ocean? How did I resist your spider's web? Did you *see* what I was doing?"

His eyes scanned me like windows onto a dilating infinity. He breathed, "There is something…"

"I can give it to you, but you must let Maria and the baby go."

"Show me this stone."

He stood. I said, "I need your word." I glanced at Tom. He threw me the pendant. I caught it left-handed because my right hand was in my jacket pocket. It was a hunch. Maybe it was a conviction or a belief. Maybe it was knowledge. I don't know. I probably never will. But as I caught the pendant, I held it by the leather thong and slapped it onto his chest. As I did it, I pulled out the torch and rammed it over the stone. First I hit the EMP button. His eyes bulged and he glowed bright green. As he did, I pressed the laser button and burned the stone into his heart.

An enormous heat radiated from him. I dropped the light and grabbed Maria, dragging her away from the sofa. There was a roaring sound, like the turbine on a jet engine. I turned my back and shielded Maria and our child with my body. There may have been a scream—or I might have imagined it. I saw Russell and Hook shielding their faces. I saw Tom turn his back and cover his head. Then there was a wild churning and turning, as though a twister had been unleashed. Maybe it had. Lamps fell. Tables overturned. One curtain was torn from the window. Doors slammed and glass shattered. Chairs and ashtrays were smashed against the walls. Then there was stillness.

We waited in silence. I released Maria and searched around the room. It was a wreck. Russell and Hook were lowering their arms and peering about, too. Outside the window, I could see sheet lightning in the gathering clouds.

I stood and went out to the driveway, staring up into the turbulent sky. I felt Maria's arms encircle me. Russell and Hook were standing in the doorway, also looking up. Tom was just beside me. There was a kind of madness in my heart, a wild fury mixed with a wild joy. Somehow, I knew the sky was looking back down at me, and I bellowed, "We are free! Do you hear me? We are *free*! You know what we have in our veins, you motherfucker? We have *hot blood* in our fucking veins!"

There was a distant roll of thunder, as though Thor were chuckling at this human upstart. The first drops of cool rain fell from the clouds, and it grew into a steady downpour that bathed my face and my aching body. Russell and Hook and Tom went inside, but I took Maria in my arms and we held each other close and we kissed, long and deep. Above our heads, storms of electrons spread in wild chaos and abandon across the sky, and the heavens roared. I didn't know if in envy, in rage or in joy, and frankly, I didn't give a damn.

Epilogue

The waves sighed as though they were exhausted then thumped onto the sand and dragged themselves out to sea. They never learned their lesson, though, because no sooner had they done it than they repeated the whole process again, lifting themselves with a huge effort, teetering a moment, sighing and thumping back down.

The seagulls thought the whole thing was a disaster because they kept circling overhead and crying out, "*Oh, fuck! Oh, fuck!*" They were riding a wind that had picked up off the Atlantic and was whipping the spray in off the waves and snatching our words from our mouths and casting them away into the vast blue dome of the sky.

Maria was barefoot, standing on the shore with the waves washing around her ankles. I crossed the sand, and stood behind her and wrapped my arms around her. My right hand cupped her breast. It already felt fuller. She hugged my arms and I kissed the top of her head. She said, "This is where it all began. Right on this spot."

"I will never forget."

She giggled. "Not even born yet, and look at the trouble he's caused. Chip off the old block."

I chuckled. "How are you feeling?"

She turned and faced me, slipped her arms around my neck. "I'm good. More to the point, how are you?"

I nodded. I looked down at her beautiful face as I had seen it so many times in my mind – my mandala, my symbol of hope that had given me strength and kept me going. "I'm good. They'll be here soon. We should go up."

We held hands and crossed the sand to climb the steps,

hewn out of the living rock, to our cottage above, overlooking Bedruthan Bay. We'd had three weeks of peace and rest on our own – sleeping late, walking on the beach, eating at quiet country pubs, loving each other with no distractions, and I had begun to grow strong again. Now, I was ready to meet Russell and Sinead and talk.

I lit a fire in the drawing room and Maria went to the kitchen to make a huge avocado and tuna salad and warm garlic bread in the Aga. I put two bottles of white Tempranillo in a bucket of ice on the table, and fifteen minutes later they arrived. As I watched them climb out of Sinead's car, it struck me that there was something different about them, but I couldn't place what, and I dismissed it as my imagination – as not having seen them for a few weeks.

None of us seemed very keen on discussing what had happened, so it was only after lunch, as the sun was making its way down toward the ocean and we were sitting over the last of the wine and a cheeseboard, that Russell finally broached the subject.

"I see the raid on the power station has been put down to the Holy Jihad."

I laughed a small laugh. "I guess they couldn't really put it down to the SAS."

"Quite so. The government has appointed a joint committee to decide what happens to the power station. The committee will be chaired by the Duke of Suffolkshire." I pulled a face and nodded. He stared at his cheese then went on, "I suppose it will be a relief for you to get it all off your chest."

It was his way of inviting me to be debriefed. That was why he was here. I smiled. "I guess it will, at that."

We moved to the drawing room, settled ourselves in front of the fire and I told them everything, from my arrival at the cottage by Lyn Celyn to the killing – if that's what it was – of Tor Sheh. Russell seemed especially interested when I mentioned the amulet that Sinead had given me. He asked her what it was but she just shook her head and told me to continue.

It had grown dark outside and Maria rose to close the curtains. Sinead asked, "Do you still feel joined with him?"

I shook my head. "No. It passed as soon as I went outside and it started to rain. It was like he was literally washed out of my system." I hesitated, then asked, "How come you were asleep?"

She shrugged. "He must have put me out. I just remember you walking in the room, giving me a strange smile, and I was out. Remember, he is my master. He created me. I may rebel, I may fight him, but he will be my master as long as I am a Seraph."

I turned to Russell. "What about you and Hook? You just stood there, staring at me."

"It took me completely by surprise, dear boy. We were totally paralyzed. I'd like to know if he could do that to me if I *hadn't* been taken by surprise. My defenses were down, you see."

Sinead shifted in her chair. "What did you do to him, Liam?"

I shrugged. "Like I said, I put the stone—"

She cut across me, shaking her head. "No, that wouldn't do it. You must have done something else. How did the idea occur to you?"

I stared into the fire and thought about it for a long time. I said, "I don't really know, Sinead. Whatever the stone was, it was very powerful. Twice it allowed me to overcome whatever it was he was doing to my mind. The third time, I don't honestly know what the outcome would have been if McGuire hadn't come along when he did. But I know the stone was there, nagging at me to remember Maria and the baby."

I glanced at her then back into the flames. The wood crackled and spat into the warm silence. I said, "McGuire was okay in the end. He was misguided about some things, but in the end, he was true to his beliefs. Without him, I am not sure if we would be here now."

257

I turned back to Sinead. "The answer to your question is, I don't know. I was desperate, and I knew that the stone had the power to counteract whatever it was he did with his mind. Some kind of intuition told me that if I blasted it in with an EMP then burned the stone into his heart with the laser, it would kill him." I shrugged. "And it did, apparently." I sighed. "I'm sorry I destroyed it." I looked her in the eye. "What was it? Where did it come from?"

She smiled then she burst out laughing. It was the first time I had ever seen her laugh. It was beautiful. She stood then came and sat next to me and took my hands in hers. Her eyes were dancing. "You humans are truly remarkable. And among humans, Liam, you are extraordinary. The stone was a stone I picked up from the drive at the house in Wiltshire. I bound it with silver and gave it to you. All the power it had – all the power to defeat Tor Sheh, the power to kill his body and send him back to where he came from? All of that came from you, from your belief – not from the stone at all."

The fire burned low. Russell and Sinead went up to their rooms and I stepped out into the garden and sat on the doorstep. Maria sat next to me. She brought with her a pack of Camels, my Zippo and two glasses of Bushmills. There was not a cloud in the sky. We sat in the dim amber of the firelight, where it spilled out onto the grass through the open door, and we held each other and gazed up at a trillion tiny specks of ice against the depth of eternal space, two tiny sparks of humanity in the infinite void of the universe.

The Deepest Cut

Excerpt

Chapter One

The call came at four a.m.

I groped for my phone. "Murdoch."

The geothermal disturbance on the other end was Russian Pete. "Murdoch...is Peter."

"Pete. It's four a.m. What do you want?"

"I need speak with you."

"Now?"

"*Da.* Now..."

* * * *

It was raining. It was always raining these days—damp and warm. I sat in the darkened car, listening to the liquid drumming and thinking of Maria, lying warm and soft in our bed. It would be first light in just over an hour. She wouldn't be up for another two. I pushed open the door and stepped into the dark road. Wet light rippled on the tarmac. Holland Park was on my left. Across the road on my right a terrace of Georgian houses slept with blind eyes behind the amber streetlights.

I loped through the tepid rain toward the black bulk of the park gates. The momentary glow of a cigarette told me one of Pete's men was waiting there for me. When I drew level, he dropped the butt in a puddle where it hissed and died. I said, "Where's Pete? What's this about?"

He jerked his head toward the interior of the park, among the black shadows of the trees. "Better Pete tell you."

I followed him through the big iron gate, wondering how he came to have a key. Then he led the way into the shadows under the great horse chestnuts. Our feet made damp crunching noises on the gravel.

He said, in his Russian baritone, "Be gentle with Peter. He is weeping lot this morning."

"Weeping?"

He just nodded silently and we went deeper into the woodland, where the rain was just a drizzle on the leaves above our heads.

They were at the statue of Lord Holland, over the wooden bridge by the pond—a small huddle of them—Russian Pete and two of his henchmen, three big black silhouettes surrounded by the glimmer of the rain and the puddles. And there was something on the ground. It looked like a bundle of saturated rags. Pete turned to face me as I approached. Even in the darkness, I could see his eyes were swollen and his face was wet. It wasn't from the rain.

I pulled out my Camels and offered him one. He shook his head. I lit up and blew smoke into the spitting drizzle. The bundle of rags was a young woman, lying on her back in the mud, staring up into the trees. Her coat was rumpled and twisted. Her arms were laid symmetrically by her sides and her legs were straight. A red rose rested in her mouth. The black handle of a large kitchen knife protruded from her left breast and there was a gaping, bloody hole where her belly should have been. Whoever had killed her had taken the trouble to lay her out there with care. I stood smoking for a while.

Eventually, I flicked ash and said, "Who is she? She family?"

Nobody said anything for a long moment. The guys just stood looking at Pete with the rain on their faces.

Finally, Pete said what I had already guessed but didn't want to believe, "She is my daughter, Eva."

I nodded. I knew what this meant, why I was there, and I didn't like it. "Who did it? Do you know?"

He shook his head. I looked again at the body, the way it was laid out—the rose, the knife in her heart, the savage wound in the abdomen. "Someone trying to scare you, move in on your patch…?"

He shook his head again. "Nobody."

I dropped my butt into a puddle. It hissed and winked out. I crouched down by her side, pulled out my pen torch and played the beam over her face and neck. Under the raindrops, her skin was gray-blue. There were blotches of purple bruising on her throat, like she'd been choked, but her blouse was saturated with blood, so she hadn't been strangled to death, just enough to make her unconscious and pliant.

I moved the beam down to her belly. I've seen some pretty nasty things in my time. I've even done a few of them myself when the occasion called for it. But this was about as horrific as it got. Her entire abdomen had been torn out. There had been no surgical precision here, just raw, brutal animal ferocity. I heard Pete choke and sob behind me and I switched off the torch.

I stood and said, "Who found her?"

Pete had turned away, his face hidden in his hands.

The guy who'd met me at the gate piped up, "Park policeman on his rounds. Half pass three. He recognize her because she come to park in mornings for coffee and see the paintings exhibition. She like this park."

I said, "A cop? Why didn't he—?"

He knew what I was going to ask and interrupted me, "Cops know Russian Pete, da? He pay their mortgages…" There was some stifled laughing. Pete turned to face me, wiping his face with the back of his sleeve. His voice was raw. "They know that anything of interest to me, they report to me. It is courtesy. Chief constable is good friend of mine. You know…"

I nodded. I knew. That explained the keys. Anyone who was anyone in this town was in Russian Pete's pocket.

I said, "So, where are the cops now?"

"On their way. We have twenty minutes."

I stared at him. "For what? What do you want from me?"

He held my eye a moment then jerked his head toward what was left of his daughter. "If police investigate, maybe it is years before killer is found. And when they find him, what?" He shrugged his huge shoulders and looked around at the dark woodlands. "Maybe he go to prison for twenty years, to secure wing with psychologists to help him." He shook his head and spat on the ground. "No…you find him. You are smart, Murdoch. You not limited like police. You have no rules. I give you any help, any money—no matter. I get you what you want. I want man who did this. You find him."

"And when I find him?"

"Better you don't know."

I nodded. "Okay, Pete. I'll do what I can. When the cops are done, I want the forensics report. And I don't want the cops to know I'm involved."

His face began to crumple again and he pointed helplessly at Eva, at the gaping hole in her belly. "What is this, Murdoch? Why? Why he did this to my baby…?" His voice was weird, twisted with pain.

They led him away through the woodlands into the darkness beneath the trees, and I made my way back through the paling, gray light and the drizzle, toward my car, thinking that most times, what really hurts is not understanding why. Pain never hurts so much as when it's meaningless.

I got deep like that sometimes.

* * * *

Maria was still in bed when I got back. I opened the door and looked in the room. The curtains were closed but the window was open and a cool, damp breeze made the drapes waft softly and brought in the splash and splatter of the rain. I stepped over and sat on the edge of the bed. Her hair was rumpled. Her face was pale with sleep and I could just make out the few freckles on her cheeks and nose. I stroked away a strand of hair from her forehead. Her eyelids fluttered and she opened her eyes. They were sleepy, but she smiled. I glanced at the clock. It was seven a.m. She stretched with her arms above her head and I had a sudden impulse to hold her and feel her body, small and supple, against mine.

She said, "Where were you?"

"Pete called. Four a.m. He had a problem."

"Pete? Russian Pete?"

I nodded.

She frowned. "Didn't you say you weren't going to do jobs for him anymore?"

I bent and touched her lips with mine. She held my face with her small hands and the gentle peck grew into a long, lingering kiss. I felt the heat stirring inside me. She pulled away just enough to rub the end of my nose in an Eskimo kiss.

Her eyes were huge and dark. "Don't change the subject, big guy. Didn't you?"

I gave her my best lopsided smile and said, "It's not that easy, Maria."

She held my gaze for a long moment, smiling. Her eyes were warm, lids half closed. She whispered, "You want to make love?"

My belly was on fire and I could feel my heart pounding. I said, "You know I do."

She patted my cheek with her hand. "Well, this is how easy it is, Liam. No. See? Easy." She pushed me back and swung her legs out of the bed. "I'm going to have a shower. You want to put the coffee on?"

I went to make coffee. And, in just a few minutes, she came into the kitchen barefoot with wet hair, wearing a purple Japanese kimono with a golden dragon on it. She sat at the pine table and I poured her coffee. Black, no sugar, the way I took it.

"Pete is a very bad man, but he's been a good friend to me."

She was buttering toast but glanced up then back down and kept on buttering. I sighed. I meant what I was saying, but I couldn't find a way for it not to sound lame.

"I can't walk away from my whole life overnight, Maria. It's going to take time."

She bit into her toast and chewed, watching me. "How much time?"

I shook my head. "I can't tell you that."

"You made me a promise, Liam. You going back on your promise?"

"No."

"So?"

I looked down into my coffee. It was real black. "His daughter was murdered last night. She was twenty-three. Eva. A nice kid."

She put down her toast. Careful, like it might have consequences if she set it down the wrong way. "I'm sorry."

I nodded. "Yeah. He'd taken care not to involve her in his life. She was a good student, just finishing a psychology degree at UCL. Like I said, a nice kid. Closest thing I ever had to a niece."

She was silent a while, staring at her plate. "Was it gang related?"

"No..." I rubbed my face with my hands. "I can't make much sense of it. It looked..." I shrugged, staring at the table but seeing Eva lying in the mud with her dead eyes staring at the trees above her, raindrops sitting on her pupils. "It looked ritualistic. He swears nobody is trying to move in on him. Nobody would be that crazy. He's too powerful and too dangerous. Even the cops stay clear. It doesn't make any sense. Unless..."

She was watching me carefully. She said, "Unless?"

"Unless whoever killed her didn't know she was Russian Pete's daughter."

She sat back in her chair. "But, then what would the motive be?"

I drained my coffee and pulled a Camel from the pack. I tapped it three times on my Zippo and finally said, "No motive."

"You're talking about—"

"A serial killer."

"That would account for the ritualistic elements."

"Yeah..."

"Liam?"

I searched her eyes. I knew what she was going to say. "What does Pete want from you? Why did he call you this morning at four a.m?"

"He wants me to find who did it."

Her face went rigid. She picked up her cup, stopped with it halfway to her mouth, then put it down again. "That's what the cops are there for. You *promised* me. You promised me that you were *not* going to get involved in this kind of thing anymore. It was a condition of our living together, Liam."

"I know."

"So? What are you saying to me?"

"Maria, will you please stop talking and listen to me for a moment?"

She was staring at me. Her eyes appeared black.

"I'm doing it, okay? I'm changing. Between you, you and

265

Russell are dragging me onto the straight and narrow." I gave her my lopsided smile, but she just kept staring at me, waiting. I sighed. "I'm making it happen, baby. But you have to understand that you can't just walk away from a guy like Pete."

"So what are you saying? If I live with you, if I make a life together with you, I'm making a life with Russian Pete, too? Like some kind of mad Russian mother-in-law?"

"No…"

"That's the word, Liam. Only instead of saying it to me, you should be saying it to Pete."

"You don't want me to do that."

"Excuse me?"

"Stop provoking me, Maria, and simmer down. I'm going to do this my way and I'm going to do it right. That way it stays done. If I do what you're asking me to do, all I get—all *we* get—is a lot of trouble and grief. I do it my way and it stays done and everybody's happy. And besides… I want the bastard who killed Eva."

She was silent for a moment. Then she said, "So what are you going to do?"

"I won't take payment for finding him. I'll tell him my payment is that he doesn't use me anymore."

She nodded. "But it has to be for real, Liam. I don't want to spend the rest of my life with gangsters breathing down my neck."

We didn't say anything for a long while, just watched each other.

Then, I said, "Everything I do is for real. You know that. Now take that damned kimono off."

* * * *

An hour later, I lay listening to the rain outside. It had slowed to a damp patter. Her head was on my shoulder and her breath gentle on my chest. Her breasts were cool on my skin, and where she had her leg over my thigh, I could feel the soft brush of her hair. I let my hand explore the curve of her back and her hip, but my mind was drifting. All I could see was Eva, staring with dead eyes into the rain.

My thoughts followed the beam of my pen torch. The red rose against the pale gray of her skin. The gray-purple of her parted lips and the stem of the rose with its cruel thorns inside her mouth. It was a strange echo of the kitchen knife plunged into her heart, the beautiful, rich red flower in her mouth. Maybe it symbolized the loving words the killer had never heard from a mouth that was full of thorns — sharp, cutting, cruel words.

And the knife. The big, cold-steel blade of a kitchen knife, plunged deeply into her heart. Again, that curious juxtaposition of symbols — the heart, the universal symbol of love. The kitchen, the hub of any loving family, the smell of baking, Mom's apple pie, Mom smiling in her apron, giving food, giving love. All brutally killed with a single plunge of that large blade.

But the knife and the rose were almost surgical in their precision, as though the rage and hatred behind them were somehow controlled by grief, by a secret, enduring hope for love, as though somehow he didn't really want to do what he was doing — as though he didn't want to kill her. He only wanted to silence her and change her heart.

Maria stirred in her sleep, squeezed me and pressed her belly close against my side. Her belly. I reached for my Camels, fished one out single-handed and lit up, blowing smoke at the ceiling. The belly was all wrong. It was almost like it had been done by somebody else. There was no symbolism here, no surgical precision, no grief or restraint. Her entire abdomen had simply been ripped out, torn away from her body. And there was no trace of her organs — no gore, no blood, no spatter.

So maybe she had been killed somewhere else and taken to the park. The forensics team would establish that. But even if she'd been killed elsewhere, that didn't explain the radical difference between the placing of the rose and the knife and the savage, bestial attack on her abdomen. I lay and smoked and wondered why it mattered.

I carefully removed Maria's head from my shoulder, slipped my arm out and swung my legs off the bed. Then I made my way to the kitchen and brewed some coffee. As I sat naked, smoking and drinking, I thought that it mattered because it showed two completely different motivations. One was tortured but craving redemption. The other was uninhibited, bestial and destructive.

Like two different people.

More books from
Totally Bound Publishing

Book one in the Heat series

For Murdoch, women are bad news. Trying to stay alive in war-torn Andalusia, tracking a vanishing femme fatal, hunted by The Brotherhood, the last thing he needs is love…

Allegra always knew that nothing good could come of waking up in police custody.

TJ VARGO

BAD COMPANY

The fight for happily-ever-after starts
now—and this time it's to the death.

Curtis has found a soulmate in Julia, but happily-ever-after
endings don't happen in Tombs without a fight — and this
time it's to the death.

Frozen then awakened after a thousand years, Kell is unprepared for modern life. Allie is only supposed to help him adjust. But some things, like falling in love, never change.

About the Author

Conor Corderoy

Conor Corderoy was born in England in 1957. He spent his childhood on Formentera, the smallest of the Balearic Islands among intellectuals, artists and writers. He had no formal schooling, though he had a governess for four years who became an alcoholic and disappeared when he was twelve. He spent his teens in Cordoba, southern Spain, where he got his first job aged sixteen, breaking in wild horses. He has since done more jobs than he can remember, including free-lance writing, law, hypnotherapy and psychotherapy. He now divides his time between England and Spain. He is an Incorporated Linguists, a barrister, a psychologist and a Master Practitioner of NLP.

Conor Corderoy loves to hear from readers. You can find contact information, website details and an author profile page at https://www.totallybound.com/

TOTALLY
BOUND

Home of Erotic Romance

www.ingramcontent.com/pod-product-compliance
Lightning Source LLC
Chambersburg PA
CBHW021519240626
47154CB00002B/700